BROOKLYN
Bombshells
PART 2: RED CHARLIE

Melodrama Publishing
www.MelodramaPublishing.com

FOLLOW
ERICA HILTON

www.melodramapublishing.com

Library of Congress Control Number:1620781005
ISBN-13: 978-1620781012

First Edition: April 2019

Printed in Canada

BROOKLYN Bombshells

PART 2: RED CHARLIE

Chapter One

It was a beautiful September afternoon with cloudless skies, a slight breeze, and a warm and friendly sun above. Pyro wasn't in the best mood as he ordered two cups of hot coffee from the café downstairs from the rehabilitation facility. Mateo had been transferred to the best rehab center in the city, and Pyro was footing the bill. It had been a long few months with Mateo lying up in critical condition, and his progress was excruciatingly slow.

Pyro made his way back into the facility, strolled through the busy lobby, and took the elevator to the sixth floor, where Mateo was fighting to regain his life day by day, minute by minute, second by second. Although Mateo was awake, he wasn't showing signs of major improvement. But Pyro couldn't and wouldn't give up on his friend—his brother from another mother. He needed Mateo by his side as his business partner. They had plans. They had a lot to accomplish together, and this wasn't the end for the duo. Pyro wanted to believe that. He had to keep his head up and hopes high, especially in front of Chanel.

Chanel was a faithful and loyal girlfriend, and Pyro had nothing but respect for her. She refused to leave Mateo's side in his darkest hour, and she was willing to take care of him. It was a love that Pyro wished he had.

When he got to Mateo's room, Pyro saw Chanel by his bedside, praying for her man—the man she was truly in love with. It wasn't fair.

They were supposed to be honeymooning in Hawaii. Now it seemed like that dream of paradise wasn't going to come true—not anytime soon.

"How you holding up?" Pyro asked her.

"I could be better," Chanel replied, sadness coloring her eyes and tone.

"Don't worry about him, Chanel. My dude is a fighter. Believe me, he ain't going anywhere. He's too stubborn and vain to die at his age." Pyro held up one of the cups and said, "I bought you some coffee."

"I'm not thirsty."

Pyro took a sip from his coffee and nodded, the weight of the situation bearing down on him. He had taken on a lot since Mateo was shot. Pyro was solely running their business, paying for Mateo's hospital and rehabilitation bills, and keeping Chanel and her mother booked in the luxury suite at The Manhattan hotel. The expenses were a small fortune. He wanted to keep Chanel safe because Mateo would have done the same for him, but he knew the money would have been put to better use on the streets or in the stock market. Still, with God and Charlie out there, Pyro felt he had to keep Chanel somewhere out of their reach.

"Why him?" Chanel muttered sorrowfully.

Pyro approached closer and placed his hand on Chanel's shoulder. "I don't know, but I know this—he's gonna make it out of this, Chanel. He came too far to lose now. He gonna be a'ight, you feel me?"

His words carried strength to Chanel, but inside Pyro was broken up seeing his friend lying in that bed, looking nearly lifeless. Mateo had this perpetual blank stare on his face with minimal signs of recognition. Every now and then he would squeeze someone's finger or attempt a half-smile. Pyro knew that his boy was still in the race, fighting to get his life back.

Chanel was trying to be the rock that Mateo needed her to be, but Pyro could see in her eyes that she needed just as much support as Mateo. They both were hurting over Mateo's condition.

"Where's ya moms?" he asked.

"She's back at the hotel," Chanel replied, her eyes still glued on Mateo.

Of course, Pyro thought. Bacardi barely came to support Chanel and Mateo. What she cared about was living the life of luxury via someone else's misery and troubles.

Chanel turned to Pyro. "And speaking of that, the hotel is way too expensive for you to keep spending all your money on. It's not necessary, Pyro. I want you to know that I appreciate all you've done, but it feels wrong to me. I don't want you to think I'm taking advantage of you."

Pyro agreed, but staring into Chanel's chestnut brown eyes and seeing her pitiful demeanor, he just couldn't say it out loud. "Nah, you good, Chanel. Don't worry 'bout me, ma. Just be there for my nigga like you been doin' and help him get better."

But Chanel wasn't having any of it. She wasn't a user. She didn't want Pyro to go bankrupt or in debt because of her plight with God and Charlie. Besides, Bacardi was the main one luxuriating in the perks. Room service, housekeeping, spa days and nights, and the heated indoor pools, her mother loved every bit of it. Meanwhile, Chanel was at Mateo's bedside ten to twelve hours a day.

Chanel had already asked her friend Mecca if she could stay with her for a while, until she figured out her next move. Mecca told her that she could spend a few nights there, but her parents wouldn't allow more than that. Their hearts went out to Chanel after Mecca told them about the robbery, rape, and Mateo's shooting, but to them it spelled trouble for their daughter. They had moved uptown to avoid such things. First, Mecca had gotten detained by the police at Chanel's place when that cop was murdered, and now this. It was too much for Mecca's parents. They felt that Chanel wasn't as innocent as she claimed to be—getting mixed up with street goons and gangsters.

"You've done enough for me, Pyro. I'm a big girl and I can handle myself. I don't want to become a burden on you. You have enough to deal with too. Besides, I found a place to stay for a week or two. I'll be at Mecca's in Harlem."

It wasn't contemplated, but the words unexpectedly spilled out of his mouth. "Mecca, nah, it's not safe there. Look, I have a spare room in a safe building. No one will know you're there . . . unless you tell them. You can stay until Mateo gets better and back on his feet. And you're right; it would save me some paper."

Chanel thought on it for a moment. "Can I tell my mother?"

Pyro shook his head—hell no. "You can tell her that you're safe, but that's it. She could slip up and let someone know your whereabouts. I mean, your sister is a grimy bitch, and until that nigga God is handled, you'd be puttin' my life in danger too."

The thought frightened Chanel. "I won't. I promise."

"You said the same thing to Mateo, and now he's fucked up," he said to Chanel without thinking. Pyro didn't realize he had some pent-up animosity toward her for running her mouth to her sisters and getting his best friend shot in the head.

All along, Chanel had felt exactly what Pyro said—it was her fault. His statement made her burst into tears, and she ran out of the room.

Pyro knew he had fucked up. He felt guilty for letting that statement out, and he immediately ran after her. He caught up to her by the elevators. She was pressing the button rapidly, looking to dash inside and escape somewhere.

"Chanel, I'm sorry for what I said back there. It's not your fault, so don't put this shit on you, you feel me?" he apologized sincerely. "And like I said, my place is safe, and you're welcome to stay there for as long as you like. I know Mateo would want that for you—for me to keep you safe."

She stared at him, wiping away the few tears that trickled from her eyes. She nodded.

Chanel stepped out of the elevator and into the plush hotel hallway. She still looked depressed from her time at the rehabilitation center. From Mateo's condition, to her life being in danger, Chanel had so much on her mind that some days she didn't know if she was coming or going. She felt like a ghost as she walked down the hall to her room. The Manhattan hotel was luxurious, but it wasn't home. It didn't give Chanel any comfort.

Chanel entered the hotel room to see her mother walking around in a long robe and downing a glass of champagne. Bacardi greeted her daughter with the nicest smile, but Chanel didn't smile back. It was nice to see that someone was having a good time on Pyro's dime. Her mother was making herself at home.

"How is he doin'?" Bacardi asked.

"His condition is still the same . . . nothing changed," Chanel replied.

"All we can do is keep prayin' for him," Bacardi said. "But I ordered some room service. I didn't know you'd be here, but it should be enough for both of us."

Chanel had to break the bad news to her mother, and there was no way to sugarcoat it. "Look, Ma, check-out time is noon tomorrow."

Bacardi stopped what she was doing and stared at her daughter as if she had heard her wrong. "Say what now?" she replied.

"We need to go—pack our things and leave here. Pyro has done enough for us, and I don't want to keep taking advantage of his kindness."

Bacardi had the saddest look on her face. Her life had never been so good. She looked like someone had pulled the rug out from under her. Her Cinderella moment was over.

Her sadness transitioned into anger. "That cheap muthafucka just gonna kick us out?! Where we 'posed to go, huh? How the fuck he gonna do us like that, especially you?" she ranted. "Where we gon' go now?"

Bacardi didn't want to leave the palace she had been in for the summer—living the high life like a fat hog. Shit, she felt Pyro could afford it. He was a rich nigga getting that street money.

"I got somewhere to go," Chanel mentioned.

Bacardi looked shocked. "You do? Where?"

"I'm going to stay with Mecca in Harlem for a stint. She doesn't mind. But we can't stay here any longer. It's getting too expensive for Pyro. Between Mateo's high medical bills and rehabilitation bills and this room with your constant room service, it's too much on him," she stated.

Too much on him? Shit, he offered, Bacardi thought.

"We need to be out by morning," Chanel said, moving around the room and gathering some of her things.

"Fuck it. I'll be packed," Bacardi replied. "But I'm leaving this fuckin' place with a bang."

"As long as we leave," said Chanel.

Bacardi didn't say it, but she thought it. This was all Charlie's fault, and her first-born would pay.

Chapter Two

*C*harlie took repeated pulls from her cigarette and stared off into the distance, looking at nothing but thinking about everything, including everyone who had wronged her. She stood on the gravel rooftop of her project building, aimlessly gazing at the floodlit city from a distance on a breezy, fall night. Charlie wasn't in any rush to go inside. Instead, she continued to relish the comfort of being alone on the rooftop— contemplating and plotting.

She felt she had nothing left; everything had been taken from her. She seethed and found herself in self-preservation mode.

She had killed a man—not some stranger, but a man that she had once deeply loved. She convinced herself that it had to be done. *But why?* She really didn't know. He committed a laundry list of infractions against her in the past. He beat her. He cheated on her. He fucked her sister. She couldn't bring herself to say the word—to say that her man *raped* her little sister. She had known that prior to the murder and, evidently, she could live with it. To Charlie, her little sister brought the misery on herself.

So, if none of that made her consider murdering him, what made her snap?

A little voice inside her said it was her ego. Her ego couldn't take hearing God say that Kym had some good pussy and Chanel had better pussy than hers, even though he uttered those words while heavily influenced by the drug she had given him. How could God say such a vile thing to her—after everything she did for him? She was his ride-or-die bitch for years, and she had even killed for him. She hated the fact that Chanel had fucked her man. God was her man and nobody else's.

In Charlie's eyes, everything was Chanel's fault—why she was forced to kill her man and why she now had nothing. Her day for revenge would come.

But first things first, Charlie had to put all her ducks in a row. What if the police found trace evidence she had overlooked in the apartment and decided to believe Kym's story? Kym would surely plead her innocence and tell them that she didn't kill God.

There were so many what-if's in Charlie's mind, it was becoming overwhelming. She was becoming paranoid, and if anyone got in her way, she was ready to violently cut them down.

Charlie was determined that her story wasn't about to end. She wasn't about to rot in some prison cell while her sister remained free and breathing and living her best life. She didn't want to fade into obscurity and be forgotten.

After being gone for several days and spending hours on the gravel rooftop, Charlie finally walked through the front door to her parents' apartment. Her foul mood was matched by Bacardi's—like mother like daughter. Her mother was seated on the couch smoking a cigarette. Charlie, who was still haunted with hallucinations about murdering God, wasn't in the mental state for chitchat. But the moment she closed the door, Bacardi got up and hurried over to her, almost looking for a confrontation.

"Where the fuck was you, Charlie? Shit is gettin' fuckin' crazy out here and you got time to disappear and not tell anyone where the fuck you were at?" Bacardi chided. "And where the fuck is my rent?"

Charlie cut her eyes at her mother. "What are you hollering 'bout now? I'm not in the fuckin' mood, Bacardi."

Charlie begrudgingly tried to push past her mother, but Bacardi was adamant in confronting her. Charlie remained defiant as she stood in the hallway across from the kitchen. A few feet from her bedroom, she noticed them. Padlocks. "What the fuck is this?" she asked.

Bacardi smirked at her daughter's sudden bewilderment and taunted, "Yeah, bitch, shit done changed up in here. From now on, rent is due on the first of the month, and everyone is to contribute toward food. Ain't no more free rides in my place."

Charlie twisted up her face. She felt everyone wanted to take advantage of her and disrespect her while she was down. She wasn't having it.

"Are you fuckin' serious?! You really wanna go there and talk 'bout free rides? I carried you and this fuckin' family for years!"

"You either pay rent or you can get the fuck out!" Bacardi retorted.

"Bitch, I ain't goin' no-fuckin'-where!" Charlie screamed back.

They no longer looked like mother and daughter, but two strangers shouting in each other's faces with erratic hand movements going back and forth.

The loud shouting brought Claire out of her bedroom. She had gone along with the program and started paying her mother rent. She didn't have a choice since she didn't have anywhere else to go. While Bacardi was living the lavish life in Manhattan with Chanel all summer, Claire had begun to get her life together. She was working part-time at TJ Maxx and attending community college. Things were copasetic until Charlie's return brought hell back into the apartment.

"Ma, you trippin' right now," Claire said.

"Stay the fuck outta this, Claire," Bacardi yelled.

"I ain't payin' you shit, bitch!" shouted Charlie.

More heated words were exchanged, and Claire desperately tried to play the peacemaker between them. Bacardi wanted $300 a month toward rent from both of them, and she wanted $200 a month for food. However,

Charlie didn't have a dime to her name. She was hungry, tired, and she wanted everyone to get out of her face.

"If you think I'm paying you five hundred a month for a project room, then you a dumb fuckin' bitch. Like I said, you ain't gettin' shit from me. All that money and shit me and God gave you, and this is how you fuckin' repay me!" Charlie shouted.

Hearing God's name spew from Charlie's mouth did something to Bacardi. On top of Charlie's self-righteous tone, it made her go ape shit. She unexpectedly lunged at her daughter, attacking Charlie like she was a bitch in her prime. Charlie got hit with a series of blows, but her mother attacking her unleashed the beast inside of her. The two were going pound for pound inside the living room, knocking pictures off the walls and sending glasses and ashtrays smashing to the floor.

"Fuckin' bitch!" Charlie screamed, grabbing her mother's hair and trying to knot it around her fist and pull it out by its roots.

"Get the fuck off me, bitch!" Bacardi growled.

At that point, it would have been a draw between them if someone had been calling the fight. But then Bacardi got a second wind and started to handle her daughter like an OG. She went ham, her fists repeatedly smashing into Charlie's face, bruising it and spilling some blood.

A mortified Claire saw the blood and tried to pull Bacardi off her sister, but she couldn't control her mother's rage. Charlie continued to holler, and when it looked like Bacardi was going to kill her, Claire decided to jump in instead of trying to break it up. Her fists went hammering away at the back of her mother's head, and now it was two against one.

"Get off her!" Claire screamed out, her emotions on overload.

"Y'all bitches wanna fuckin' jump me!" Bacardi shouted.

It didn't take long before the sisters got the best of their mother. Years of disrespect had come full circle, and soon it was Bacardi hollering out for help.

Butch arrived home just in time to see Claire and Charlie beating on his wife. He was sober and immediately came to his wife's rescue. Quickly, he assessed what was really in motion and angrily started to throw blows at Claire and Charlie. It was unreal. Had things gotten that dysfunctional with the family?

"Get off ya mother!" he bellowed.

His punches were solid. Nobody fucked with his wife, and nobody was going to disrespect their home. For a minute, it was a hurricane of hostility as both factions released hatred and aggression onto each other. Butch uppercut Charlie and she went crashing to the floor in a daze. It almost felt like he knocked out her tooth. Claire rushed to her sister's aid and, miraculously, the fight ended. But not the hostility.

"Fuck you both! I hate y'all! Fuckin' die, fuckin' fo' real!" Charlie screamed hysterically.

Bacardi matched her daughter's outrage and screamed back, "You a trifling red bitch, Charlie, and you gonna burn in hell for what you did to ya sister. How could you set Chanel up and let God fuckin' rape her!"

The accusation leveled the whole room. Bacardi expected the guilt that was now written all over Charlie's face, but when she looked to Claire, she saw the same thing in her eyes.

"You knew too!"

Claire tried to avoid eye contact. As Butch tried to process what his wife had said, Bacardi started tossing her daughters' belongings into the hallway. She was done with them.

"Y'all bitches get the fuck outta my house!" she shouted.

"What? Are you serious? I just paid you rent," Claire challenged. "Give me my fuckin' money back then."

"Bitch, you ain't gettin' shit back!" Bacardi retorted.

While Claire was fussing with her mother, Charlie was in the hallway trying to gather her things so they wouldn't get stolen, knowing there were thieves in her building. The commotion inside their apartment had the entire floor coming out of their apartments to see what was happening. Cell phone cameras were out and recording. It was always something going on with that family—never a dull moment in the Brown household.

Butch went along with the program and helped Bacardi with tossing his daughters' shit out. When Charlie tried to go back inside the apartment, Butch stormed into the kitchen and grabbed a sharp knife and held it up threateningly to Charlie as Bacardi continued to throw out clothes, shoes, and personal items.

Claire was now in tears, but Charlie refused to cry. She held her own and scowled at her parents and threw threats their way. *Fuck that!* She wasn't embarrassed and she wasn't about to break down and look weak in front of the neighbors. She refused to give them that satisfaction.

Looking on at the ruckus at Bacardi's apartment door with the other neighbors was Landy. She was mesmerized by the ordeal going down right next door to her apartment.

Seeing Landy gazing at her, Charlie immediately asked, "Bitch, you just gonna stand there and watch, or you gonna get me some fuckin' trash bags?"

Landy went into her apartment and shortly returned to the hallway and tossed two black trash bags at Charlie. It was all the help Charlie was going to get from her. Shit, trash bags cost money, and Landy wasn't about to create any issues with her own family, especially her mother. A few other neighbors tossed garbage bags at Charlie like she was some charity case and it gave them a reason to stay in the hallway and be nosy.

After Bacardi tossed out what she wanted to get rid of, meanwhile keeping the good stuff for herself, she slammed the door shut on both her daughters, turned around, and looked at Butch. She knew she had some explaining to do.

Chapter Three

Chanel rode quietly in the backseat of the Uber and gazed out the window. Everything was changing, and it wasn't for the better. It felt like she was cursed from the day her mother gave birth to her. When something good came into her life, it didn't last. *Why?* Why couldn't she experience happiness without it being ripped from her? Chanel remembered more frowns than smiles, more hurt than joy, and more hate than love. But Mateo loved her, and she loved him, and she had to hold on to that.

She had gathered her things from the hotel and was on her way to Pyro's condo in a posh area in the Bronx. When she arrived, Pyro was waiting for her downstairs. He smiled when he saw her in the Uber he had arranged for her. Chanel climbed out of the backseat with her bags and released a sigh. This was it. She hoped staying with Pyro wasn't going to be yet another burden on him.

"So, this is it, huh?" Chanel asked, looking up at the building and then fixing her eyes on Pyro's.

Pyro took her larger bags and replied, "This is it. You'll be safe here. C'mon, let's go up so I can show you around."

She followed him through the lobby and into one of the two elevators. It ascended with them riding in silence before it came to a stop on the eighth floor. Pyro stepped out and Chanel followed.

Pyro smiled, slightly, as much as he was used to doing and he started to show her around his place. It was spacious and it was beautifully furnished with a large TV mounted on the living room wall. The spare bedroom where Chanel would be sleeping was cozy with expensive bedding on the king size bed and beautiful artwork on the walls. The walk-in closet was empty except for an area rug that covered the hardwood floor.

"You can put all your things in there. There's enough room," he said, placing her bags on the rug.

"Okay."

Pyro continued to show her around the apartment. There was a roomy kitchen for her to cook in, if she decided to. As she drank in her surroundings, Chanel recognized that everything had a place; things were lined up painstakingly. She wondered if he had a housekeeper. Pyro was neater than both her and Mateo, and that was saying something. The labels on his canned goods in the cupboard were lined up precisely, sparkling water in the fridge the same. His clothes were placed a certain way inside his closet. His sneakers and shoes were organized, and it seemed that there wasn't a speck of dust anywhere. It seemed like he had a bit of OCD. It was a bit awkward, and she worried a little. She didn't want to feel awkward in his home.

Thankfully, the bedrooms and bathrooms were on opposite sides of the condo.

After a quick tour of the place, Pyro went into his bedroom to change clothes.

"You're not staying?" she asked when he came back into the kitchen.

"Nah, I gotta take care of something," he said.

She was still frightened to be alone. She stared at him, and he picked up on her uneasiness.

"Chanel, you're gonna be okay. I keep a low profile and nobody comes here like that. You have everything you need to be comfortable, and security is tight downstairs. No one can come up without you giving the okay," he said with assurance.

She still felt a bit uneasy, but she nodded. Pyro smiled at her and she weakly smiled back. He turned and left the apartment. The moment he was gone, Chanel made sure all the locks were secured. Now alone, the place felt much bigger than before. She had a nasty vision of God climbing into the apartment through an open window, even though they were eight floors up, and once again coming for her. She shivered from the thought.

When night fell, Chanel still remained apprehensive even with the TV and lights on. She stayed glued to the couch and stared at the door each time she heard some kind of movement or the elevator door opening and closing. She was on edge, though she tried not to be.

By three in the morning, her eyes started to get heavy, and no matter how hard she tried to stay awake, it was becoming a losing battle. Chanel decided to retire into the bedroom. To make herself feel more secure, she pushed the dresser against the bedroom door and went to sleep with her clothes on.

Eight hours later, Chanel's eyes popped open to the sun shining through the bedroom window. It was a new day, but she was still living her same life with the same predicament. She got up, moved the dresser from in front of the door, and stepped out into the rest of the apartment to find no sign of Pyro. She wondered if he had come in late and left early. She went to his bedroom door and knocked gently, but there was no answer. Since the door was ajar, she opened it and went into his room. Everything inside seemed undisturbed.

This bothered her greatly. She hoped that she wasn't keeping him from his own home. She didn't want to be a burden on him, but she didn't want to be alone either.

Chapter Four

*Y*ou should have told me, Bernice," Butch shouted, the veins in his neck bulging and pulsing with his heartbeat. "I should have known about this shit sooner!"

"Well now you know," Bacardi snapped back.

"It's a little too late now," he said, pacing around the kitchen. "My own daughter. Charlie—how could she do something like that to Chanel?"

Bacardi placed her hands on her wide, robust hips and paused to contemplate the question. But there was no valid explanation. "Don't worry, Butch. She'll get hers."

He stopped pacing for a moment to look Bacardi in her eyes. "They all will."

Butch hated to be kept in the dark, especially when it came to his daughters. His youngest set up by her own sister. He couldn't comprehend it. Every time he thought about it, his heart would race to the point that his chest hurt, and it was becoming harder for him to calm down and not think about it.

"That shit ain't right!" He continued to walk the floor, anger and guilt eating away at him. He had invited the man who attacked his daughter into his home and treated him like his own son.

For the first time in over twenty years, Butch and Bacardi had the apartment to themselves. Usually, the kids leave the nest for college or marriage. Their kids left the apartment from trauma and deceit. Butch had a hard time believing that Charlie could do something so serious to her little sister. And God? He wanted to wrap his hands around that fool's neck and snap it like a twig.

Sitting down at the kitchen table, Butch growled, "I'ma kill that nigga, Bernice. What he did to our daughter, he needs to pay."

"He will pay."

Butch wasn't immune to violence. Back in his day, he dealt with his share of goons. And although he wasn't on the best terms with his kids, he was still a father and he was still very protective over his daughters—even Charlie. But she crossed that line.

Bacardi recognized the look Butch carried in his eyes, and they were on the same page. They both wanted to implement justice for their little girl.

"We just can't get caught," she said, reading his thoughts.

"We won't."

They continued to talk about murder over bacon and eggs. They both were serious and knew once the wheels started to turn to their plot, there would be no turning back. It was going down.

"We allowed that nigga into our home and he betrays our family like this," Butch continued to grumble. "I'ma empty my clip in that fool."

Bacardi told him that this wasn't an excuse to start drinking again. Butch had been getting a monthly injection of Naltrexone, a drug used to block the pleasurable effects of alcohol. So far he hadn't relapsed.

He downed his pineapple juice and slammed the glass on the table. "It's why I'm staying sober. When I shoot that piece of shit, I don't wanna miss."

The knock at the front door interrupted their murder plot. They both fixed their eyes on the door and wondered the same thing. Was it their daughters trying to come back home?

Bacardi pushed her chair back from the table and went to see who it was. When she looked through the peephole, she frowned and glanced at her husband. "It's that dumb, white, wanna-be-black bitch, Landy."

"What she want?"

"Like I fuckin' know."

Bacardi hadn't seen Landy around since that cop got shot in the stairwell of their building. Puzzled, she cautiously opened the door. "What the fuck do you want?"

Landy ignored the rudeness and eased into the apartment uninvited. "Hello, Mr. Butch and Mrs. Bacardi," she greeted warmly.

Bacardi rolled her eyes and eyed Landy up and down. "Why you got ya hair in them braids? Who you 'posed to be, Alicia Keys?"

Landy decided to let her comment go. She had known Bacardi for a long time and knew how petty she could be. She kept her amicable performance going by saying, "I came by to see if y'all needed anything from the grocery store. My parents are sending me to Stop & Shop in a Lyft. I could go shopping for you too."

Bacardi smirked again and asked, "You buying?"

"Well, no, but I would shop for y'all if you needed anything and you wouldn't have to contribute to the Lyft or pay me for my time."

Butch looked at his wife and mocked, "Well, ain't that mighty white of her."

Landy made herself comfortable by taking a seat at the kitchen table. She was a bold one. Bacardi and Butch shared a puzzled look.

"So, how's Chanel? I haven't seen her around lately."

Bacardi knew what was up. It was said that the second thing a person brings up is what they really wanted. Landy wanted to be nosy and Bacardi was ready for her.

"Since when do you give a fuck about Chanel?" she retorted.

Landy's eyes widened. "Excuse me?"

"Bitch, you heard what the fuck I said. You ain't go visit my baby in the hospital not once! You was walking around here like ya black until those cuffs got put on you. And then you turned back into Elandy Slogenberg."

Landy coolly replied, "I only asked because there's a rumor going around that Charlie had set up Chanel to get raped and murdered. Is that why you kicked Charlie out?"

The heat came over Bacardi rapidly. She knew that there wasn't a rumor, because Charlie being part of it had been under wraps until yesterday. The project walls were paper thin, and their neighbors were too damn nosy. Landy sat there looking like she was some reporter for CNN.

"You got-damn white trash bitch!" Bacardi shouted.

A fuming Bacardi went lunging after her, but Landy was quick on her feet. She sprung from the chair and flitted around like a housefly trying not to get smacked down. When Bacardi tried to grab her, Landy slithered out of Bacardi's grip, bolted for the front door, ran down the hallway, and took flight down the stairwell—never looking back. She had escaped by the skin of her teeth, but she had what she needed. Bacardi's anger was confirmation that it was true.

Bacardi tried to give chase, but she was no spring chicken.

"Don't fuckin' come back here no mo', you white trash bitch!" Bacardi screamed into the hallway.

She slammed the door and pivoted toward Butch. "This shit is gettin' outta hand, Butch. We gotta do something. Our family's reputation is on the line."

"We will, Bernice. We will," Butch assured her.

Chapter Five

*I*t was either a coincidence or a sign that karma was coming to bite her in the ass. At this turbulent moment in her life, Charlie's hooptie refused to start. She shouted and cursed the old car and even slammed her fist against the steering wheel.

Claire sat in the passenger seat quiet and confused. *Is everything gonna be all right?* Had she made the right choice by defending Charlie and leaving home with her? Right now, Charlie looked like a lunatic and Claire thought her head was about to spin around and green slime would soon spew from her mouth.

"Fuck! Fuck! Fuck! Fuck everything!" Charlie shouted heatedly, banging her fist against the dashboard and against the window.

"What we gonna do, Charlie?" Claire asked.

"I don't fuckin' know, Claire!" Charlie snapped at her.

Just then, a few rapid taps on the driver's side window startled Charlie. She was about to spin around and shoot with her hand reaching for her gun, but she quickly recognized who was at her window. It was two neighborhood drunks, Mike and Cooler. Charlie rolled down her window to see what they wanted—probably looking for a handout.

"What y'all two lowlifes want?" she asked impolitely.

"We heard ya car not starting. Want us to take a look?" Mike asked. He had a wide, hopeful, innocent grin that said he could be trusted. But he couldn't. The hood nicknamed him "Smash and Grab Mike," because if he was experiencing alcohol withdrawals he was known to pick up a bottle and smash someone—anyone—across the head and grab whatever cash and valuables they had on them. A few smash-and-grab licks in, he preyed upon the wrong target. Sixteen-year-old Kaizer emptied his clip into a man old enough to be his granddad. Mike's bony body drank in those hot slugs and miraculously survived.

"What, you a mechanic now, Mike?"

"I worked on many cars back in my heyday," he replied.

"A'ight, see what you can do," said Charlie, popping the hood. "Don't try no shit, Mike. I'm watchin' ya slick ass."

Mike and Cooler, the two parking lot mechanics, went to see what they could do to bring the old junk some life—maybe work their magic on the engine for some spare change.

Charlie leaned back into the seat and turned to her sister. "We ain't got nowhere to fuckin' go, Claire. Even if they do get this started, what next?"

Claire pressed her lips together, almost as if she didn't want to bring something up.

"What? You got something to say, Claire, then say it!"

"I might know a place for us to go."

"Where?"

"I can call a friend."

"Then what you waitin' on? I'm not trying to sleep in this car tonight," Charlie said, sitting up in her seat.

While Mike and Cooler desperately tried to get the car started, Claire pulled out her cell phone and dialed a number. Charlie didn't take her eyes off her sister. She hoped that Claire could come through for her. Charlie had burned all her bridges and she had no one to call.

"Give it a go, now, Charlie," Mike said to her.

Charlie turned the key, trying to bring the engine to life, but the car continued to stall. It was coughing and choking. It damn near sounded like it was dying.

"Fuck!" cursed Mike. "We gon' try this one more time."

While they were doing that, Claire had gotten in touch with her friend. They were chatting on the cell phone and Charlie was listening to the conversation closely. It would be gravy if Claire could find them somewhere to stay until she could make some moves.

Claire ended the call. Her expression was flat. Charlie didn't know if it was going to be good news or bad news.

"So, what she say?"

"She said it's cool."

A slight smile appeared on Charlie's face. "That's what's up."

Mike and Cooler approached the driver's side window. The look on their faces indicated that they didn't have any good news to give Charlie.

"What?" Charlie asked in a gruff voice.

"Bad news," Mike started. "It looks like either one of two things— your alternator or your transmission. Either way, this car is dead in the water."

"Fuck!" Charlie pounded the steering wheel again.

"Can we get a few bucks for trying?" Mike asked.

Charlie flashed a scowl. "Nigga, get the fuck away from my car!"

Disappointed, both men scurried away from the vehicle.

Charlie had to call a cab to get them to their destination. The last thing she wanted to do was travel through the busy city with their belongings in several black garbage bags. But they didn't have a choice.

The taxi dropped them off in a posh Brooklyn area called Clinton Hill. The sisters stood outside a nicely developed five-story building. They would be staying the night with Melanie, a classmate of Claire's. Claire and Melanie had several classes together, and they would frequently study and talk on campus, but they didn't hang out together. They weren't friends by anyone's definition, but when Claire called her out of desperation, Melanie agreed to help her out. But it was just for one night, and it wasn't out of altruism. Melanie simply wanted to be nosy.

Dragging the large garbage bags, the sisters entered the building and climbed three flights of stairs. Claire knocked on the door and it soon opened with Melanie looming into their view. The look on the girl's face spoke volumes to the sisters. Seeing the trash bags they carried, she blocked their entrance into her apartment and said, "I thought I said you could spend one night. What's up with all these trash bags?"

Charlie didn't like her attitude. She was ready to go off on her, but Claire spoke first, saying, "It is. But we couldn't very well leave our things in the hallway or outside. Come sunlight, we'll be gone. I promise, Melanie. Do me this solid and I'll owe you one."

Reluctantly, Melanie moved to the side and allowed the sisters into her home.

"This is my sister, Charlie," Claire introduced her.

Both women sized each other up and nodded acknowledgement. Claire hoped that her sister played nice.

They walked into Melanie's large, one-bedroom apartment and they instantly grew jealous of her. It looked like she had hired an interior decorator. There were blue, green, and gold colors, large area rugs, costly looking vases, large paintings with glided frames, and a baby grand piano. The large white sectional with lots of throw pillows was the room's anchor. It looked so perfect that they didn't want to sit down anywhere.

Claire and Charlie dragged their bags to the corner, and they instantly became an eyesore in the lavish looking room. Melanie exhaled and thought, *It's only for one night.* She was kicking herself for inviting Claire to stay, but it was too late to ask them to leave.

"So, do y'all want a drink?" she offered to try and take the edge off.

Charlie wanted a glass of Hennessy. She needed something strong after the day she'd had, but when Claire saw Melanie frown, she knew not to ask for the same. Melanie wasn't a thug bitch. She came from a different world far from theirs. She was classy. She had dreams and carried herself a certain way.

Melanie went into the kitchen, which was connected to the living and dining room. She mixed up some appletinis and grabbed a plate of sushi rolls she had just made. The food was out of the girls' league. Charlie wanted to be stubborn and refuse the sushi, but her stomach was growling like a lion. Charlie and Claire dug into the sushi, and surprisingly, it was delicious.

"You play the piano?" Charlie asked her.

Melanie nodded. "I do."

"Wow, that's what's up. I always wanted to learn how to play the piano," said Charlie.

Claire was stunned by the confession. *When was this?* she wanted to ask. But she decided to keep her comment to herself.

"I can teach you someday," Melanie said.

Charlie didn't look interested in furthering the conversation. If she did want to learn to play the piano, it was a long time ago. She was just making conversation with Melanie, trying to size her up and feel her out.

"That would be cool," Charlie replied nonchalantly.

As they continued to make conversation, the sisters found out that Melanie also decorated her place, she was an A-student, and she was a good cook, making them think of Chanel. She was attractive, but Claire and Charlie's beauty didn't go over her head. Melanie resembled a younger version of Halle Berry, but not as pretty. Maybe she could be a distant cousin.

Once the alcohol began to flow through their systems, the mood started to loosen up. After several more cocktails, all three of them started to act like old pals. They laughed and joked and started to get to know each other more. Melanie was a nosy one. She wanted to know all about the sisters. They were intriguing.

"Y'all from Brooklyn, huh? Brook-lyn in the house," she enunciated with an urban tone.

Claire and Charlie laughed.

"What part y'all from?" asked Melanie.

"The really rough part that will eat you alive," Charlie responded.

Melanie laughed. "Well, I need to not go there!"

More drinks were consumed and the living room became ground zero for them. The sun had set and the night was young. Melanie tossed back her glass, smiled, and said, "I got another question for y'all. Are y'all half-white?"

"No," Claire answered.

"Oh really? Because y'all can maybe pass for white," Melanie pushed.

"Well, we're not. We a hundred percent black," Charlie chimed.

"Black Lives Matter, right?" Melanie joked.

"They don't where we come from," Charlie answered.

"So, are you in college too, Charlie?"

"Nah."

"So you got your degree in the streets, right? I'm not hating on that."

Charlie shot an awkward glance at her sister. At first, it was fun and laughs between them, but it seemed like Melanie was mocking them.

"So, I have to ask—why did your parents throw you two out?"

Charlie frowned at the question. She quickly spoke up, noticing that the bitch was being extra nosy, and she didn't want Claire spilling any of their family's tea. It wasn't any of the bitch's business, even if she was providing them with a place to stay tonight.

"It's personal," Charlie replied tersely.

"I was just asking. I wasn't trying to intrude in your business."

"Then fuckin' don't," snapped Charlie.

Melanie felt slighted and insulted, but she kept quiet about it.

"Well, I guess enough about talking about y'all lives. Do y'all want to hear about mine?" she said with gleefulness in her tone.

Charlie really didn't, but it was her place and Melanie wanted to boast about her ambitious life. She was lording over the sisters and loving it. Meanwhile, Charlie was listening intently and she was also scheming on the naïve bitch. She wondered how Melanie could afford to live like this. The rent alone was steep, and Charlie estimated the furnishings cost at leave five to six thousand dollars per area. The bedroom set, living room and dining scenery, it was all high-end. The only downside to the apartment was that you had to go through Melanie's bedroom to get to the one bathroom.

"I just love nice things, as you can see," Melanie said proudly.

"Yeah. I can see that," replied Charlie with a fake smile. "Can I use your bathroom?"

"Of course. It's through my bedroom."

Charlie excused herself from the room, leaving her sister and Melanie to chitchat.

Inside the bedroom, Charlie quickly rummaged through the closet. All she saw were labels—rows and rows of designer labels. She smirked. *There is no way this bitch could afford all this shit on her own at twenty years old,* she thought. *No fuckin' way!*

The high-end items were starting to make her pussy wet. She had seen enough.

Charlie came back into the living room and sat down with something to look forward to. It was about to become a new day for her and Claire. She smiled at Melanie, thinking it was going to be a huge payday for them if they handled it right.

Melanie was trying to be cordial to her guests, but she felt that she needed to repeat that come sunlight they were gone. Charlie listened as she laid down some more rules. She didn't allow anyone to sleep on her couch and remarked that it cost her five thousand dollars at Ethan Allen. Charlie was tired of the bitch bringing up how much her shit cost.

The night was growing late and it was time for everyone to retire to bed. As Melanie was in her linen closet pulling out sheets and blankets for her guests to sleep on the hardwood floors, Charlie decided to walk with her full appletini, and she "accidently" tripped on something and spilled the green liquid on the expensive white couch.

It was a typical hater move. "Oh shit! I'm so sorry!" Charlie yelped with a fraudulent apology.

Melanie spun around and burst onto the scene, only to see a nightmare before her eyes. Her eyes widened with shock and disbelief. The sight of her pricey couch now stained with green liquid made her burst into tears—almost hysterical. All three girls jumped into action and started blotting the fabric to stop the mess. Fortunately, some of it came out, but the cushion was ruined.

"Melanie, I'm so sorry . . . believe me, it was an accident," Charlie apologized.

Melanie didn't know what to believe. It could have been an accident, but she doubted it.

Inwardly, Charlie was laughing her ass off. She hated the bitch.

Although Charlie repeatedly proclaimed that it was an accident, Claire and Melanie knew it was done on purpose. Melanie also knew that you can't be nice to scum bitches like her. She wanted them gone early tomorrow morning.

Charlie couldn't sleep. She didn't want to sleep. She stayed awake thinking and plotting. Melanie wanted them gone in the morning and that was only a few short hours away. Charlie saw opportunity there, and she didn't want it to go to waste.

At a little after two in the morning Charlie heard Melanie creeping from her bedroom to go to the door. She assumed that the sisters were sleeping and the light from the outside hallway came flooding in and then quickly went dark.

From her position on the floor, Charlie pulled the covers over her head and pretended to be asleep. She peeked out and observed a man carrying a small brown duffel bag. Melanie and the stranger hurriedly disappeared into the bedroom, and the door closed. Charlie could hear them whispering about something.

Claire was still asleep and she didn't stir. Charlie's little sister wasn't astute like her. She got too comfortable when they shouldn't be comfortable at all because they were homeless and broke.

Charlie didn't know the stranger who went into the bedroom with Melanie, but she knew he was a hustler. She could easily sniff one out. He and Melanie spent about twenty minutes in the bedroom doing whatever. Charlie assumed they were fucking, but the door opened back up and Melanie walked the guy out without the duffel bag.

Charlie smiled.

Charlie was up bright and early a few hours later. She got into the shower first. As the water cascaded down on her, she couldn't stop thinking about that duffel bag she saw come into the apartment. She knew something precious was in it, and she planned on not leaving Melanie's place without it.

While Charlie was taking a shower, Melanie heard the water running. She glanced at the time and saw it was a quarter to seven. *Thank God*, she thought. She wanted the sisters gone. She had important things to take care of today. She remained lying in bed staring at the ceiling, counting the minutes on the clock until she drifted back off to sleep.

About an hour later, Melanie woke up to a strong smell coming from the bathroom. It was the smell of disinfectant. She wondered why she was smelling it. *Are the ghetto girls cleaning up?*

The cleaning didn't stop in the bathroom. Melanie could hear the dishes being washed. Curious, she opened the door and peeked into the living room and saw that Charlie was up, dressed, and cleaning all surfaces. Her pile of sheets and blankets were picked up and the space was spotless, except for Claire. She was still sleeping.

Melanie was impressed. Maybe she had Charlie figured out all wrong. She smiled warmly at her and uttered the words, "Good morning."

Charlie smiled broadly and said to Melanie, "We'll be gone soon. I just wanted to say thank you by cleaning up for you."

Melanie nodded her approval.

Charlie then asked, "I hate to ask, but do you mind if I use your cell phone? My battery went dead, and I need to make an important phone call before we leave here."

Melanie didn't see any harm in it. She handed Charlie her cell phone but wondered why Charlie didn't just use her sister's cell phone or ask to use a charger. She didn't want to appear like she was some petty bitch, though, so she kept her questions to herself.

"What's your security code?" Charlie asked.

Melanie had forgotten her phone was locked. She felt strange giving out the code. She had personal things on her phone, like most people.

Charlie noticed that Melanie seemed apprehensive about it. Thinking hastily, she reiterated, "I just want to make a few important phone calls and confirm where me and my sister are going to sleep tonight. I know you don't want us here."

It was understandable. Melanie gave her the pass code and said, "Take your time. I want y'all to be okay tonight."

Charlie smiled. "We will."

Melanie turned and walked back into her bedroom. Her instincts told her to lock her door, and she listened. Melanie jumped into the shower and then got dressed. She was ready for this bogus merrymaking with the sisters to be over with. Once they were gone, she could breathe again and relax. She played nice because she and Claire were cool at school, and the young girl was intriguing. Melanie had wanted to do her good deed for the week. It felt nice to feed the homeless. It was her presumptuous way of thinking.

Dressed and ready to say goodbye to Claire and Charlie, she unlocked her bedroom door and stepped out. Rapidly, Melanie was met with a gruesome fate. From out of nowhere, Charlie viciously struck her in the head with a hammer. Melanie released a loud shriek that Charlie tried to silence by striking her in the head again. Melanie collapsed against the floor, copious amounts of her blood pooling around her head.

Melanie's screams woke Claire up. When she picked herself up from the floor and finally realized what was happening, she flipped.

"Charlie, what the fuck did you do?"

"Just chill out and shut the fuck up! I got this!" Charlie replied.

Claire watched in horror as her sister sprung into action. Melanie was badly beaten, bleeding profusely, but she was still alive—barely. Wearing yellow dish gloves, Charlie stuffed a rag into Melanie's mouth and dragged her into the bedroom. Charlie was moving quickly, like she was a professional at this. She tied Melanie's hands behind her back with a silk scarf. Melanie, still conscious, was frantically trying to free herself, but then Charlie marched over and struck her again with the hammer, and again, and again until she was still.

Charlie said to her sister, who was now frozen with shock, "Claire, listen up, put these gloves on and bag up the linens we slept in and start wiping down everything we touched in here."

Claire stood there looking like a deer caught in blinding headlights.

"Claire, get dressed and do it now!" Charlie barked, snapping her sister out of her shocked state.

Tears started to stream down Claire's face. "Charlie, this is going too far. What are you doing? I don't wanna go to jail," she fretted.

"You won't if you just listen to me and do what I say. Don't come back into this room and give me your cell phone. Now, Claire!"

Claire sprung into action and did what her sister told her to do. Charlie pushed her out the bedroom and closed the door. Immediately, Charlie focused on the cell phones. She deleted all of her sister's history from the phone and removed the SIM card. Next she meticulously went through Melanie's phone, reading her text messages. There wasn't anything to delete except Claire's call to her the previous day. Melanie did mention to some nigga named Scott, who appeared to be her brother, that she was allowing a friend to sleep over. She never mentioned Claire's name—which was great. Scott had texted her back, stating that he would be over her place that same night to make a quick drop. He was actually her brother and not some nigga she was messing with.

Charlie went into Melanie's closet and found the brown duffel bag stashed in the back. She crouched down and opened it, and, as she predicted, it was filled with cash. From her estimate, she figured there was nearly $80,000 inside. Charlie beamed. *Bingo!*

Melanie was still hanging on to life by a thread. Surprisingly, the preppy bitch was tougher than Charlie had assumed. Now it was time for Charlie to clean up her mess. Melanie was a liability and Charlie couldn't afford to leave behind any witnesses. She went over to where Melanie was lying bound on the floor and placed a plastic bag over the girl's head. She coldheartedly finished what she started by bashing the girl's skull in with the hammer. It was brutal. For good measure, Charlie held a pillow over her face for a few minutes. Melanie Jones was dead.

When Charlie emerged from the bedroom, Claire was fully dressed and methodically cleaning the apartment. Charlie didn't want her sister to see the body, so she closed the bedroom door. They locked eyes, but they didn't speak. Claire didn't want to know what happened to Melanie inside the bedroom. She expected the worst. Everything felt still inside there.

Charlie grabbed two trash bags and went back into the bedroom. She started tossing essentials and anything worth taking into the bags—designer bags, jewelry, shoes, and most importantly, the money. She also tossed the linens into trash bags. Now they had more bags than they had come with, and it was becoming a burden for them. How were they going to drag all these bags out of the building without looking suspicious?

With the apartment thoroughly cleaned out, it was time to make their escape. Claire knew in her heart that they would eventually get caught. Melanie wasn't some loser or some bum that you can easily make disappear. She had a lot going for her, and the detectives assigned to the case would be zealous in solving her murder. She was upset with Charlie for getting her mixed up in murder and robbery but, as usual, she didn't say anything.

Charlie grabbed two baseball caps and two light jackets that belonged to Melanie. She and Claire both tucked their distinguishing red hair under the baseball caps, and then put on the largest pairs of sunglasses that Melanie owned. They painted their lips with dark colored lipstick and even gave themselves exaggerated eyebrows and moles. It was time to leave in their disguise.

"Look, we need to be careful and on point. I'll start taking the bags down the stairwell and out the backdoor so we won't be seen," said Charlie. "It's still early, so hopefully we won't run into many people. You wait a few minutes and then bring the rest."

Claire nodded, her stomach doing somersaults.

Charlie grabbed three full trash bags and acted like she had the strength of five men. She was determined to not get caught and not be seen. She left the apartment leaving Claire behind. The only thing to do was to be careful, smart, and patient.

It didn't take long for them to remove the bags. They moved with urgency to leave the area. Before they knew it, they were outside waiting for the Uber Charlie had arranged from Melanie's phone to show up. When their ride arrived, they sprung into action, asking the driver to pop the trunk. They quickly tossed the garbage bags in the trunk and climbed into the backseat. Charlie told him their destination.

"We're going to Harlem."

The Amsterdam Houses was a place that the sisters weren't connected to. Once there, Charlie took the trash bags filled with their clothes and tossed them into the nearest dumpster, along with the bag containing the linens from Melanie's apartment. Claire objected, but Charlie had to remind her that Bacardi had kept all their good shit and all that was in those bags was junk.

Charlie had seen too many bitches living better than her—the women she helped rob and kill with God and Fingers, her sister Chanel, and now this bitch Melanie. Charlie hated to see others having more than her. She vowed that from today on out, she would be upgrading her life.

With two bags left in their possession, mostly containing Melanie's things and the money, the girls walked to the nearest train station and took the A train to 125th Street. There, on the busy street lined with fashion boutiques, nail shops, fast food places, and more street merchants than you could count, they purchased two extra large suitcases on wheels.

"We need to get right," Charlie told Claire, walking quickly with the bag in one hand and rolling one of the suitcases with the other. "C'mon."

Claire followed behind her sister like a stray puppy. She was terrified and jumpy, and her eyes darted all over the place. She felt that a swarm of cops was going to swoop down on them and haul them away at any moment.

The sisters came to a stop on a side block with strangers coming and going. Quickly, Charlie packed the suitcases and they discarded their baseball caps and shades in a nearby trash can and wiped off their makeup. Charlie exhaled, feeling confident that they were going to get away with murder. So far everything was going smoothly, and as long as Claire didn't freak out, they were on the right path to a new life.

"Now we need to find a place to stay," said Charlie.

Charlie booked them a room for a week. It was a decent hotel room in Midtown Manhattan, where they could relax and get their minds right.

Claire hopped into the shower and lingered under the hot water for what felt like forever. She wanted to wash away everything that had transpired in the past twenty-four hours. She wanted to scrub away her sins. *What have I gotten myself into?* she kept asking herself. It was a nightmare that she couldn't wake up from.

After stepping out of the shower and toweling off, Claire stared at herself in the foggy bathroom mirror. She didn't like what was staring back at her. Out of the blue, she started to cry.

Who is Charlie? she thought. Her sister was a lunatic. She had seen that firsthand this morning. There was no defending Charlie anymore—the bitch was pure evil. She had set Chanel up, and Mateo was shot in the head and nearly died. Now Melanie. Charlie had made her an accessory to first-degree murder. Melanie was her friend—sort of. And even if she wasn't, she didn't deserve to die like that. All the layers of Charlie were being revealed. She had been robbing and killing people all along. Claire deduced that all those gifts Charlie had brought home were there because someone had died. The revelation of her sister's wicked lifestyle hit her like a Mack truck, and she started to slip into a deep depression again.

That night, Charlie tried to get her sister to cheer up and stop moping and crying, but Claire couldn't stop. She was afraid, and she felt betrayed. She wouldn't talk. She wouldn't eat. She would only sit there and weep and sleep. There wasn't anything Charlie could do to cheer her sister up. She couldn't bring her back from where she had come from and what she had seen—the devil and almost hell itself.

The next day, Charlie left Claire alone in the hotel room to go out and make some moves. She wanted to unload the stolen merchandise and put the money in a safe place. It was risky walking around the city with $80,000. Plus, she was tired of hearing her sister's whining and seeing her cry and stare off into space.

Charlie hoped Claire didn't become a weak link. Charlie saw an opportunity and she decided to take it. If she hadn't, they would be broke and homeless, and most likely staying at a shelter or sleeping on park benches. There was no way Charlie was going to go down that miserable road. Besides, she had just killed God, so in her mind, she had nothing to lose and nearly $80,000 to gain.

There was one thing that puzzled her about God, though. Why hadn't the streets heard about his murder yet? It had been days since Kym was arrested, yet, nothing—no word on the streets about his death.

She didn't know if that was a good thing or a bad thing.

Chapter Six

*P*yro stepped out of the elevator at 4am and approached his apartment. He was coming from an old flame's place after a heated night of fucking and sucking on each other. While lying in Lisa's bed, Pyro couldn't stop thinking about leaving Chanel alone for a week when he should be there guarding over her. He got dressed and left Lisa's place in the middle of the night. Lisa was left puzzled by his action.

At first, Pyro thought he was doing Chanel a favor by sleeping over with his females. He wanted to give her some space and he wanted her to feel at home at his apartment. He also knew to set firm boundaries when he was there with Chanel. He would never come out of his bedroom unless he was fully dressed, and he would go out of his way to make her feel comfortable and, most importantly, safe. Pyro also knew to keep Chanel from seeing the shadier side of things—of him; drugs and guns. He figured she had probably heard stories, but that was all he wanted her to hear. Mateo did his best to keep his woman out of that life, so who was Pyro to expose her to what his friend fought to keep her away from?

When he entered his apartment, everything seemed quiet and still— maybe too still.

"Chanel?" he called out.

She didn't answer him.

"Chanel, where you at?" he called out again.

Still, there was no response. He figured she was sleeping, but he grew slightly nervous and removed his gun from his hip. He started to feel guilty for leaving her alone for so long. Pyro didn't want to crowd her, but now he questioned if his absence made her feel more uncomfortable and more afraid.

Cautiously, with his gun parallel to his side, he advanced toward the second bedroom and carefully peeked inside. He sighed with relief to see Chanel sleeping in the bed under the covers and looking peaceful. She was even snoring. She had endured some long, tiresome, and trying days, and it was good to see her sleeping like a baby.

Pyro faintly grinned and closed her bedroom door. He went into his own bedroom to get undressed and to stay the night. This was going to be his first night sleeping in his own bed since Chanel had moved in. Sleep was desperately calling his name. Pyro climbed into his comfy, large bed wearing only his boxers, and he was fast asleep a minute later.

A few hours later, Pyro heard a slight tap at his bedroom door. Groggily, he called out, "Who?" even though he knew the answer.

"Hey, it's me. Good morning. I'm glad to see you're home. I just wanted to let you know that I'm cooking breakfast for us," she said sweetly.

He wasn't a breakfast type of dude. The only reason his fridge was stocked was for Chanel.

"I'm not hungry," he shouted back.

"C'mon, everybody loves breakfast. It's the most important meal of the day," she said.

"Just go away!" he yelled, pulling the covers over his head.

Chanel sighed and left from his door. It was easy to see that he wasn't a morning person. In the kitchen, she made herself pancakes with crispy bacon and peppermint tea. She sighed while sitting at the kitchen table. Pyro finally spent the night at his apartment and she still felt alone there.

He slept for ten hours and woke up to the late afternoon sun seeping through his bedroom window. He emerged from his bedroom fully dressed to a very clean apartment and a downtrodden Chanel. She had already been to visit Mateo, and now she was sitting in the living room watching HGTV. Noticing Pyro was awake and dressed, she faintly smiled at him and he realized that she was lonely.

"You okay?" he asked her.

"Yeah. I'm fine," she replied matter-of-factly.

Pyro stood in front of her, looking handsome in his street clothes.

Seeing him fully dressed, she then asked him, "Are you gonna be back for dinner?"

Dinner? Pyro survived on protein shakes, vegetable smoothies, and fast food. Having someone cook him dinner wasn't in his program. But the cheerless look on Chanel's face made him rethink leaving so abruptly.

"You know what? I got time to chill," he said, pulling off his hoodie and kicking off his Yeezys.

"I thought you were leaving?"

"Nah. I'm in no rush." Pyro plopped down on the couch quite close to Chanel and got comfortable.

Chanel moved over, widening the space between them, and replied, "You don't have to stay because of me, Pyro. I'll be okay."

"I know. But I wanna stay. It's cool."

He decided to hang out with her for a while. She was watching an episode of *House Hunters*, the beach house edition.

"You like this show, huh?" he said.

"Yeah. It's fun to watch rich people live their lives so freely and spend money on something like a summer home on the beach. Coming from the projects, we can't even fathom that. But hey, if you got it, you got it, and why not spend it on what makes you happy?" She shrugged.

"I feel you."

Chanel asked him, "I'm curious. What makes you happy, Pyro?"

"Making money," he replied.

She chuckled. "And that's it?"

"What else?"

She didn't push any further. Pyro was an intriguing guy. He kept to himself, kept a low profile, was extremely clean, and he was a loyal friend. Chanel knew there were demons deep inside of him and he had a violent past, but overall, he was a nice guy.

They continued to watch the show and chitchat a bit. It didn't take long for Pyro to become somewhat captivated by watching families, mostly white, searching for a new home with the assistance of a real estate agent.

"Have you ever thought about buying a house?" she asked.

"Nah, not really."

"It would be a good investment for your future."

"I guess. But I live alone, so who would I buy a house for? Shit, I do fine living in a nice apartment and doing me. A nigga like me ain't tryin' to be boo'd up." He laughed.

When he smiled Chanel realized how large and perfectly round his eyes were. He had innocent, pronounced eyes that were deceptive, whereas Mateo's eyes were small, slightly slanted, and sexy.

"You wanna be a bachelor all your life?"

"Right now, I'm not really looking. But if something right comes along, I might rethink it."

She smiled. "Someone will, Pyro. You're a nice guy—handsome too. You'll make some woman very happy."

"Right now, I'm trying to make all of them happy as long as they're making me happy," he joked.

"You're so stupid," Chanel giggled.

Pyro sat for two hours watching four episodes of *House Hunters,* and that was enough for him. It was time to go. He stood up to leave, and

Chanel right away asked him, "When are you coming back?"

He shrugged. "I don't know. Why?"

She sighed. "This apartment is still new to me, and some nights I get scared."

He moved closer to her with a compassionate look on his face. He didn't want her to be scared. He sat next to her briefly and said, "Chanel, you good here. There's nothing to be afraid of. You're safe here. Believe me; I won't let anything happen to you."

"You're right. I just need to get my nerves in check."

She said it, but he knew that apprehension still swirled inside of her from being alone at night. Having gone through what she went through, Pyro understood. She needed time to heal and to cope.

"Look, from now on I'll make it back at night to make you feel safer," he said.

She smiled.

As promised, Pyro made it home that night and slept in his own bed, but he also brought some female company back with him. Chanel didn't mind. She wasn't alone, and that was all that mattered to her.

Over the next several days, Chanel figured out that Pyro was a player. His bed was a revolving door. He had about four main women who all thought they were "the one" for him. The one thing the girls had in common with each other was that they all hated that Chanel was staying with their man, and they treated her with disrespect out of earshot of Pyro. They didn't care that she was Mateo's woman. They wanted the bitch gone.

Chapter Seven

Stern banging on your apartment door is a familiar yet frightening sound when black and living in the ghetto. There was always something happening in the projects that brought the NYPD with either questions or warrants.

Bacardi and Butch were lounging in the bedroom when they heard that stern banging. Bacardi jumped out of bed and put on a robe to see who was knocking like they were the police. *Maybe it is the police*, she thought. If so, she and Butch hadn't done shit—not yet. They both guessed that this was somehow connected to the fight they'd had with their daughters.

While Bacardi marched toward the door, tying her robe together, she griped, "I swear, Butch, if those bitches pressed charges on us, I'ma fuck them up fo' real this time."

She swung the door open to see two plainclothes detectives standing in the hallway. They immediately flashed their New Jersey badges and announced who they were.

"I'm Detective Meroe, and this is my partner, Detective Flinch. We're here to ask you some questions."

Bacardi stood there confused. "What kind of questions?"

"Can we come in?" asked Detective Flinch.

She wanted to tell him no—hell fuckin' no—but she relented and ushered them into her home.

"What's this about, detectives?" she asked.

By now, Butch had joined her in the living room. Seeing the detectives made him tense.

"Sorry to bother you, but we have a victim in the morgue who was murdered a couple weeks ago in New Jersey. His name is Godfrey Williams, and we need someone to formally identify his body. From our understanding, this is his last known address," said Detective Meroe.

Bacardi and Butch were shocked. God was dead?

"He's dead?" Bacardi asked.

"Yes, ma'am."

"You said murdered?"

"There seems to have been some kind of domestic dispute, and we have his girlfriend detained on Rikers Island until her next bail hearing," Flinch answered.

Girlfriend? "What girlfriend?" Bacardi asked.

"Um . . . a Kymberly Stephens."

Bacardi and Butch exchanged a look. They didn't want anything to do with God, and they certainly didn't want to identify his body. They were glad that he was dead, and they hoped he was rotting in hell. Bacardi's mood shifted, and she became upset that the detectives came to their door with this shit.

"We're not his fuckin' parents and that muthafucka raped our daughter. So fuck him!"

The detectives were shocked by the revelation and right away started to take notes, as if they were going to arrest a dead man. They left shortly after, but Butch was mad he didn't get to kill God himself.

"I can't even get revenge for my daughter's rape," he grumbled. "I wanted to feel his life drain from my own hands."

"It's karma, Butch. That nigga is gone and he's never coming back," Bacardi said.

Bacardi immediately got on her cell phone to tell Chanel the good news. She no longer had to worry about God and she could come home now.

Chanel felt like a huge weight had been lifted off her shoulders. Her mother's phone call with the unexpected news about God made tears drop from her eyes. The evil monster was dead. God was gone—murdered. She didn't know by who or why, but he was no longer a threat to her. She needed to tell Mateo and Pyro and let Pyro know that it was safe for her to go home.

She wanted to tell Pyro right away, but he was preoccupied with female company in his bedroom at the time. She heard them fucking. It was one of his main females, and she knew not to disturb him. She got dressed and left the apartment to visit Mateo at the hospital. She figured by the time she came back, Pyro wouldn't be too busy to hear the news.

Chanel sat by Mateo's bedside and exhaled. She took his hand into hers and looked into his eyes with a smile.

"He's gone. He's dead, baby," she said to him. "God is dead."

She could tell that it registered. Mateo had heard every word she said. He gently squeezed her hand and almost had a look of relief to him.

He managed to squeeze out one word. "How?" His voice was extremely low and raspy.

"Someone murdered him in New Jersey. We don't have to worry about him anymore," she added.

Chanel knew that even in his condition, Mateo was still worried about her. It was a bittersweet visit despite the news. God was dead, but Mateo was still on a long road to recovery. There wasn't much Chanel could do but sit at his bedside and talk to him and pray for him and show him love and support.

She spent nearly two hours with Mateo, talking to him and feeling nostalgic about how they first met. She wanted to feel his arms around her again and see his bright, wide smile. Mateo's love for Chanel was evident and undeniable. Every time Chanel would walk into a room, he would light up.

With it getting late, Chanel decided to end her visit. She smiled down at Mateo and kissed him lovingly on his forehead and then his lips.

"I love you, Mateo. Get well, baby. I need you."

An hour later, Chanel made it back to Pyro's apartment just as he and his girlfriend were finished eating Chinese takeout. Pyro was in a good mood. She figured pussy did that to a nigga. He was glad to see Chanel.

"Hey, where did you go?" he asked.

Chanel was all smiles. "I went to visit Mateo. It was good. We talked."

"How is he?"

"He's gonna get better. I know it. I can see it in his eyes. As we were talking, I saw so much life in them," she said, nearly bouncing around with an upbeat attitude.

Pyro could tell that something was different about her. He figured it had to do with Mateo's progress.

"I'ma slide through tomorrow and bring him some food from La Madres."

"Thanks, Pyro. He loves your visits."

"So, what's good? You look and seem different right now," said Pyro. "I mean, I'm not complaining. It's good to see some life coming back into you."

"It's just—I'll tell you later," she said, looking past Pyro and gazing at his girlfriend Dior, who was standing behind him with her arms folded across her chest.

Dior rolled her eyes at Chanel. To her, "later" meant when she wasn't around.

"So our party just gonna stop the minute she comes here, Pyro?" Dior asked him with her lips twisted up.

"Say what?" Pyro questioned. "Why the sudden attitude?"

"I'm just saying, we were chilling and doing us, and now you actin' funny because she's here."

Dior glared at Chanel, sizing her up. She knew the type. Dior despised Chanel's soft voice, how she never kept direct eye contact, and how she was always cooking and cleaning for Pyro. The docile, humble persona that Chanel projected was just an act in Dior's eyes, and she was irked that Pyro didn't see it.

Chanel lowered her head a touch. "I'm sorry. I didn't mean to start any trouble between y'all. I'll be in my bedroom," she said, walking away from them.

"Ain't no need to be sorry, Chanel." Pyro's eyes lingered on Chanel walking away.

Dior peeped it. "Why your eyes more on her than me?"

"She's a friend, and she's been through a lot in the past few months, Dior. Her man, my nigga, is fucked up in the hospital and we're both tryin' to be there for him, and I'm tryin' to be there for her because it's what Mateo would want me to do. I ain't got time for your fuckin' jealousy," Pyro barked.

"Jealousy?" Dior screamed. "Nigga, how long you knew me? When have I ever been jealous?"

"You know what? Just leave."

Dior looked shocked. "What?"

"Just get out!"

"Are you serious?"

"Yeah, like cancer."

"Look, you're being extra right now. I didn't mean to overreact," Dior explained. "I just wanted us to spend some quality time together."

"Yeah, well that can happen some other time. I got shit to do anyway," he replied unemotionally.

"Really? You got shit to do after I done fucked you?"

"Listen, I'm not tryin' to argue with you or be an asshole. You need to leave, though," he said sternly to her.

Dior didn't want to leave, but Pyro rushed her out the door while she tried her best to do everything to stay. But his mind was made up. Besides, she wasn't really his girlfriend.

With Dior finally gone, Pyro went to Chanel's bedroom door and knocked. He was curious about what *later* news she wanted to tell him. She opened her door and smiled. Once again, she started to apologize for interrupting his quality time with Dior.

"I'm so sorry, Pyro. I didn't mean to start any trouble . . ."

"Nah, you good, Chanel. Everything's good. You didn't start any trouble," he said with a smile. "I wanted her to leave anyway."

Chanel came out of the bedroom and into the common area. She was still cheerful about something.

"What was it you wanted to tell me?" he asked her.

"Good news. He's dead. God is dead. My mother called and told me this morning," she stated.

It was astonishing news, but Pyro felt ambivalent about it. He wanted to be the one to tell Mateo that he had killed Fingers and God. Still, he was glad that the rapist was dead. Killing one out of two wasn't bad.

"I can go home now," Chanel said. "He can't hurt me again."

Home. She was right about God not posing a threat to her anymore. But there was one thing he felt she was forgetting. Charlie. He had become Chanel's protector, and he didn't want her in the same apartment with Charlie, the mastermind. Pyro felt that bitch was a wicked sociopath to set her own sister up to get robbed and raped by her own boyfriend, and then make her live through the trauma of her fiancé being shot in the head. Charlie was more ruthless than any bitch Pyro had encountered before.

He stared at Chanel with some concern. "Maybe you shouldn't rush to go back home. I would feel more comfortable if you stayed here until Mateo gets better. And then y'all can both move on with your lives."

"You're worried about Charlie, right?"

"That bitch is wicked, Chanel. Sister or not, you can't trust her, and she needs to get got."

"Pyro, promise me that you won't do anything to her," Chanel said, locking eyes with Pyro.

"You still want her breathing after what she did to you?"

"She's still my sister, and I don't want any blood spilled in my name."

Pyro didn't want to make her that promise, but Chanel continued to hold his gaze and he could only relent. "I promise you that I won't touch that evil bitch."

Chapter Eight

The hotel in Midtown Manhattan had quickly turned into Charlie's place of business. Working with two cell phones, she had merchandise to move and connections to reach out to. She called a few frenemies to see if one of them could pick her up in the city and run her around to do her errands. She paced around the hotel room with her cell phone glued to her ear and talking a mile a minute—trying to run game on someone to help do her bidding.

Unfortunately, one by one, each person she reached out to gave her a chilly reception and blew her off.

"Nah, I'm good, Charlie. Word around town is that you bad news right now," one of them said.

"What the fuck you mean, I'm bad news?" she yapped back.

"I'm just sayin', you hot right now." He hung up.

Charlie stood there dumbfounded by his remarks. She didn't know what was up, but she figured it had to do with how she and God had fallen off lately. She was no longer up to putting her used hooptie in the shop or waiting on anything because she had money now. She had room to breathe and stretch out her legs with eighty large. She thought about renting a car, but she liked the perks of being driven around, especially through rush hour traffic. But it wasn't looking promising. Every person she called had something negative to say.

Fuck it! Charlie said to herself. She decided to Uber around town. Time was money and money was time.

Charlie carefully secured every bit of cash into the rolling luggage. She left the room, leaving Claire in bed under the covers without saying goodbye.

When the Uber driver arrived downstairs, she got into the backseat with her things and right away asked him, "How much would it cost me to rent you for the day? Flat fee."

The driver, a young and clean-shaven white male turned around. Charlie knew he was sizing her up. He replied with, "Fifteen hundred, plus tolls."

Charlie laughed at his ridiculous price. "You gotta be a fuckin' comedian," she mocked, followed by tossing him ten dollars for his time.

"Get lost!" she added, climbing out the backseat.

Everyone was a crook.

Charlie sighed. First things first, she needed to secure the cash. She walked to the nearest Chase bank to open a safety deposit box. The bank wasn't too busy in the early morning. She met with a bank representative and filled out the necessary paperwork, and he escorted her to a private vault. She kept out four thousand for expenses and stashed the rest of her newfound fortune in several safety deposit boxes without any questions or raised eyebrows. To everyone inside the bank, she was a casual businesswoman looking to protect her assets.

Next, she went to the bank teller and paid her Chase credit card bill, which would include the hotel fee, and subsequently dropped $500 on her debit card. There wasn't much pocket money left, but it was more than she'd had in a long time. She wondered how Claire was going to feel about not having access to the money. It was a thought that was short-lived. Charlie didn't give a fuck how Claire felt. It was her money and she kept things moving.

She marched back to the hotel and went into the room to find Claire just as she had left her—lying in bed, moping, and doing nothing. Charlie glanced at her sister but didn't ask if she was hungry or anything. Charlie didn't have the time, nor did she want to console her sister. She was in business mode, and she wasn't about to let Claire hold her back.

Charlie pulled out her cell phone and decided to call her favorite client, Mona. A few rings later, Mona answered her phone.

"You busy? I got some really nice shit for you to check out."

"If it's worth my time, come through."

"It's definitely worth your time," Charlie guaranteed.

"Cool. Meet me at place. You got the address, right?"

"No doubt."

Charlie smiled. Money. Money. Money. That's what it was about—making money and lots of it. She was a one-woman show—the headliner who attracted the crowd. Charlie had a ton of stuff to profit from, and she was ready to eat like a hungry, hungry hippo.

She called for another car. She was eager to get to Mona's place and show her everything she had for sale. Mona was good peoples, someone Charlie could rely on to help unload her merchandise. With two suitcases of shoes, jewelry, designer shades, and fashionable clothes with the tags still attached, Charlie estimated cost was at least over thirty thousand dollars. She was willing to sell everything to Mona at a huge discount.

The ride to Westchester County was pleasant. The cab came to a stop in front of a friendly looking two-story house on the peaceful, suburban street. The white vinyl house had a fire engine red door with a brass lion's head doorknob. Parked in the driveway was a burgundy BMW with tinted windows. The area was a direct contrast to Brooklyn. Charlie liked the manicured lawns and ornamented porches and front steps.

After she removed her two suitcases from the backseat and paid the driver his fare, Charlie strolled toward the front door and knocked. The front door opened, and the first thing that stood out on Mona was the NYPD badge attached to her hip along with her holstered weapon—a Glock 19. She smiled at Charlie and invited her inside.

"So what you got for me?" Mona asked, ready to get down to business.

"Shit that's gonna have muthafuckas envious of you," replied Charlie.

Charlie took a quick survey of Mona's place, and the woman had the best that money could buy. In Mona's living room was one of the largest flat screen TV's Charlie had ever seen—an 80-inch. The décor in the living room was topnotch with a leather sectional, a distinguished coffee table, a pricey area rug, and modern artwork. Lying on the sectional was some shirtless thug—probably some nigga Mona was fucking. It wasn't Charlie's business.

Mona was a detective at the 77th Precinct in Brooklyn. She was in her late thirties and grew up in the Gowanus Houses in Brooklyn. Mona was a tough and streetwise woman who had seen it all and been through it all. She had two sons who were being raised by her mother in the Bronx, and she had just finished recovering from a fat transfer to her ass and a tummy tuck. Her waist was now snatched and you could balance a bottle on her round, protruding ass. She called it her mommy makeover. Her peers at the precinct called it a mid-life crisis, but the hustlers and thugs called Mona their Serena Williams. Though she was a cop, her friends were boosters, cokeheads, thugs, and some of the grimiest niggas from the streets. She was known around the way to be a down-ass bitch for a cop. Mona had a thing for bad boys, and those same niggas loved that she had a badge.

"You got time, right?" asked Charlie.

"Bitch, I wouldn't have told you to come over if I didn't," Mona said.

Charlie placed the two suitcases on the floor near Mona's feet and unzipped them both. Mona's eyes lit up with delight. "Damn, bitch! Who you robbed, Kim Kardashian?"

"Damn near," Charlie joked.

Mona started going through the items like a fat kid in a candy factory. She already knew that she wanted it all. She loved fashion and what Charlie presented was high-quality shit.

"Fuck it, how much for everything?" asked Mona.

"For real, you want it all?"

"Bitch, didn't I just ask you that?" she mocked.

"I got you. For everything, give me seventy-two hundred."

"Good."

Charlie beamed. Mona never disappointed. She remained in the living room while Mona disappeared into another room. So far, Charlie was turning her tragedy into a profit. She was a natural-born hustler and she wanted to pat herself on the back. There weren't too many people who could get grimy with it and survive by any means necessary like she could.

Mona came back into the room and handed Charlie a wad of cash, mostly hundreds and fifties. While Charlie counted it, Mona started to remove everything from the suitcases, but Charlie said to her, "Yo, you can keep the suitcases, too."

Charlie wasn't about to drag back any empty suitcases to the city.

Accomplished is what Charlie felt after the transaction with Mona. She was $7,200 richer. She felt unstoppable. She briefly thought how Mona's place would be the perfect lick if she ever became desperate. Charlie subtly took an inventory and it was a pretty penny. But it wouldn't be easy, though. Mona was a tough, cautious, and shrewd bitch, and she kept either a .357 or a .45 at arm's length, plus her holstered Glock. Mona was one of a small few that Charlie knew not to even think about fucking with.

Climbing into the backseat of the Uber, Charlie wondered where Mona was coming up with so much cash, especially being on a cop's salary.

Charlie walked into the hotel room carrying Chinese takeout and feeling like a million bucks. She realized that Claire hadn't eaten anything in almost twenty-four hours, and if her sister didn't eat, she was going to die.

Claire looked comatose on the bed. It looked like she was spaced out and didn't care to live at all. Charlie had grown annoyed about her sister's behavior. She had seen enough. She marched toward Claire scowling and angrily pulled away the covers from her body.

"Claire, this shit needs to stop right now. What the fuck is wrong wit' you?"

"You know what's wrong with me!" Claire snapped back.

"She was nobody to you—nothing! That bitch looked down on us, and you lying here feeling sorry for her."

"What did we do, Charlie? What did we do?"

"We got paid! That's what we did," Charlie shouted. "Shit, we were getting our asses kicked out there. I did something about it. And besides, we ain't do shit but get kicked out an apartment. So don't start running your mouth off 'bout sumthin' that ain't happened."

Claire's expressionless gaze lingered on her sister. "You believe that, don't you?"

"Yes. I believe it. She's not dead, Claire."

"She's not?" Claire then asked incredulously.

"No. So you think I'm a monster?"

"I don't know what you are."

"I'm your sister and I didn't kill your friend. She's fucked up, but she's good," Charlie continued to lie.

The look on Claire's face spoke something odd to Charlie. Her little sister was bugging. Did she really believe that she didn't murder Melanie? If so, Claire was funny-farm crazy. But Charlie went along with the program. She was willing to do and say whatever it took to bring some life back into Claire and to get her eating and drinking again.

Little by little, Claire started to eat and drink something. Charlie continued to keep her little sister company, mostly monitoring her every move. Claire reached for the remote control and turned to a movie on HBO. After a while, the crazy delusion she had sold to Claire seemed to be wearing off.

Charlie wondered when Claire officially lost her mind. Was it the cheating scandal? Was it the fact that she pretended to be someone that she wasn't for all those years? Were the clues somewhere in their childhood? Claire had a case of Kanye West, spewing to everyone how much of a genius she was until she got exposed.

Either Claire would prove to be a crazy genius like Van Gogh, or she would become a psycho bitch and hurt those around her like Charles Manson. Whatever the outcome of Claire's state, Charlie was still going to get paid and do her.

Chapter Nine

The city was alive with the early afternoon sunshine on what was turning out to be a beautiful October day. Chanel climbed out of the cab on Amsterdam Avenue on the west side of the city and took in the scenery. It felt good being outside and not having to look over her shoulder anymore. She was in that part of town to meet with Mecca. Chanel wanted her life to get back to normal again, and that meant seeing Mecca in public.

Mecca had gotten a full scholarship to Columbia University, and everyone was extremely proud and happy for her, including Chanel. She always knew her friend could do it. She had what it took to succeed. Mecca had a stable home environment. She was focused and smart, and she knew what she wanted out of life.

The two decided to meet up at a local eatery close to the university to catch up on things. Chanel walked into the quaint restaurant with a full bar and mostly undergraduates taking time out from their studies. Chanel joined Mecca at the outdoor patio, knowing warm days like this were becoming far and few between.

"Hey girl!" Mecca excitedly hollered at Chanel.

The two girls hugged for a moment and started to praise each other.

"You look good, Chanel."

"Thanks. And so do you."

"I'm so glad that you finally came out."

"Shit. I needed some time out. It feels good," said Chanel.

"I know it does. But I got you, everything's on me."

"No, that's not right—"

"Listen, after everything you've been through, it's the least I can do," Mecca said with finality.

Chanel smiled. She didn't argue with her friend. They took a seat at the round table and ordered some drinks. Right away, the laughter, the gossip, and the enjoyment of seeing each other took over. Mecca started to tell Chanel about her experiences in college.

"I love it here, Chanel. It's perfect for me."

"I bet it is."

"And I'm thinking about joining a sorority," Mecca said, taking a sip of her Coke.

"Are you serious?"

"Yeah, they have connections, especially after you graduate. Girl, I can't wait for you to enroll into college. Maybe we can join the same sorority," Mecca said with enthusiasm.

But Chanel didn't feel the same enthusiasm in attending college and joining a sorority like her friend. She wasn't ready to get back into the public and focus on college yet, not until Mateo was better.

"You're gonna love college, Chanel. You'll see," Mecca added.

"Your major is communications, right?"

"Business and communications."

Chanel smiled. "That's what's up."

"But enough about me. How's Mateo doing?"

"He's doing so much better, Mecca. I mean, every day is a battle, but Mateo is a warrior and the progress he's made these past few weeks is phenomenal," Chanel happily stated. "He's talking in a low, raspy voice and his physical therapist is pushing him hard to get his coordination back. It's just a matter of time."

"I'm so glad to hear that. Ohmygod, I want to see you happy, Chanel. You and Mateo, y'all are like the perfect couple. I adored y'all two together."

"We're getting there."

The two ordered their food, and their waiter, Joseph, was mad cool. Mecca and Chanel both had the chicken melt, and before they knew it, it was almost time for Mecca's next class.

"Girl, I gotta go. I can't be late for class," said Mecca, lifting herself from her chair and preparing to pay for their meals.

She pulled out a fifty-dollar bill and placed it onto the table. It would cover the check and a healthy tip for Joseph.

"How are you getting back home?" asked Mecca.

"Pyro is picking me up."

Mecca looked shocked by the news. "Pyro?" she questioned with a raised eyebrow.

"Yes. I'm staying with him temporarily," Chanel informed her.

"Oh really?"

"Nothing like that, Mecca. He's simply a friend looking out for me right now, that's all."

"Okay. I'm not judging you. I thought you were still at a hotel."

"It became too expensive."

The girls exited the eatery just in time to see Pyro arriving in his sleek Benz. He pulled to the curb and got out of the car with a smile.

"Y'all two ladies good?" he asked.

"Yeah, we're fine, Pyro," Mecca returned with a warm smile his way. "It's good to see you again."

"Likewise," said Pyro.

"I didn't know you were looking after my girl like that. That's what's up."

"You already know. She's family."

"Yes. She is," Mecca replied.

She couldn't stop grinning and flirting with Pyro. He came through in his classy CLK Benz with his diamonds glistening and a fresh haircut under a dark blue Yankees fitted. He looked like money.

Pyro hadn't planned on staying in the city long, but he took one look at Mecca and decided to change his plans. The young college student was looking extra sexy in her autumn attire. The apple bottom she carried in those tight jeans was calling out to him. When she started talking about Columbia University, it piqued his interest.

"So, what you been up to lately, Pyro?" Mecca asked him.

"Busy . . . taking care of business," he replied.

"I can see that." She grinned.

He smiled.

It didn't take a rocket scientist to see that there was some chemistry building between the two of them. Yes, Pyro and Mateo were drug dealers, but they were also smart young men and shrewd investors who wanted to build a legitimate empire.

"Listen, I need to use the bathroom before we leave," Chanel chimed.

She turned and went back into the eatery, giving Pyro and Mecca some time alone. When she returned, it was time for them to leave. Mecca and Chanel both promised to speak more. Hugs were exchanged.

Pyro and Chanel climbed into his Benz, but before they pulled off, Mecca said to Chanel, "Call me." They left for home, while Mecca headed back to the university, knowing she was going to be late for class. It was worth it.

Chapter Ten

Bacardi sat by the kitchen window staring down at the street below her, watching the interactions of drug dealers and drug fiends on the block, along with the comings and goings of residents from her building. She liked some of them, but there were a whole lot of people she wanted to slap. It was no secret about what happened to Chanel and who was responsible for it. The gossip was spreading rapidly from block to block like an airborne disease.

Bacardi sipped on her glass of spiced rum with a heavy mind. She and Butch were dead broke and rent was due next week. With their three breadwinners out of the apartment and the both of them not working, money was nonexistent. She needed to do something.

It took everything in her not to call Chanel to see if she had any money to lend them. She definitely wasn't calling the two bitches who had the nerve to put their hands on her—especially that sneaky bitch Claire. Bacardi never expected that from Claire. Charlie wore who she was on her sleeve, as did Chanel. But Bacardi believed Claire to be a sneaky-ass Scorpio, and she still fumed about Claire hiding what she knew about the assault. She itched to jump on her crazy-ass daughter for that shit.

She downed the spiced rum and poured herself another glass. Butch sat at the kitchen table looking gloomy himself. It looked like he had aged a decade in the past few weeks.

"What we gon' do, Bernice?"

"I don't know, Butch. I'm still tryin' to come up wit' something. Shit!"

"It needs to be quick. We broke."

She picked up her glass and slammed it back down on the table. "You think I don't fuckin' know that? Muthafucka, I'm sittin' in the same fuckin' apartment as you, goin' through the same muthafuckin' problems."

"What about them clothes in the closet?"

"What about them?"

"They gotta be worth something, right?"

Bacardi scowled at the thought of it. She wanted them for herself. She thought she would wake up one day fifty pounds lighter and twenty years younger and be able to wear it all.

Butch pleaded with her to do the right thing. "Our only option is to start selling them clothes, Bernice. Our hands are tied."

She knew he was right. The clothing she kept would most likely pay their rent for a year and then some.

"Fuck it. I'll sell 'em off," she relented.

Bacardi got on her cell phone and called one of Charlie's old friends, Wanda. She was a pickpocket and a booster, and Bacardi told her about the items she had for sale. Wanda told her that she would be over there on the first thing smoking. She knew that Bacardi calling her meant two things were true—she had some expensive shit and then there was some dirt to hear.

It was early evening when Wanda knocked on the apartment door. Bacardi swung it open and smiled at Charlie's friend.

"I brought some gifts," said Wanda, holding up two blunts.

"My kind of bitch," replied Bacardi with a grin.

The two sat in the living room smoking and drinking, and business was put on hold as they talked, got high, and sipped on brown juice.

Wanda told her about the rumors she had heard floating around about Charlie and Chanel. Even high, Bacardi didn't want to talk about it. She made a mental note to beat that little white bitch Landy down for spreading gossip about her family.

As the two were finishing off the bottle of Hennessy, Wanda continued to press the issue about Chanel and Charlie. She wanted the inside scoop. She had gotten comfortable with Bacardi, calling her Momma B, and she stayed for hours. Finally, Bacardi opened up and started to spill the beans about what happened.

"Charlie's a foul fuckin' bitch," she muttered.

"That bitch is," Wanda agreed.

"Everything is fuckin' true, Wanda. My own daughters are fucked up, and now God was killed by some bitch. I got fuckin' detectives comin' to my door with questions about his murder and gonna want me and Butch to identify that muthafucka's body. Dem fools must be crazy, after what he did to our daughter," Bacardi slurred.

It was all news to Wanda. She was getting all the tea.

"Charlie always been a foul bitch, Momma B, real talk. The only reason I ain't go after that bitch after the shit she did to me is because I got respect for you," Wanda proclaimed.

"And I always thought y'all were friends."

"If she's a friend, I would hate to see my enemies."

"That bitch ain't got no friends."

"She sure don't. But anyway, I'm ready to see what you got for me, Momma B."

"I damn near forgot that I called you here for business. Bitch, you got me high and running my mouth," Bacardi joked.

"It's because we're cool like that." Wanda smiled.

Maybe, Bacardi thought. Though she was high and tipsy, she was still on her guard and about her business.

Bacardi removed herself from the couch and disappeared from the living room for a moment. Wanda sat there and took another pull from the blunt, her eyes like slits from the potent weed.

Bacardi came back into the living room tugging multiple black garbage bags. She dumped everything out onto the floor for Wanda to look at. The tags were still on the clothes, the shoes were topnotch, and the belts, earrings, and bracelets were high-quality.

"Shit! Charlie left all this shit behind?"

"Bitch ain't leave shit behind. I *took* her shit," Bacardi corrected.

Wanda grinned. "I know she was mad."

"And? Like I give a fuck 'bout that bitch's feelings."

Wanda loved it. She took a look at the clothes and said to Bacardi, "I definitely have some clients for these clothes. I can have everything sold by the morning."

"You serious?"

She nodded. "Yup! Charlie always had the best shit. The people I know will eat this shit up."

Bacardi grinned. It was music to her ears.

They started to place everything back into the trash bags. Wanda was eager to leave with the merchandise and get down to business—maybe too eager. Before she could step foot out of the living room, Bacardi grabbed her arm, her grip like a vise. Her fixed stare at Wanda meant that what she was about to say was serious.

"You better not fuck me over, Wanda, cuz I swear, I'll fuckin' find you and fuck you up so bad that ya own mama won't recognize ya ass. You understand me?"

Wanda nodded submissively. She understood.

Bacardi's tightened jaw transformed into a smile. "Ok then, girl. I'll see ya tomorrow!" Bacardi released her tight grip from Wanda's arm and allowed her to leave with the expensive merchandise.

Chapter Eleven

I'm not gonna lie, Chanel, you can definitely cook your ass off," Pyro said as he devoured a thick slice of her French toast.

Chanel smiled. "I'm glad you like my cooking."

"I love it. I'm mad at myself for missing out all this time. Damn, this is almost better than sex," he joked.

Chanel laughed. "You're so silly."

Pyro finished off his plate and made himself a second helping of French toast, sausage patties, and scrambled eggs. Pyro had started eating Chanel's breakfast on the regular and was making it home for her dinners. He had fallen in love with her cooking. Someone to cook for, shelter, and conversation—it was what Chanel needed.

That night, Pyro stuffed his face with spare ribs, macaroni and cheese, cornbread, and string beans. It felt like he was about to gain fifty pounds. Chanel had made his bachelor pad into a home with her home cooked meals and laughter between them. But behind the smiles, the cooking, and the joyous conversation, he was worried about her.

Pyro looked at Chanel and genuinely asked, "You ever thought about going to see a therapist?"

"A therapist? Why?"

"You know, to talk and let shit out. You've been through a lot, Chanel, and I want you to be okay. I don't want you to stress yourself."

"I'm fine, Pyro."

"It's good to see that you're going out in public and doing you, but I want you to get active in something. You need to keep yourself busy. You ever thought about applying to college?"

"Honestly, I'm not ready for college. I just wanna take care of Mateo right now."

"That's cool. But Mateo would want you to function at your highest level. I know you care about him, but you still gotta live your life, Chanel."

He wanted her to succeed, not just let days go by waiting on Mateo to make a full recovery.

"You care too much. You know that, Pyro?"

"I'm supposed to care. You're family, and it's what Mateo would want me to do."

"I know, and I will do that—live my life when the time comes. But my main priority is Mateo. He's been there for me and now I need to be there for him."

"No doubt. And if you don't want to see a therapist, then you know you can talk to me about anything. I can be your ear, and I won't charge you a hundred dollars an hour," he joked.

She laughed. "Oh, you would be that expensive?"

"Shit, for listening to peoples' problems on a regular and then having to deal with your own shit afterwards, a nigga better charge a hefty fee."

"Well, black people don't go to therapy; they go to church," she teased.

"Shit, with some of the churches and pastors they got out here today, there's more shit going on in there than in the streets."

Chanel laughed. "I know, right?"

Pyro patted his stomach.

"You want some more?" she asked him.

"Yo, you trying to fatten me up or something? You gonna have me wobbling instead of walking."

"Maybe you need to gain some weight."

"Okay, I see your plan—feed me and feed me and make me unattractive so that you can have me all to yourself." He laughed.

She swatted him away. "You wish."

Their joking and merry conversation continued into the living room. They played cards and Pyro's favorite, backgammon, and grubbed on some munchies.

In the middle of a game of rummy, Chanel said, "You're right, Pyro."

"About what?"

"About me getting out there more and maybe applying to some colleges."

He smiled. "Now that's what I like to hear. Mateo would be proud."

"Yeah. He would."

Nights with Pyro were fun. When he was home, it seemed like time flew by for Chanel. He was good company and she appreciated that he was taking the time out to make sure she was okay.

"You're a nice guy, Pyro. So when are you gonna find you a really nice girl to hold you down?" she said.

"It's crazy out there. It's hard to find a shorty with a good head on her shoulders."

"They're out there."

He raised an eyebrow. "Maybe she'll come along unexpectedly," he replied.

"She will."

Pyro came strolling into Mateo's room just after 2pm the next day carrying a small leather duffel bag. Mateo was watching college basketball—Duke versus North Carolina—and Pyro immediately felt nostalgic. His missed his best friend. As soon as Mateo saw him, his eyes lit up as they gave each other dap.

"What's up? You lookin' better," Pyro cheerily announced.

Mateo struggled to sit up straight. Unassisted, he gripped the handrails on his twin bed and propped himself up. Both knew that Pyro was forbidden to help per the instructions from Kyle, the physical therapist.

Finally, Mateo replied, "I'm good. I'm stronger."

"I see that," Pyro agreed. "But you lookin' a little rough. You scarin' all the women."

Mateo grinned, and his hand slowly went up and touched his facial hair. Since the incident, his short hair had grown into a small man bun, and he was sporting a full beard and mustache. Pyro opened his duffel, where he kept his clippers. He wanted to cut off Mateo's locks and remove all his facial hair.

Mateo watched Pyro like a hawk and quickly noticed that he didn't add a comb to his clippers.

"I'ma give you a quick buzz cut, and when you get outta here Bolo gonna hook you—"

Pyro couldn't finish his sentence before Mateo was shaking his head. "No, leave it."

Pyro stood with the trimmers in his hand looking perplexed. "Bruh, why I'm here then?"

Mateo didn't answer right away. Sometimes it took longer than usual to reply to questions as his brain searched to form his sentences. He knew what he wanted to say, but it was like he had to line his words up and then spit them out. Eventually, he replied, "Just hit my edges and sideburns and shave this beard off."

"Have you seen ya hair?" Pyro pulled out a hand mirror and handed it to Mateo. "You lookin' a little metro wit' that girl bun."

Mateo heard Pyro loud and clear, but he was too busy checking out his reflection. "Chanel likes it."

Pyro chuckled. "Whatever, man."

As Pyro tightened up Mateo's hairline, he was stopped every few minutes. Mateo kept taking mirror breaks to make sure he wasn't fucking it up.

"C'mon, Miss America!" Pyro joked. "I got this."

The two conversed about their business, the stock market, and how Chanel was progressing while Pyro's sharp razor and steady hands shaved off Mateo's beard. When he was done, he felt like he had surpassed his own expectations. He handed Mateo the mirror and then stood back to admire his handiwork. The man bun, sideburns, and mustache worked for him. His soft, jet-black hair, chiseled jaw line, and thick eyebrows made him look like a different dude, Pyro thought. Still thuggish, but not street.

"Damn, you pretty," he admonished. "You might be onto something wit' this hair shit."

"They all gonna want me, Pyro," Mateo bragged. "But my heart belongs to one woman."

"Shit, give 'em to me then."

Pyro stayed well past ten that night. He got them dinner and came back, but the staff had to insist that he leave once they realized that he had sneaked in a bottle of Hennessy, even though Mateo didn't partake in the brown juice.

Pyro promised Mateo he would come back in a couple of days. Leaving was always bittersweet.

Chapter Twelve

*C*harlie was feeling like her old self again—getting that money and not giving a fuck. She took the initiative to get her shit together. One week at the hotel was a full month's rent in some neighborhoods. So, early one morning she went out apartment hunting. What Charlie wanted was a place that would rival Melanie's and Chanel's. She wanted something to show off. It didn't take her long to find something in Clinton Hill not too far from Melanie's place, which was a bold move. It was a one-bedroom within her price range. After Charlie provided her with fraudulent information and a sizable cash down payment, the landlord was happy to hand over the keys to the place.

"Enjoy it," said the landlord.

Charlie smiled. "Believe me, I will."

Right away, Charlie started decorating the place with a woman's touch, wanting so badly to emulate Melanie.

Claire was dumbfounded that Charlie had gotten them an apartment, and in the same neighborhood where Melanie lived—or used to live. Whatever she believed.

"Are you serious, Charlie? Here?"

"Why not? I like the area. Besides, we ain't got shit to hide, right?"

Claire stared at her sister with that continued bewilderment. It looked like she was hesitant to walk into their new apartment.

Charlie was in no mood to deal with her sister's strange and crazy behavior. "Claire, this is something new for us, so don't be bringing that crazy shit up in here. Okay? The past is the past, so let it be. I found us this place so we can live in peace. If you not wit' that, then you ain't gotta move in wit' me. Go be on your own."

Charlie gave her a tour. The apartment would have been perfect except Claire was expected to sleep on the pullout sofa.

"Where's my room?"

Charlie sucked her teeth. "Claire, don't start ya shit."

"How am I starting? You got a room, right? Shouldn't I have one too? I'm grown, Charlie. I need my personal space."

"I got what I could afford. Your selfish ass should be happy I'm puttin' a roof over your head."

In almost a whisper, Claire said, "I want my own room, Charlie."

"We all want things, Claire. You get what I give you! And right now I could only afford one bedroom."

"But I work. I can pay my share."

"Uggggh, I can't anymore. You're so selfish. I've been sacrificing for you, Chanel, Bacardi, and Butch all my life making sure the bills were paid, and this is how you thank me? You whine about something so fuckin' petty!"

"You actin' like you raised me! And let's not pretend that you'd have any of that money if it weren't for me. I brought you to Melanie. That was me!" Claire hit her own chest with force and had a deranged look in her eyes, which were quickly darting left to right. The murder of her schoolmate was weighing heavily on her. Charlie got spooked for a moment. Her sister seemed like a nut, able to snap at any second. But Charlie knew she couldn't show fear to loony people.

"Okay, listen. I'm already locked into this lease for a year. When the lease is up we can get a two-bedroom, and if you ever want to sleep in my room that's cool."

Having nowhere else to go, Claire acquiesced to her sister's compromise.

Charlie didn't give Claire any of the money that she had killed for, and Claire went back to her life of school and work to keep herself busy. She needed to keep herself from going insane. But at school, her classmates were broken up about what had happened to Melanie; the news of her gruesome death had spread like wildfire. While students and staff were heartbroken, Claire remained quiet and aloof.

While Claire was dealing with the grief at her school, Charlie grew angrier each day about her parents not calling her to apologize and to give her back her expensive shit. Bacardi had no right to keep any of her things. And then she heard from an unlikely person.

"Who the fuck is this?"

"Hi, Charlie. This is Landy."

Charlie smirked. "Landy? What the fuck you want?"

"I was trying to get in contact with Wanda."

"Wanda? Then why the fuck you hittin' my jack? You know I don't fuck wit' that bitch."

"Really? That's odd."

"Odd? Bitch, what the fuck do you want!" Charlie roared

"Well I don't have much money, but my parents gave me a hundred dollars to buy the red bottom sneakers you're letting Wanda and Bacardi sell for you."

"Bacardi got Wanda selling my shit?"

"You didn't know?"

"Bye, girl."

So Bacardi was selling her good shit. Her mother had disrespected her, and Charlie couldn't swallow that kind of disrespect. She was ready to confront her mother and pop off.

The next day, Charlie got out of the cab in her old neighborhood and marched into her old building with a heavy scowl like she was a soldier ready for war. She left Claire at home. Charlie didn't need her sister holding her back or trying to give her a conscience. She wanted to handle their mother on her own. She stepped into the pissy elevator and pushed for the fourth floor. She rode it silence, bubbling like a volcano. She was ready to spread her destruction like hot molten lava.

She rushed toward her mother's apartment door with her hands clenched into tight fists. She was on a mission to get her shit back, even if it meant beating her mother down.

"This disrespectful bitch," she growled to herself.

She banged on the apartment door like she was the police, knowing it would get her mother's attention and piss her off. Moments later, the door flung open with Bacardi looming into Charlie's view.

"Bitch, what the fuck is wrong wit' you banging on my got-damn door like that!" Bacardi shouted.

"Where my fuckin' shit?! I want all my shit back, you triflin'-ass bitch!" Charlie retorted.

"I know you ain't come here for *my* shit, bitch. You better leave from this fuckin' door 'fore I beat yo ass down again," Bacardi shouted.

Bacardi's eyes shot around the hallway, and she saw that her oldest daughter had come alone. Of course, Claire didn't have the balls to handle another confrontation with her.

"I ain't goin' no-fuckin'-where until I get all my shit back," Charlie shouted. "You out here tryin' to sell my shit."

"Yo shit? Once it's in my place, it becomes *my* shit!"

"Fuck you! Ain't shit belong to you," Charlie screamed.

Charlie was seeing red. In her eyes, it wasn't her mother that she was arguing with; it was a foul, disrespectful bitch. Their argument echoed through the apartment and the hallway. It was looking like round two between mother and daughter was about to start. They both were ready for the conflict—ready to tear each other apart.

"You dumb bitch, get the fuck away from my door!"

"I ain't goin' any-fuckin'-where until I get my shit back!"

While they argued in the doorway, Charlie glanced past her belligerent mother and noticed something odd. There was some pretty, young bitch walking back and forth like she lived there. She was wearing a long, white T-shirt and leggings, and she stood in the middle of the living room staring with bafflement as Charlie argued with her mother like they were strangers on the street.

Unbeknownst to Charlie, Bacardi had gone online and listed the two bedrooms for rent. It was against the housing authority's rules, but everyone was doing it. Bacardi was surprised by how quickly she started receiving messages from potential tenants. So many people were looking for a cheap and reasonable place to stay. Bacardi could have rented both rooms, but she was selective, or prejudiced, or both and then some. She only wanted pretty girls—black women, no whites allowed. She told Butch this, and he agreed.

The women had to be fly like her daughters and represent. Once Bacardi got the second room rented, she and Butch could live like retirees, and they were both just in their forties.

But Bacardi's plan didn't sit too well with Charlie.

"Who the fuck is that bitch?" Charlie growled.

"She's none of ya fuckin' business," Bacardi shouted back.

Charlie was about to lose it. "I know you ain't got that bitch up in here sleeping in my fuckin' bed, the same bed that God and I paid for!"

They cursed each other some more, and then the elevator chimed. Charlie couldn't believe who stepped out of it. She stood there in shock, feeling like she was outnumbered.

Chapter Thirteen

*C*hanel and Pyro sat in his Benz outside the project building on another beautiful autumn day. Chanel felt antsy about being back in her old neighborhood. It had been a long while since she had been back to the projects. There were so many memories she wanted to forget.

Pyro promised her that he had her back and wasn't going to let anything happen to her as long as he lived. Still, Chanel looked a bit on edge.

"Look, we don't have to go up there," Pyro said.

"I need to a get few important things. I've waited too long," she said.

"Well, I'm ready when you are."

She nodded and smiled at Pyro. He had become her protective angel, and she didn't know where she would be without him.

The two climbed out of the Benz and walked toward the lobby. Chanel moved with her head held up high, feeling like she could take on anything right now. She was different. She looked and walked differently. The meekness and low self-esteem that once ruled her was long gone.

Pyro allowed Chanel to step into the elevator first, and the stench of urine was something she did not miss.

"Nasty muthafuckas," Pyro griped at the smell. "Niggas ain't got no fuckin' home training. Like, who the fuck takes a piss in the elevator?"

Chanel pressed for the fourth floor and they rode up in silence. Moments later, the doors opened to the commotion in the hallway. Seeing Charlie arguing with Bacardi made Chanel stop and frown. She wasn't expecting Charlie to be there, but she wasn't about to run from her sister. Things done changed.

Hateful glares were exchanged between the sisters. Charlie's angry attention quickly shifted from Bacardi to Chanel. Charlie was overtaken with jealousy and embarrassment. Chanel looked good. In fact, she looked better than ever.

How? Charlie thought.

Her nigga was almost dead—or brain dead—and still, Chanel looked like she could walk the runway at a fashion show. Her outfit looked like she had money, and her hair was long and sensuous, flowing down her back. Seeing her with Pyro triggered something in Charlie.

"So, you fuckin' him now?" Charlie spewed with contempt. "Y'all gettin' off the elevator all boo'd up!"

Pyro stood in front of Chanel protectively with his eyes narrowed into angry slits. He was ready to slap the shit outta Charlie.

"Leave her alone, Charlie. You fuckin' done enough!" Bacardi yelled from the doorway.

"Apparently, I didn't," Charlie replied in a gloating, antagonistic manner.

Her words stung like a thousand bees. Chanel furiously fixed her eyes on her older sister and something came over her—a feeling that possessed her like a raging hell. She eased from around Pyro's protection like a panther on the hunt and abruptly pounced on Charlie with ferocity. She punched Charlie so hard in the mouth that her head jerked back.

It was on!

Chanel viciously punched her sister again and again, but Charlie wasn't going down without a fight. She swung back with a fierce jab, striking

Chanel, but Chanel wasn't that weak and meek little sister anymore. One hit wasn't about to intimidate her. They fought pound for pound, cursing, yelling, and carrying on.

"You fucked up, bitch!" Charlie shouted.

Charlie thought she was going to get the best of Chanel. She believed that she had more experience and more rage, but she underestimated her baby sister. Chanel's anger was nuclear. A right hook to the side of Charlie's face stunned her and she started to stumble. It felt like she'd been hit by a brick. Swiftly, Chanel was on top of Charlie wailing away. While she attacked her sister with a barrage of punches, she repeatedly screamed, "He raped me! He fuckin' raped me! You let him rape me!"

"Get this bitch off me!" Charlie hollered in near defeat.

The hallway was once again teeming with neighbors with a front-row seat to the main event. There was never a boring moment at Bacardi's apartment. Seeing Charlie getting her ass beat, the neighbors started to yell, "Kick her ass, Chanel! Fuck her up!"

Another resident shouted, "Trifling ho!"

"Grimy bitch!"

It was obvious who they were rooting for. Folks were tired of Charlie and her deceased boyfriend God. They had terrorized people for too long, and now karma was biting back like a grizzly bear.

It nearly looked like Chanel was going to kill her sister. "He raped me!" she continued to scream.

Bacardi was about to flip out, seeing that everyone was in her family's business, but she stood by. Charlie was getting what she deserved—a proper beatdown.

"I fuckin' hate you!" Chanel shouted.

During the melee between the sisters, Charlie's gun spilled from her jacket, and she was left completely defenseless. Seeing the pistol on the floor, Pyro snatched it up. If there weren't so many witnesses around, he would have killed Charlie with her own gun. But he kept his composure and allowed Chanel to do her thing. He didn't know she had it in her.

Chanel clearly won the fight. She proved that she was no longer going to be anyone's victim. When Bacardi finally pulled Chanel off Charlie, it looked like Charlie had fought a bear. Her nose was bloody, her eye was black and blue, and her hair was in disarray. She had a hard time catching her breath as streams of sweat rolled off her body. She smelled like a wet puppy. Charlie, who was once worshiped and feared around the projects, was humiliated.

"That's what I'm talking about, Chanel! You fucked that bitch up," someone said with amusement.

Inside the apartment, Chanel paced back and forth in the living room, cursing and amped up. She needed to calm down. Tears trickled from her eyes. Her chest heaved up and down. It looked like she was going to have a panic attack.

"Fuck that bitch, right!" she exclaimed with extreme emotion.

On the one hand, she felt elated that she had the courage to fight Charlie and she actually won. On the other, Charlie was her older sister and it hurt Chanel deeply that she played a part in what had happened to her and Mateo. Whatever possessed her to stoop so low, Chanel would never know.

"Calm down, Chanel. You did good. You did what you needed to do," Pyro reassured her. "You finally put that bitch in her place."

Butch and Bacardi agreed.

Still, Chanel didn't want to be the bad guy. She didn't want her anger to control her. Yes, Charlie did her dirty, but she wanted to be better than the tragedy.

Meanwhile, Bacardi's tenant stood in the background in silence, not knowing what to expect next. She was new to the apartment, and seeing mother and daughter and then two sisters fight each other like they were in the UFC was mind-boggling to her.

Chanel finally noticed the stranger inside the apartment. Her frown transitioned into a warm smile toward the girl. She went over and said, "Ohmygod, I'm so sorry that you had to see that. I apologize. My name is Chanel."

She extended her hand for a handshake.

"I'm Jacqueline," the young woman replied.

The two shook hands. Chanel had become a different person for Jacqueline. Actually, she became her old self—friendly and warmhearted.

In Chanel's eyes, Jacqueline seemed nice and pleasant. She was a part-time legal assistant, and she went to NYC Technical College at night. She used to live with her mother in the Linden Houses, but it was a rocky environment for her, with her mother being strung out on drugs and continuously smoking up the rent money and stealing from her. Jacqueline decided it was time for her to leave.

Chanel noticed that the apartment was clean, the fridge was stocked with food, and Butch was still sober. It was an entirely different place. *Where was this place a few years ago?* Chanel thought.

Butch was delighted to see his youngest daughter again, as was Bacardi. The days of treating her like trash were over. Oddly, Butch hugged her and proclaimed how deeply he missed her, and Chanel was taken aback by the action.

In no rush to leave, despite what had happened earlier, Chanel and Pyro took a seat in the living and chitchatted with everyone. Chanel lied to her parents and told them that she had been staying at Mecca's place. She didn't want Bacardi to get the wrong impression of her moving in with Pyro, even though it was temporary and they were friends. She also filled them in on Mateo's progress.

"He's doing so good," Chanel mentioned.

"I'm glad to hear that," Bacardi said.

When Bacardi brought out refreshments for them, Chanel needed to pinch herself. *Whoa—what the heck has this place turned into?* she thought. Bacardi was doing everything in her power to make the two of them feel at home.

"Look, it's getting late. Chanel and I need to go," Pyro said, standing up from the couch.

Butch and Bacardi stood too. Bacardi shot her daughter an inquisitive look that Chanel averted. Before his exit, Pyro reached into his pocket and removed a large wad of bills. He peeled away five hundred dollars and handed it to Bacardi.

"That's for you," he said.

She was pleased. Receiving money for doing nothing was her forte. "Thank you."

"I know Mateo would have done it," he said.

He gave the middle-aged woman a hug and left the apartment. Chanel shot a warm smile at her parents with thankful eyes, and she followed Pyro out the door.

When they left, Bacardi stood in the foyer baffled. They were behaving more like a couple than friends. And she didn't like it.

Chapter Fourteen

*C*harlie looked in the mirror and grimaced at what she saw. She was becoming tired of seeing bruises. Her meek little sister actually beat her down. Shit felt surreal. If there was one thing the hood respected, it was power, and everyone witnessed her looking powerless and humiliated. Charlie wanted payback. She needed to get back on her A game and show niggas and bitches how powerful she really was. If they wanted to call her grimy, then she was going to show them just how grimy she could be.

She seethed at her reflection. "Fuckin' bitch." She spun around and marched out of the bathroom.

Claire was sleeping, and Charlie didn't want to wake her up. She threw on some clothes and left the building. It was time to implement her plan. It was time to go to the extreme.

She left the apartment and climbed into the backseat of an Uber. She needed to head to the city and get her cash from her Chase stash box. She gave the driver her destination, sat back, and marinated in her anger.

After the bank, she headed to a used car lot in Bay Ridge, Brooklyn. The dealership on 4th Avenue had some of the best cars that money could buy. Charlie walked onto the lot with $70,000 on her. Right away, her eyes landed on a candy red Mercedes Benz SL. It stood out.

"She's a beauty," the dealer said loudly.

Charlie turned around to see a short white man in a gray suit approaching her with a smile.

"Say what?"

"I said she's a beauty. Red must be your favorite color," he said.

"I just like the car."

"I do too, but unfortunately, I'm gonna have to part with it today because it looks like you like it a lot more than me," he replied.

She did. She loved it. It was like love at first sight.

"My name is Benjamin," he said, holding out his hand for a shake.

"Charlie."

"Well, Charlie, I already know you have good taste because you came here."

"How much?" She motioned toward the Benz.

His thick smile continued. "For you, we'll work something out, since you love this car more than me. It goes for ninety thousand—"

"Ninety?"

"Yes, but like I said, we can work something out."

"Yeah, we need to, cuz I'm willing to pay cash for it right now."

"Cash? You have cash on you right now to buy this car?" he asked.

Charlie unzipped the bag she had come with and had him take a peek inside. He smiled wide and said, "Well, um, let's get started on the paperwork."

"First, how much?"

"Straight cash? Sixty-five thousand, and that's because you and I have the same taste, and I like you, Charlie. You're my kind of woman," he complimented.

She wasn't much for the brown-nosing, but he was humorous. Charlie followed him into the main building to fill out the paperwork. An hour later, she had the keys to the Mercedes Benz SL. She slid into the driver's seat and took a strong whiff of her new car. It was two years old, but it still had that new car smell. Now she was the one smiling brightly.

"Enjoy it," said Benjamin.

"Believe me, I will."

Fuck Chanel and her Range Rover, she said to herself.

Charlie tuned the radio station to Hot 97, and Davido's "If" started to blare through the car. She drove the Benz off the lot and bopped in her seat as she headed home. When she got there, she left the Benz idling and called Claire. Several rings later, her sister finally answered her phone.

"What, Charlie?"

"Come downstairs. I wanna show you something."

"Show me what?"

"Just come downstairs, Claire," Charlie said with a little more force.

Claire sighed and hung up the phone. She exited the building with an attitude. In fact, she had several and was keeping everything pent up inside. She eyed the candy apple red convertible Mercedes Benz and knew it was bought with the blood money Charlie didn't share with her.

"What's this?" she asked.

"This me," Charlie replied with a huge grin. "You like it?"

"What happened to your old car?"

"That piece of shit? You can have it."

The remark infuriated Claire. *Am I only worth that piece-of-shit car? Does that make me a piece of shit too?* she thought. Even after Charlie made her an accessory to murder? She felt Charlie was belittling her.

"So, do you like it, sis?" Charlie asked her again.

Claire frowned. "Are you serious right now? You spent all that money on this?"

"Yeah. It's a status symbol—let everyone know that I'm makin' a fuckin' comeback," said Charlie.

"Comeback?" Claire chuckled. "And what do you plan to do about parking, huh? This whole area is a huge no-parking zone. You're gonna get ticketed or towed."

"Claire, stop being so fuckin' negative. Shit! We need to go out and celebrate. Look at what we accomplished since our parents kicked us out."

"You mean what *you* accomplished, Charlie. I'm not in your world and you damn sure don't include me in it and when you do, it's some fucked up shit," Claire shouted. "And it was a stupid thing to spend *our* money on."

"What the fuck is wrong wit' you? Damn it, Claire, why can't you act right just for once, and be fuckin' happy 'bout something?"

"Because I can't," Claire yelled.

"You know what? I'm out. I tried to put a smile on your face and all you do is fuckin' complain. A bitch is tired of hearing it," Charlie griped.

Claire still frowned. "Bye!"

Charlie sighed. With finality, she spewed, "Get ya shit right, Claire, or get left behind. And as for parking, I'll figure it out. I always figure shit out and get shit done."

Claire pivoted and went back into the building with her negative attitude.

Charlie shook her head and sped away. She had better things to do than coddle her little sister. She drove her new toy straight to her old neighborhood to show it off and announce to the haters, *I'm back, bitches—and better than ever. Y'all can't keep a bad bitch down!*

Chapter Fifteen

*I*t was nearly noon, and Chanel had spent a lazy morning in bed. She was gently awakened by the sun seeping through her window. She had a good night's rest and she was ready to start her day by making herself a breakfast fit for a queen. She had to put the fight with Charlie behind her. There was no reason to dwell on it. She was moving on, but the beatdown she had given Charlie was therapeutic for her. Chanel didn't even know she had it in herself.

She climbed out of bed, put on a long T-shirt and shorts and some fuzzy animal slippers, and walked out of her bedroom feeling like a blossoming flower. Finally, it felt like she was winning—like she was getting back on track. Mateo was improving and so was her life. Chanel had support from Pyro and, surprisingly, her parents. She never thought that would ever happen. She always believed that hell would freeze over before Bacardi and Butch would ever have her back. But they did, so the devil must have had frostbite. It was an amusing thought.

In the kitchen, she started to prepare breakfast for herself and Pyro, if he was hungry. She heard him last night with company. Pyro kept himself busy with the ladies, but it didn't bother her. At least someone was having sex.

Hearing Pyro's bedroom door open, Chanel smiled. She was happy to cook for him and his female guest. But when she saw who came out of his bedroom, her entire expression changed. Mecca reluctantly walked out behind him wearing one of his button-up shirts, her long, shapely legs showing underneath. The look on Mecca's face clearly indicated that Pyro had given her a really good night.

Mecca gave a hesitant smile. She knew she had some explaining to do.

A million emotions were going through Chanel. She didn't understand why, but she suddenly felt betrayed by them both. However, she kept her expression blank. She didn't want to make an issue of it. She went back to making breakfast when Mecca walked over with an apologetic look on her face. She attempted to help, but Chanel snapped, "I got this. I can do it without your help. And since when did you start cooking?"

Immediately, Mecca looked around to see if Pyro had heard the remark. Of course, Mecca didn't cook, but she would pretend to be whatever type of woman she needed to be to catch and keep Pyro's attention.

"Chill out, girl," Mecca whispered to her. "Just let me help you with breakfast."

Chanel eyed her friend with doubt.

Pyro saw them cooking and went over to say, "Hey, we're not staying for breakfast."

"We're not?" Mecca shot him a puzzled look.

"Nah, I got shit to do. We'll just grab some takeout on the way out."

"Oh." Mecca scurried back into his bedroom to throw her clothes and shoes on.

Chanel kept quiet. She tried not to be care whether they stayed to eat or not.

Mecca quickly hugged Chanel. "I'll call you."

Chanel shrugged. "Sure, cool."

"I'll see you later, Chanel," said Pyro, giving her a kiss on the cheek.

He left with Mecca. Chanel stood in the kitchen feeling ambivalent about their situation. *Why should I care?* she asked herself. They were both her friends—friends who happened to find each other. But seeing them together did bother her.

Chanel knew everything about Mecca, including her schedule, and she decided that she needed to have a word with her friend. In fact, she wasn't even hungry anymore. After she put the breakfast food away, she went back into her bedroom and shut her door. She went back to bed to get some more rest and to do some thinking.

Chanel decided to catch up with Mecca outside her job at a clothing store on Third Avenue in Downtown Manhattan late the next evening. She was somewhat nervous about talking to Mecca, but she was determined to do so.

Mecca walked out and looked at Chanel with an uneasy smile.

"Hey," Mecca started. She sighed and continued with, "Look, I apologize for yesterday morning. I didn't want you to find out like that."

Chanel nodded. "So, you and Pyro—how long has that been happening?"

"We exchanged numbers that afternoon when he came to pick you up at the restaurant, and we started talking and texting each other. I thought you would be cool with it. I really want your approval of us, Chanel. It would mean a lot to me."

"Why would you keep this from me? I'm supposed to be your best friend."

"And you are, Chanel. Why are you making this a thing? I honestly thought you knew," she lied. The truth was, Mecca didn't want her relationship with Pyro exposed until she was sure she wasn't a fling.

Even though she had once wished for it, for some reason, Chanel no longer wanted them together. Her eyes stayed fixed on her best friend and she asked that question—the question she already knew the answer to.

"Did you sleep with him?"

Mecca nodded. "I did."

Chanel shook her head. "Listen, I'm going to keep it real with you. Pyro is a player. He's a womanizer, and I see him bringing a different woman to his bed almost every night. So, believe me, Mecca, when I say this to you—you're no different than the others. The only thing he sees in you is a booty call," Chanel proclaimed.

Mecca listened, but she didn't understand why her friend was telling her this. Her eyes started to well up. "You're supposed to be rooting for me, Chanel, not going against me."

"I'm not going against you; I'm only looking out for you, Mecca. I know Pyro, and he's gonna use you."

"It sounds like you're hating on me," Mecca countered.

"Hate? I'm telling you the truth—trying to protect you."

It was a shock to Mecca. "Protect me? You know who you remind of right now? Charlie and Claire."

Now that was a gut shot for Chanel. "Seriously? You're going to compare me to my sisters? I'm nothing like them."

"You could have fooled me. And you shouldn't be telling Pyro's personal business like that, especially after he opened his door to you and is allowing you to stay there rent-free."

"I thought I was looking out for you—being a friend, you know?"

"No. I don't know. And why should I tell you my business when you can't be honest with me?"

"What are you talking about?"

"I'm talking about how you were lying to me about where you were staying. I thought you were in a hotel all that time, but come to find out that you were shacking up with Pyro—and while your man is in the hospital. And now you're telling me not to mess with him. Why? Because you want him too?"

Chanel was completely taken aback by the accusation. "No! Hell no! We're just friends."

"Well, you could have fooled me, because right now your actions are speaking much louder than your words. I thought you were my friend and that you would be encouraging. Obviously, I was wrong," Mecca retorted.

Chanel didn't want to argue with Mecca, but it was too late. Mecca stormed off, leaving Chanel behind looking dumbfounded.

What just happened?

Chanel walked away from the scene. She started to feel some guilt about the exchange between her and Mecca. She thought about Mateo, knowing she needed to be there for him. He was who truly mattered to her, right? So why the animosity over Pyro and Mecca being together? Was Mecca right? Had she developed feelings for Pyro?

Chapter Sixteen

*C*harlie's bright red Mercedes Benz SL was eye candy and a status symbol cruising through the Brooklyn neighborhood. It was like a flashing marquee that screamed, "Y'all muthafuckas thought I was down, but look at me now, bitches!" As she made her rounds through Brooklyn with her music blaring and the top down despite it being a breezy fall day, Charlie felt like a goddess—and a boss. She wanted to be seen and heard. She may have been knocked down, but she wasn't staying down.

Whoop! Whoop!

Charlie cursed and scowled at the sight of the police lights flashing behind her, but she kept her cool. She was legit, but she still didn't trust police at all. She hoped it was a routine traffic stop, but she wondered why they were pulling her over. She hadn't violated any traffic laws, and she knew everything on the Benz was functional.

A troubling thought raced through her mind. What if they had found her DNA at God's murder scene? The situation had been lingering heavily on her mind, and until Kym was convicted and sentenced, Charlie would remain uneasy about the investigation.

That feeling of panic quickly subsided when Charlie saw Mona exiting the unmarked Crown Vic, along with her partner Ahbou. Her expression remained deadpan as her eyes stayed fixed on Mona and her partner through the rearview mirror. Still, Charlie didn't trust anyone.

Ahbou and Mona approached the driver's side, and Mona had a wide grin on her face. Charlie exhaled in relief.

"Bitch, where did you cop this sweet ride from?" Mona asked.

"None of ya business. Don't hate on a bitch," Charlie replied jokingly.

"I think I'm paying you too much money for your product," quipped Mona.

"Shit, a bitch gotta eat, right?"

"No doubt."

Charlie climbed out of her Benz and they started to chitchat on the Brooklyn street like Mona wasn't a cop on duty. Ahbou was immediately smitten by Charlie. The pretty redbone had his undivided attention.

"That last load you sold me, it was on point. When I go out, everybody asks me where I got my shit from," Mona said.

"I told you, I get nothing but the best. I'm glad you loved it."

"I did. So, when will you have some more items like that coming in?"

"Give me a week or two, and I'll have some new shit for you."

"I like the sound of that," said Mona. "Oh, this is my partner, Ahbou."

Ahbou reached out and shook Charlie's hand. "How you doing?"

"I'm doin' fine."

"Yeah, that you are," he flirted.

Charlie smiled politely his way. He was average height, lean, and dark-skinned with a low cropped haircut. Nothing stood out about Ahbou but his badge.

"SL Benz, candy apple red—what that run you, like eighty K?" he guessed.

"Close. I see you know your cars," Charlie replied, leaning back on her car.

"I know nice things," he countered, smiling slyly at Charlie, "And I'm looking at something really nice right now—a lot more attractive than the car. You're a beautiful woman, Charlie."

Blunt. She had to respect that. "Thank you," she returned with nonchalance.

"Keep it in your pants, Ahbou," Mona warned. "She's a friend."

"I know. I'm just being cordial," he said.

"Yeah, and I know your kind of cordial."

Charlie laughed at their quick exchange. It was comedic, but something about Ahbou was intriguing to her. He wasn't really a handsome man, but his boldness and demeanor were somewhat attractive.

"Hey, you need to come to the house more often," Mona mentioned to her.

Charlie raised a brow. "Oh, you're inviting me to your place? Business or personal?"

"We can entertain both," said Mona. "But I would like to see you come by. You're cool. And my partner likes you."

Charlie grinned. "Thanks."

"Listen, we need to run. But think on it," Mona added.

Mona and Ahbou started to walk back to their unmarked car. Before climbing into the passenger seat, Ahbou shot one final glance at Charlie.

Charlie didn't know what to think. The friendly traffic stop by Mona left her somewhat perplexed. She wondered if she should trust it.

Charlie didn't really have any friends, and she decided right then that she would take Mona up on her offer. Mona was a valuable ally to have on her side. Charlie needed all the resources and connections she could muster. She was building something big, and the foundation had to be strong.

A week after the traffic stop, Charlie parked her red SL Benz on the suburban street in Westchester County and got out the vehicle looking like she was going to a nightclub instead of an intimate gathering at a friend's place. She wore a short skirt that was more leg than skirt and a halter top that showed how perky her breasts were. Though Charlie was from the streets and she was tough, she couldn't shake the uncomfortable feeling of knocking on a cop's door to hang out. It didn't make her a snitch, but it was an awkward feeling.

The door opened and Mona was all smiles. "Hey, bitch! I'm glad you decided to come through. Come on in."

Charlie entered the home, believing there would be other people inside, but it was only her and Mona. Charlie took a seat on the couch, and Mona started to roll up a blunt. Shit, Mona was more hustler than cop.

In no time, the two women got high on the potent Kush and were gradually draining a bottle of Grey Goose.

Mona laughed and slapped the arm of the couch. "Hey, you know my partner really likes you," she mentioned. "That fool couldn't stop talking about you that day."

"So you want me to fuck a cop?"

"He damn sure wants to fuck you, but I keep telling him that you're off limits. Are you?"

"Oh, so what you asking? Do I wanna fuck him too?" asked Charlie.

Mona shrugged. "He just wanted me to put it out there. But Ahbou's cool people. He's definitely about his business—definitely nobody to fuck with."

"I'll think about it."

"That's all you can do."

It didn't take long for them to finish off the bottle of Goose, and Mona rolled up their third blunt for the evening. Charlie was having a good time with her. For her to be a cop, she got high like a ghetto bitch, and she was able to go drink-for-drink with Charlie in alcohol consumption. They were both tipsy, but not drunk—not yet.

"Charlie, I got a question for you. You got that nice car, nice clothes, nice jewelry—is stolen merchandise the only thing you're selling?" asked Mona.

"And why ya asking?"

"Just curiosity, that's all. Bitch like me believes you're moving coke."

"Coke? Wow. You tryin' to set me up?"

Mona laughed. "Fuck outta here. You know me—"

"Yeah, you're cool, but you're still a cop," Charlie replied.

"I'm not tryin' to get in your business; I was just asking."

"To answer your question, no, I'm not moving any coke or any drugs. The only thing I'm selling is merchandise."

"I really like you, Charlie. You're smart and you got heart. Real recognizes real," Mona proclaimed.

"No doubt."

Mona was more than a decade older than Charlie, but neither cared about age. It felt like they had known each other for a long time. Their backgrounds were similar and their mentalities were identical—get money by any means necessary and stay respected in the game.

Mona opened another bottle of Grey Goose and poured both of them a glass while she continued to pull on the blunt.

"So, you feeling my partner or what?" she brought up again.

"I told you, I'll think about it."

"Yeah, do that and let me know soon, cuz I'm gonna smack Ahbou if he don't shut up 'bout you," Mona stated.

Charlie laughed. "Damn, it's like that with him?"

"Yeah. Pussy-craving muthafucka."

Charlie and Mona started to hang out on a regular basis. It started at Mona's place and then it shifted to Mona coming over to Charlie's

Brooklyn apartment. Mona was impressed with the place. Charlie had taste. It became common for the two of them to get high and tipsy—and sometimes asshole-drunk—together.

Claire hated them together. Not only was Mona was taking her sister's attention away, but Mona was loud and always came to their apartment with a gun—or guns. Something about Mona rubbed Claire the wrong way. The look in Mona's eyes was shifty, and Claire felt she was bad news. When she was alone with Charlie, she continuously pleaded with her to leave that woman alone. Claire felt the fact that Mona was a cop was even more of an incentive not to mess around with her.

"Don't trust her, Charlie. You need to leave that bitch alone."

"Stay out my business, Claire," Charlie rebuked.

Soon, Ahbou started to come along, and the trio would get high and drink. Ahbou was an intriguing guy. His personality was magnetic and he was humorous just as much as he was dangerous, something that captured Charlie's attention. The streets were saying that he was a killer with a badge, but his dirty jokes were hilarious.

"What comes after 69? Mouthwash," Ahbou joked.

Everyone laughed. Ahbou was a natural comedian. Even Charlie couldn't hold it in, bursting out laughing like she was at a *Def Comedy Jam* show.

"One more thing, ladies, if you ever get bored, do this—text the message, 'I'm pregnant,' to random mobile numbers and see what comes back," he said.

"He is too much," said Charlie.

"That's why I love him. He keeps my day interesting," said Mona.

Charlie and Ahbou locked eyes. He was attracted to her red hair and young beauty, and she was attracted to his charisma.

It didn't take them long to fuck each other's brains out in the bathroom. With the door locked, Ahbou curved Charlie over the bathroom sink, pulled down her jeans, ripped away her panties, spread her legs, and quickly thrust his hard dick inside of her. He was fucking her roughly in the doggystyle position while he watched their debauchery in the bathroom mirror. Charlie enjoyed having him inside of her. He was an average size, but he worked his dick like he was a giant, and he manhandled her body like it was a stop-and-frisk—cupping and squeezing her tits, massaging her clit, smacking her ass, and taking charge of her pussy.

"Ooooh, fuck me!" she cried out.

"Damn, you got some good fuckin' pussy!"

He made her come, and she made him come. He loved every minute of it, and he wanted Charlie to be his main bitch.

She was down for it. There was something about Ahbou that Charlie enjoyed. It was easy to see that he was infatuated with her. Right away, he was willing to do anything for Charlie. Meanwhile, she saw an opportunity in fucking with a cop like Ahbou—give him some pussy, suck his dick, and he would become her protection with a badge on the streets.

It didn't take long for Charlie to have Ahbou eating out of her hands. She freaked him like she was a porn star, sucking his dick in the front seat of the unmarked car and giving him pussy in the backseat or on the hood. It was their thing—fucking outdoors. Having sex in public turned him on, and Charlie used that to her advantage.

She used Ahbou to fuck with her enemies and her frenemies. She was giving him the names of her former friends and soon after, front doors were being kicked open by the police and raids were being carried out.

Wanda was one of them. Cops raided her place like she was a drug kingpin and found all kinds of stolen shit that she couldn't explain. They placed the handcuffs on her and arrested her.

When Charlie found out that Landy was the first to spread the gossip about her and Chanel, she set her dog out on her for revenge. Ahbou was subtle with setting up the young girl with a few ounces of weed and a few ounces of cocaine. As she was walking home from the train station one night, detectives approached her and a female cop implemented a stop-and-frisk, resulting in the drug bust.

Landy became hysterical. She had no idea how weed and cocaine got in her bag. Tears ran down her face as she repeatedly exclaimed, "It's not mine, officers. Please, I'm telling you, I don't do drugs. It's not mine!"

Landy didn't want to go to jail, but the cops arrested her right there on the spot. She was put through the system and her life was immediately turned upside down.

Charlie was on cloud nine. She felt like a queen ruling over the peasants, and Ahbou was her knight in shining armor. She would give the nigga some pussy and some head, and he was at her beck and call.

Some days Charlie could be seen riding through the Brooklyn hood in the front seat of Ahbou's unmarked cop car, pulling up on people in her old neighborhood. Everyone hated the ground she walked on, and they wanted her stopped. Meanwhile, she continued to point out dudes who she knew were riding dirty. The result was a spike in gun arrests, drug arrests, and grand larceny arrests—the whole gamut.

Charlie had become a snitch, but she didn't see it that way. To her, it was only retribution. The projects had turned on her—disrespected her—and she was determined to get her revenge.

In the aftermath of Charlie's rampage, there was an onslaught of complaints filed at Ahbou's precinct, but the Civilian Complaint Review Board would never receive them. Ahbou was just one in a cluster of dirty cops in his precinct, and his sergeant was in on it too.

Chapter Seventeen

ateo's physical therapist, Kyle, was amazed by Mateo's recovery. Mateo was determined to get better. He was on the fast track to becoming healthy and whole again. As the days ticked on, he started to notice that Chanel wasn't coming to see him every day. Then it scaled back to maybe twice a week. Though he was getting better, he felt his support system fading. Mateo could see that something was wrong with Chanel, but she wouldn't tell him what it was.

Chanel's sudden distraction from him was just the motivation he needed. He began going above and beyond the expectations of his physical therapist. While Mateo was still somewhat bedridden, Kyle worked with him to strengthen his legs and upper body so he would eventually walk again.

The times when Chanel was there with him, she seemed distant all of a sudden. It was like her body was there physically, but mentally, she was someplace else. It never used to be like that. In the past, Chanel gave Mateo her undivided attention and support, talked to him, and prayed with him. Now, when he would ask her what was wrong, she would get an attitude and reply, "Nothing!"

Mateo could tell she was hiding something. He felt like he was losing the love of his life.

Chanel couldn't put her finger on why she was so upset, but the more Mecca came to the apartment to see Pyro, the angrier she became. She told herself that she was trying to protect her best friend, but even she had a hard time believing it. The good thing was that she was able to hide her annoyance from Mecca after their argument. Mecca thought Chanel was glad that she and Pyro were getting close.

Mecca was happy she had found someone worth being with. She wanted a happy ending. She had fallen in love with Pyro, and she couldn't go a day without seeing him. She wanted Pyro to put a ring on it someday.

The affection went both ways. Pyro was really digging Mecca, and not just in the bedroom. She was smart and beautiful, outgoing, and she was going places in life. She wanted to be a journalist, and she was becoming a socialite in the city.

Mecca had a charming personality and was frequently invited to big events in the city where politicians and celebrities gathered. Her well-connected Colombia University friends were opening their circle to allow Mecca inside, and she was including Pyro. Pyro loved it. His girl had connections in the city that could be very beneficial to him. The two of them could become the ultimate power couple. They both were smart, fearless, and ambitious, and it didn't take long for them to say to each other, "I love you."

Chanel heard a sudden banging on Pyro's apartment door. She was surprised that Pyro didn't hear it and go to the door, but he was a heavy sleeper. She walked out of her bedroom, tying her robe together to go see who it was. By the sound of the knocking, it didn't look like it was going to be friendly company.

She glanced through the peephole and saw Pyro's baby mama, Sheree. At first, Chanel wasn't going to open the door, but something petty came over her and she changed her mind. She unlocked and opened the door, and Sheree immediately pushed by her and made her way into the apartment.

Sheree knew that Pyro was getting serious with someone. When she saw Chanel opening the door, she figured Chanel was the one.

"Bitch, where the fuck is my baby father at? You the bitch he fuckin', right?" she shouted.

Chanel stood there speechless.

Sheree continued to curse and yell, "Where the fuck he at? I need to see him right now. Go get that nigga, bitch. You wanna fuck my baby father, then you got a fuckin' problem wit' me."

Wow! Chanel thought. The bitch was loud and crazy. She wondered how Pyro got mixed up with her.

"I'm not sleeping with him," Chanel finally said.

"Bitch, stop lying. Look at you, naked underneath that fuckin' robe and stayin' the night at his crib and answering his door—and you gonna fuckin' lie to me."

Chanel was at a loss for words. There was no talking rationally to Sheree.

Sheree was making a scene. She became so loud in the apartment that she could have woken the dead. Eventually, the ruckus caused Pyro to come out of his bedroom dressed in his boxers with Mecca following right behind him.

"Sheree, why the fuck are you here?" Pyro yelled, his hands clenching into fists.

"Who the fuck is that bitch? Oh, so you got a fuckin' nasty-ass orgy happening here, huh, nigga? I see why you can't come see ya fuckin' son," Sheree shouted.

"Yo, first of all, you need to watch your mouth, and second, it ain't like that. But how the fuck did you get into this building?"

"Don't worry 'bout that!"

"A'ight, you need to leave," Pyro shouted.

"Fuck you. I'm not goin' nowhere," Sheree replied. "Who is she, Pyro?" Sheree's head nodded toward Mecca while her eyes continued to blaze.

"My name is Mecca, Sheree. And I was hoping one day to meet you and your son because Pyro and I are together."

"My son," Sheree shouted. "You come near my fuckin' child and I will whip your ass, bitch! Pyro, is she serious?"

Chanel sat front and center as the three argued. Pyro still had no idea how Sheree had gotten into the building, but he wanted her gone. He quickly called security to come and escort her out.

Sheree continued to rant and curse. It was clear that she was extremely jealous seeing Pyro with someone else.

"Me and you aren't together, Sheree. How many times do I need to fuckin' tell you that?" Pyro said with irritation in his voice.

"Oh, it's like that, nigga? We ain't together, but you sure wasn't sayin' that the other night when you were deep in this good-ass pussy—coming inside of me raw and shit," she responded, while sexually gesturing between her legs.

Chanel gave Mecca the subtle side-eye, saying silently, *I told you so.*

Pyro clenched his jaw.

"Yeah, muthafucka, don't get quiet now," Sheree continued. "You wanna fuck me and that delusional bitch at the same time and act like you're committed to her?"

Mecca had heard enough. She was heartbroken and couldn't even look at Pyro. She spun around and went back into the bedroom, slamming the door behind her. She thought Pyro was the one—her man to love and cherish. Their relationship was clearly a lie.

Pyro shot Sheree a look that could cut her in half. "You're a crazy bitch, Sheree. That's why I don't fuck with you."

"Say that to yourself next time you eating me out," she countered.

Pyro went into the bedroom, where Mecca was hurriedly getting dressed.

"Mecca, let me explain," he pleaded with desperation in his tone.

Mecca spun around to face him and shouted, "Explain what, Pyro? You fucked her the other night?"

"Look—"

"Fuck you, Pyro!" she screamed.

Pyro was urgently trying to stop her from leaving, and while doing so, Sheree boldly stood at the threshold to the bedroom and shouted, "You keep playin' wit' me, Pyro, and I guarantee you that you will never see your fuckin' son again."

Pyro's rage was reignited, and he moved toward Sheree with a ferocity that even scared her. "I'll kill you before you take my son away!"

They continued to argue while Mecca continued to get dressed. It had turned into chaos inside the place. There was another loud knock at the door, and Chanel answered it. It was security arriving. Chanel pointed the guards to the bedroom and they moved with a sense of urgency to carry out their job.

Seeing the two men, Pyro bellowed, "Yo, get that fuckin' bitch outta here."

They grabbed an angry and bitter Sheree to remove her from the premises and she tried to resist. They threatened her, letting her know that if she didn't leave right away, then they were going to call the police and have her arrested for trespassing. Sheree didn't want to go to jail, so she reluctantly allowed the guards to escort her out of the apartment.

Mecca was right behind them, leaving in tears. Pyro was unable to stop her. She cursed at him again, and when he tried to grab her arm to get her to hear him out, she angrily jerked away from his grasp.

"Fuck you!" she cursed at him again.

He slammed the door behind her and fumed.

Chanel exhaled. She was glad that Mateo didn't have baby mama drama and a bunch of women like Pyro. Now Mecca might see Pyro for the player he was, and Chanel only had to open the door and step aside.

It had been one entertaining morning. Pyro wanted to be left alone, so he went into his bedroom and closed the door behind him. Chanel saw no reason to bother him. She felt that he had made his bed, and now it was time to lay it in. He was a real asshole for fucking Mecca and his baby mama at the same time—and without protection. She knew he was a player, but damn, not like that.

Chapter Eighteen

*C*harlie could feel the twists and turns of the moving vehicle. Then she felt the car moving at a steady speed and figured that they were on the highway now, but she had no idea where she was going. She had been blindfolded and placed into the backseat. She felt a tinge of nervousness, but she tried to keep her cool. She hoped accepting Mona's proposition wasn't a mistake.

"You'll do fine, Charlie—lots of money to be made if you fuck wit' me," Mona had told her.

"Doin' what?" Charlie had asked.

"What you've been doing—hustling," Mona had replied.

Charlie paid attention to Mona's lavish lifestyle, and she knew whatever Mona was doing on the side was paying a lot more than her police salary. Her $65,000 a year was pocket change compared to her primary source of income.

The vehicle traveled through the Holland Tunnel into New Jersey and then made its way to a warehouse on the outskirts of Newark. The car entered the spacious warehouse, and a man closed the rolling gate behind the vehicle for a clandestine meeting inside.

Still blindfolded, Charlie finally felt the car come to a stop. She heard the doors opening and right after, a pair of hands grabbed for her and someone said, "C'mon, get out. We're here."

She didn't resist. She was removed from the backseat and heard several voices. Finally, the blindfold was removed and Charlie was staring at nine high-ranking officers in uniform from various New York City precincts. Not only was she staring at cops, but she also saw tons of confiscated kilos of cocaine and heroin.

"What the fuck is this?" she asked with uncertainty.

"Relax, Charlie. This is the business opportunity I was telling you about," Mona said.

It was an awkward moment for Charlie. She didn't do too well with cops. Mona and Ahbou were an exception.

"So, this is her?" asked a sergeant. "And you're sure she can be trusted?"

"I can vouch for her, sergeant. She's good peoples and really good at what she does," said Mona.

They all stared so intensely at Charlie, she felt like she was being put on the auction block. There were sergeants, lieutenants, and even a captain in her presence. Some of NYPD's finest weren't looking so fine right now. It was corruption. Only the most trusted criminals were recruited to the inner sanctum, and once drafted, you were guaranteed a "get out of jail free" card. The cops had an elite list of hustlers on their payroll that moved their seized drugs, but there was so much to move that they needed more quality recruits.

The seized drugs were supposed to be destroyed after samples were taken for trial. However, certain members of law enforcement who were assigned to carry out the destruction of the narcotics decided otherwise. Seeing all that valuable product destroyed when it could have been making them rich made them all go against the badge. They had been making a killing for over six years and showed no signs of slowing down. The seized drugs were a cash cow and covert retirement plan.

Mona's cohorts had heard stories about Charlie. She was grimy, and that was just the kind of recruit they were looking for.

"What we do here, Charlie, is get money . . . lots of it," Mona said.

Judging from those kilos on the table, she saw it. Charlie had her reservations about dealing with more cops, but this was an opportunity to make more money than she could ever dream of staring right at her. There was no way she was going to turn it down. She wanted to get paid too.

"What y'all need me to do?" she asked.

"The arrangement is, you work for us. You move drugs for us, nothing else and nothing extra, and we'll give you points on the package. If you abide by our rules and do what we say, you will become a very rich woman," Captain Curtis Halstead, a twenty-year vet with the NYPD, said to her.

She was listening.

Lieutenant Patrick Davis, who had over a decade on the force, handed her a burner phone. "Only we will contact you through that phone, no one else. And it's not to be used for anything but to converse with the faces you see in this room today. It's clean."

Charlie nodded.

"If you happen to get arrested, you should know the drill—keep your mouth shut and one of us will get in contact with you . . . to help you out," Sergeant Whyte promised. "We have lawyers on standby, so don't panic. We've been doing this for a long time. You look like a smart woman who knows what to do in a crisis."

"I can hold my own," Charlie replied.

They all looked at her with intensity. The decorated NYPD uniforms, the badges, the holstered weapons—it all felt surreal to Charlie. Cops were telling her how to be a criminal. How ironic.

"And where would I be moving the drugs to?" she asked.

"We'll call you with locations and times," said Lieutenant Graham, who had been a cop for fifteen years.

They were meticulous with the details and instructions. The officers knew the tricks and trades of the streets, the law, and their fellow officers.

They had access to information that no one else had, from pending indictments and prosecutions to forthcoming raids on organizations and dealers. They felt that they would always have the upper hand against prosecution because they had plants in every department and they were extremely wary about who they brought into their corrupt organization.

Charlie agreed to take them up on their offer. With God and Fingers dead, she needed a new hustle. She couldn't plan and execute licks alone, but selling cocaine was just really about transportation, she believed. Who couldn't do that? The deal was that Charlie would get ten percent of the profit.

She didn't like those fractions, but she agreed to it.

"You'll be fine, Charlie. Just move carefully and always do what we say," Mona advised her.

Charlie nodded, and the deal was sealed.

What Mona and the other officers didn't tell Charlie was that her name had come up in the investigation of the murder of Godfrey Williams. Kymberly Stephens had parents in high places, and they had hired a topnotch criminal defense attorney for their daughter. They also hired an outside DNA specialist to test everything inside the apartment to prove their daughter's innocence. There were key pieces that they wanted tested, but the corrupt cops were already trying to find someone dirty in a New Jersey precinct and lab to swap out the evidence. If they couldn't find an ally and Charlie's DNA was present, their plan B was simple—murder Charlie before she was arrested. They couldn't allow her to turn state's evidence against them.

Chapter Nineteen

*C*hanel looked lost in thought when the cabbie said to her, "Ma'am, we're here. That will be twenty-five dollars," snapping her out of her backseat daydream.

"Oh, I'm so sorry," Chanel said, reaching into her purse to pay him.

"It's okay."

Taking a cab to the rehab center was easier for her than driving her Range Rover. Parking was a headache in the city, and it was expensive.

Chanel was outside the rehab facility, about to go inside to see Mateo. It was an uncertain feeling, when it shouldn't have been. In the past, she was always excited to go visit her man, ready to nurse him back to health and comfort him. Considering the traumatic incident he endured, he was doing better than expected. However, his rehabilitation was taking a long time, and it was taking a toll on her. She yearned for him to get back to normal, so they could be together like a couple should be. She wanted to marry him and move on with their lives.

But lately, she had been feeling torn about love and matters of the heart. In her spare time she would watch chick flicks or romantic comedies, and then she would find herself crying her eyes out. She was lonely.

Chanel stood at the threshold of the hospital room gazing at a sleeping Mateo. He looked so peaceful. She sighed heavily and stepped farther into the room. A slight smile crept across her face. She took a seat next to him and took his hand into hers. Her touch was what woke him. Seeing Chanel by his side, Mateo smiled.

"Hey," he greeted.

"Hey, baby. How are you?"

"Better now that you're here," he replied warmly.

She smiled.

"I love you," he said with unwavering certainty.

"I love you too, Mateo."

Mateo sat up with ease. His legs were wobbly and his coordination was still off, but his upper body strength had returned.

"Don't you look gorgeous?" He kissed Chanel's hand and patted his bed for her to sit down beside him. She did.

"Me?" she replied, "I'm starting to think I'm competing with you lately. And don't think I don't know about you and Nurse Beth."

His smile was wide. "She gives the best sponge baths."

"What!"

"She likes to pay extra attention all around here." Mateo's left hand circled his groin area. They both chuckled, but Chanel thought there was some truth to that.

Chanel saw a game sitting on the chair.

"What's that?"

"It's a game Pyro bought for me. It's called Mahjong. You wanna play?"

She perked up and shook her head. "Pyro? When was this?"

"He came by last night cryin' on my shoulders 'bout that baby mama drama. Ain't you glad I saved myself for you?"

"And I saved my . . ." her voice trailed off.

"You know that your values still stand, Chanel. Don't ever think differently. You're still the woman who saved herself for me—who is still saving herself for us, for our love. If it's taken, then it doesn't count. Remember that—it doesn't count."

Chanel nodded.

Nurse Beth came in to check Mateo's vitals just in time to break the somber turn the conversation had taken.

"Hello, handsome," she sang as she pulled out her stethoscope. Chanel peeped how she took the extra step to warm the chestpiece before placing it on Mateo's heart. To Chanel, Beth was ancient. She was at least thirty-five years old, with brown skin and natural hair. Her apple bottom was her best asset, and by the looks of how tight her scrubs were hugging her hips, Beth knew it too.

Next, she grabbed Mateo's wrist to check his heart rate. While Beth was counting, Chanel asked, "How's he doing?"

Nurse Beth's index finger quickly shot up to silence her. A couple of awkward moments of silence and finally she said to Mateo, "You have a resting heart rate of sixty, which is very good. You'll be out of here soon." She smiled again at him. "I'll be sad to see you go."

She was off to the next patient, and Chanel realized she never spoke directly to her. This contributed to her already funky mood.

"There goes your cougar." Chanel was being snarky.

"You mean panther."

Chanel rolled her eyes. "She's at least forty."

"Nah, she just a little older than me," he replied, scooting over so Chanel could lie next to him and snuggle.

She crawled into his bed, and his strong arm comforted her. "I thought black didn't crack."

Mateo loved the attention. "Ah, look at my baby. You jealous."

She smiled. "Un poquito."

"Poquito my ass," Mateo replied and then planted a kiss on her lips.

Chanel's visit with Mateo was shorter than usual. Instead of spending the majority of her day with him, she stayed for a couple of hours and then gave him an excuse why she needed to leave. He seemed understanding.

Chanel took a cab back to Pyro's place. Mecca called Chanel during the ride. She wanted to meet up and talk. Chanel was down.

When she walked into the apartment, Pyro wasn't home. It had been nearly a week since the incident between Mecca, Sheree, and him. Chanel didn't want to get involved with their drama, but it was easy to see that Pyro was hurt by Mecca leaving him. It was obvious that he really liked Mecca and he was missing her. But he didn't want to talk about it to anyone, especially not Chanel. That incident put somewhat of a strain on their friendship.

Chanel got dressed for the weather in some jeans, sneakers, and a light, pumpkin-colored leather jacket. It was late autumn with a chilly breeze outside, and the holiday season was about to be in full swing. Halloween, Thanksgiving, and Christmas—each one was right around the corner. Thinking about the holidays weighed on Chanel's spirit. She didn't want to spend them without Mateo. She wished he could make a full recovery so they could spend them together. It had been a daunting few weeks for her, but she was still moving forward, praying that she went into the New Year with high spirits and Mateo walking by her side.

She trekked down into the parking garage and got inside of her white Range Rover and headed to Manhattan to see Mecca.

Chanel walked into the modernly decorated restaurant with clear acrylic barstools and black metal tables near Columbia and spotted Mecca already there, seated at the table looking despondent. Her head was lowered and her attention was on her cell phone. Finally, she looked up and spotted Chanel coming her way. She managed to smile and stood up to greet Chanel with a friendly hug.

"I'm glad you came," said Mecca.

"Are you okay?"

"I'm doing fine," Mecca replied.

Chanel knew it was a lie. She could see it all over her friend's face, the pain and heartbreak that Pyro had put her through with the Sheree business. Chanel knew she would have felt the same way if Mateo had put her through something like that.

"Well, I'm here for you, Mecca. Let's talk."

The two sat at the table opposite each other. They ordered Shirley Temples and some appetizers.

"So, how are you holding up?" asked Chanel.

"I'm okay, Chanel, for real. You don't have to keep asking me the same thing in a different way. I'm going to always be okay," Mecca replied faintly. "Let's talk about something else."

Chanel didn't believe her. Her words were saying that she was okay while her eyes were manifesting something completely different. Their drinks came, along with their appetizers. They ate, drank, laughed a little, and talked. But after putting up a strong exterior, Mecca unexpectedly started to cry her eyes out at the table.

"How could he do this to me, Chanel?" she cried out. "I loved him."

"I know you did, Mecca."

"He's out there having sex with his baby mama and then comes and makes all these promises to me. Ohmygod, I'm so stupid," she said with a tinge of defeat and embarrassment.

"Mecca, don't stress yourself over this. We're women and it happens to everyone. Don't you remember? You told me that once when I was tripping about Mateo."

With her tear-stained eyes, Mecca looked at her friend. "But you know what hurts me the most, Chanel? It's that Pyro hasn't called me since the shit happened. And I'm embarrassed. I miss him. But I should have listened to you when you told me that he was a player."

Chanel, seeing her friend in deep pain, sighed and said to her, "Listen, I know for a fact that Pyro misses you and that he really likes you. If you want him, then you need to fight for him. And I also know that those other women don't mean anything to him. Just give it time, Mecca. I know Pyro. He'll come around."

Chanel took her friend's hands into hers and held them firmly in her grasp, while she fixed her eyes on Mecca. "Look, you're the best thing to happen to him. You're a good woman, Mecca. I know it and he knows it, and he's been searching for someone like you for a long time. And if he can't see that then he's a fool and you're too good for him."

Chanel didn't believe this for one second. In her eyes, Pyro was a womanizer and undoubtedly had moved on to the next one. But she had to say something comforting, seeing how distraught her friend was. It was all she could do other than kicking Mecca while she was already down.

Mecca managed to smile at her friend's encouraging words. She was grateful for a friend like Chanel. She sighed with some relief and the two friends stood up and hugged each other warmly. After her talk with Chanel, Mecca felt a thousand times better.

Chapter Twenty

*C*harlie steered her flashy car into the Washington Heights alleyway at dusk, traveled a few feet farther from the public street, and brought the vehicle to a stop. She climbed out of her Benz looking like the boss bitch she had become, wearing a pair of red bottoms, stylish jeans that hugged her juicy booty and curvy figure, and a pricey shearling coat. Being in a sketchy place such as a back alleyway would have been intimidating for anyone—man or woman, but Charlie carried a look of certainty that no one was going to fuck with her. And she had her reasons to believe so.

Charlie was balling out of control. Immediately, her name started to ring out throughout the New York City hoods. She was moving one to three kilos a week, netting her cut of $3,500 a ki. In one month she had stacked over $25,000. It was a healthy profit for her, but she yearned to make so much more. If the NYPD kept supplying her with the drugs, then she would become a millionaire in no time. She was making more money with cops than she ever had with criminals, including God.

Charlie's name had become synonymous with quality kilos of cocaine. She moved like a shark in the cold waters, hungry and looking for money to devour. She began to rub shoulders with big ballers and shot callers in the tri-state area and beyond. Dealers couldn't wait to make the exchange with Red Charlie, the Brooklyn Bombshell. It was her name in the streets, and the name carried weight. Charlie would come through with her mind on money—always counting the cash before relinquishing the product. She was a bold and daring bitch, willing to walk into any apartment, dark alley, or warehouse with kilos of cocaine on her.

Carrying two kilos in a leather tote, Charlie knocked on the rusty steel door that was nestled among the other shady looking entrances in the back alleyway. She remained alert with her concealed .380 and 9mm, both guns already cocked back with the safety off.

The rusty door opened up and a burly giant of a man appeared standing a hulking six-six. He glared at Charlie and her petite and curvy stature. She glared up at him and asked, "Where Mission at?"

His hard stare stayed fixed on her longer than the comfortable gaze, but Charlie didn't falter. In fact, hers matched his. He stepped back from the threshold, allowing Charlie into the building, and then hollered, "Yo Mission, Charlie here."

Charlie coolly walked inside, but remained cautious.

Mission met her out in the open with a smile. "Charlie, Charlie, Charlie, what's poppin'?" he asked gleefully. "I know you got that for me."

"You know I do, Mission."

"Always on point. I fuckin' love it," he replied.

Mission was an ambitious hustler who had come a long way from his days as a two-bit thug from Harlem. He had graduated from moving ounces and pounds to moving kilos in less than a year. He was thin, light-skinned, and motivated, and he was fortunate to have Charlie as his connect.

While the two talked, Charlie's cell phone chimed. She checked the text message and a bright smile lit up her face. It was a smile that caught Mission's attention.

"Damn, ma, I thought I was the only one that had ya attention at the moment. A nigga got you cheesing like that?" he asked.

"It's business," she replied.

"Business, huh? Yeah, I know that kind of business, and I don't mind that kind of business myself," he replied, looking her up and down. He wouldn't mind something more with the kilos he was buying, but he knew not to push up.

"Listen, I didn't come here to flirt. Let's wrap this up."

"Let's . . ." his voice trailed off.

Mission placed the cash on the table in front of Charlie. She started to count it right away.

"Damn, Charlie, this like our sixth transaction together and you still don't trust me?"

She shot a cold look at him. "I don't trust anyone."

She continued counting, not letting his remark distract her. Mission's hulking goon stood guard by the doorway, remaining silent and being the muscle that he was paid to be. When she confirmed it was all there, Charlie handed over the product. Mission was all smiles.

"Ya shit do really good out here on these streets," he said.

"I know," Charlie replied cockily.

She pivoted and left the building and got back into her Benz, but not before securing the cash inside the trunk. She picked up her phone and reread the text message she had received earlier. It brought another smile to her face. The message came from a drug dealer from Atlanta named KB.

HEY BABY GIRL, I'M BACK IN NEW YORK. I WANNA SEE YOU . . . BUSINESS AND PLEASURE.

Something about KB made Charlie want to connect with him in more ways than re-ups. KB was making serious money by copping several kilos on a regular basis from her—doing business up and down the east coast. He didn't flirt with her or show any sexual interest in Charlie at first, and if he did want to fuck her, he did a good job of hiding it. KB was a ruggedly handsome nigga, standing six feet tall with a lean and chiseled body, a narrow face, and intense eyes.

Charlie found him very attractive. He was country, from the backwoods of Georgia. He was born in the Deep South with dirt roads, trailer parks, and outhouses for bathrooms. When he talked, his southern accent was thick, and Charlie found it enticing. The stories he told her were interesting, and he was a go-getter—a nigga who earned his respect from the south to the north. Despite growing up underprivileged and coming from one of the poorest areas in Georgia, KB was intelligent, educated, and a natural-born hustler. He had pulled himself up from his bootstraps and made a nice life for himself.

"Mmmmm . . . Oh shit, fuck me, KB . . . I love that dick," Charlie purred as KB slammed his hard dick into her.

The two were taking full advantage of the hotel room KB had booked for two days. With KB, Charlie found herself in full freak mode. His dick was big and thick, and his stamina was almost unnatural. He had a perfect rhythm inside of her, pounding her pussy and getting her juices flowing. He grabbed her hips and held her still while he thrust into her, emitting a cry of ecstasy from Charlie.

Earlier, he ate her out until she came in his mouth. She was his sexy minx and KB wanted to please every inch of her. He had wrapped one hand around her neck, dragged her forward, and slammed his mouth down on hers as they were fucking in the missionary position. Now as they explored the doggystyle position, Charlie gripped the headboard and felt her pussy being desecrated in a good way.

Her cell phone chimed. She glanced at the caller ID and saw that it was Ahbou trying to contact her. Of course, she ignored him. This was much more important.

"Who that calling ya?" KB asked her, fucking her silly.

"Ooooh shit . . . nobody important, baby," she said.

KB spun her around and pushed her against the bed forcefully, making her take every inch of his big dick. It didn't take long for KB to make her come again. Her legs quivered uncontrollably and she released an ecstatic holler that echoed off the walls of the room.

Lingering on a post-coital moment, KB removed himself from the bed and went to pour himself a glass of champagne. Charlie joined him. Together, they downed champagne while naked. Charlie was business first, play later. KB had bought several kilos of cocaine from her earlier at a reasonable price, and then it was back to his hotel room for playtime.

"I want ya to come wit' me to de Bahamas," he mentioned.

Charlie was taken aback. "The Bahamas?"

"Why not? Let's just get away."

Once again, Charlie's cell phone rang. It was Ahbou calling her again. Like before, she ignored it. In fact, she turned her cell phone off completely. She wanted to spend some quality time with KB without any interruptions. His mention of taking her to the Bahamas was interesting. She barely left the city, and now he was talking about taking her out the country. But there was one problem. She didn't have a passport.

KB moved intimately closer to Charlie and took her into his arms. The way he held her and stared at her, it was like nothing she had felt before—not even from God. To KB, Charlie was sophisticated, which was a stretch to anyone's imagination. He wanted to be with her.

"Ay, ya don't need to think 'bout it. We finna do big things together, Charlie, if ya let me," he said.

She was smitten by him.

"Big things, huh?"

He smiled.

Chapter Twenty-One

A trip to the Bahamas was heavily on Charlie's mind as she and her frenemy Wanda walked through the front door of her apartment. Claire was seated in the living room with a stack of books in her face when the interruption happened. Right away, the peace and quiet she was experiencing came to a rude halt. Claire gave her sister a dry and halfhearted hello, which instantly put Charlie in a sour mood.

Claire glared at Wanda. She never liked the girl. Wanda wasn't a fan of Claire either, so neither one spoke.

Charlie, not caring what her sister was doing before her arrival, decided to turn on the stereo and blast some rap music. She then smirked at her little sister and said, "Oh, I'm sorry. Are we bothering you?"

Claire frowned. Not only was her sister inconsiderate, she was dangerous too. Claire didn't like what Charlie was into. She had found the cocaine and seen the bundles of money, and she hated the dirty cops coming and going from their apartment as if they owned the place. It all made her extremely uncomfortable.

To make the situation worse, the same project bitches who had turned their backs on Charlie were now regularly visiting and sitting in their living room drinking their liquor and eating the food Claire helped pay for. Claire strongly felt that these bitches were users and just being nosy, but Charlie wanted to show off and boast about the finer things she had in life and talk shit. Charlie was living her best life, but what was the point if nobody knew?

Claire felt Charlie was living foul and reckless, and she wanted out. It was the reason she was studying so fervently. Claire wanted to graduate, start a career, and leave her dysfunctional family behind.

"Look at this bitch. Why she still pretending to study when all she gonna do is cheat on her next test?" Charlie mocked.

The insult cut Claire deeply. It was a part of her life that she wanted to forget. She couldn't believe what she heard. But Charlie had said it, and Wanda was laughing too hard at it.

"I mean, what do my little sister think she is, an A-student or sumthin'?" Charlie continued to crack on her sister.

Wanda continued to laugh, adding insult to injury.

Claire wasn't going out like that. She responded, "And who are you? A washed up, ho-ass gangster?"

That remark coming from Claire was shocking. Wanda laughed just as hard at that as she had Charlie's joke.

"Oh, so you tryin' to call me a ho?"

"If the shoe fits . . ." Claire replied.

Claire was giving it back just as good as she took it. But she hated the tension and she hated living with Charlie. There wasn't anywhere for her to go for privacy because she slept in the living room and it was where Charlie entertained herself and her guests.

Charlie laughed and shot back, "You forget to take your medication, wit' ya crazy ass?"

Claire was fed up with bickering back and forth with Charlie. She got up from the couch and marched into the bathroom for two reasons—for some privacy and to make a phone call.

Claire planted herself on the toilet and pulled out her cell phone. It was a call she didn't want to make, but she decided to swallow her pride and reach out anyway. She dialed Bacardi's number and felt nervousness swimming around in her belly.

The phone rang and Claire waited with bottomless apprehension. Finally, her mother answered.

"Who this?" Bacardi barked into the phone.

"Bacardi, it's me, Claire."

"Why the fuck are you calling?"

"I just—I just wanna come back home. Please. I don't wanna stay here with Charlie anymore," she pleaded.

"Oh, so the grass ain't greener, huh?" Bacardi responded with contempt in her voice.

Claire was in tears as she spoke to her mother. "No. I wanna come back home. I don't wanna live with Charlie anymore. She's too much."

"Bitch, you should have thought about that when you put your hands on me."

"I'm sorry."

"Sorry ain't enough, and hell no, Claire. You made your choice to side wit' that bitch, now fuckin' deal wit' it."

"But Mama—"

"Don't fuckin' *Mama* me now, Claire. It's too fuckin' late. And not after you kept that secret from me on what Charlie did to Chanel. You must be out ya mind to think you have the right to come an' move back in wit' me!" Bacardi ranted.

"I'm sorry!"

"Fuck your apology. I don't fuckin' accept it!" she spat. "And besides, both y'all fuckin' rooms are already rented out and I'm gettin' good money for them. Don't call me no fuckin' more!"

Bacardi hung up on her.

Claire sat there crushed. She felt stuck now. Her mother was a ruthless and unforgiving bitch. Her tears continued to fall. It felt like the walls were collapsing in on her. She was out of choices, and she would have to deal with Charlie's bullshit until something better came along. But she didn't foresee anything better coming along. It felt like she was living in hell on earth.

The past two days felt like paradise for Claire. Charlie hadn't been home, and Claire was able to read, study, and relax. Her sister had up and disappeared out of the blue without saying a word to her.

Claire wasn't complaining. She needed the solitude. It was therapeutic for her. For once, it felt like she lived alone, and she was loving it. But that feeling would soon become short-lived.

On the third day of Charlie's sudden absence, Claire heard a heavy knock at the door. It ricocheted through the apartment and disturbed Claire from her reading. Whoever it was seemed very impatient.

Claire got up from her chair and went to see who it was. She looked through the peephole and recognized the person knocking. It was Ahbou.

"Charlie's not here," she said to him through the door.

"Where is she, then?" he asked with irritation.

"I don't know."

"I think you do!"

"You need to leave, Ahbou."

"I'm not going anywhere until I know where Charlie is," he replied.

He continued to bang on the door, annoying and scaring Claire.

"Please leave, Ahbou, before I call the police!" Claire threatened.

"Bitch, did you forget? I *am* the fuckin' police."

"And I'll call the real ones to report you for harassment," she countered.

"Cop or not, I know about you, and it ain't pretty."

Ahbou seethed from the other side of the door. He couldn't chance Claire calling the police and having cops not on the take find him there.

"I'll be back, and I wanna know where the fuck she is," he said, making his departure.

Claire exhaled, glad he was finally gone. The stench of Charlie's mess was starting to stick to her.

Ahbou was unshakeable. Every day, twice a day, he came to the apartment looking for Charlie and seeking out a confrontation. He had become a stalker. He was obsessed, but Claire thought she was safe from him inside the locked apartment.

After Claire got dressed for work, she stared through the peephole to make sure Ahbou wasn't lurking around in the hallway before she walked out. She didn't see anything off, so she opened the door. The moment she stepped foot into the hallway, it seemed like Ahbou appeared from out of nowhere. He argued with Claire and pushed his way into the apartment, frantically looking for Charlie.

"Charlie, where the fuck you at?" he shouted.

"I told you, she's not here!" Claire yelled.

Ahbou pivoted and stormed at Claire with a wild and jealous look in his eyes. Claire was terrified, but she tried not to show it. When a nosy neighbor came to investigate the incident, it spooked Ahbou and he hurriedly left the scene.

The following day, he came back. He banged on the apartment door to no avail and then used his badge to get the superintendent to let him in. He was done playing nice. He caught Claire off-guard. She was about to leave for work, and when she saw Ahbou inside the apartment, she screamed with fear.

"Where the fuck is she? She's with some nigga, right? She's fucking somebody else?" he shouted with rage.

"I don't fuckin' know!" Claire retorted.

Ahbou didn't like the insubordination from Claire. He felt like he should be respected. He charged toward her and forcefully grabbed her by her clothes and shoved her against the living room wall.

"You fuckin' bitch, I'll bash your fuckin' face in if you ain't telling me the truth," he threatened her. "Is she seeing another nigga?"

"I told you, I don't know. I'm not in my sister's business," she exclaimed.

He glared at her. The frightened and unknowing look in her eyes indicated to him that maybe she was telling him the truth. He knew that Charlie wasn't close with her sister. So why would she tell her anything? Of course Charlie would disappear for several days without telling anyone where she was. It was her character.

He released his grip from Claire and stepped away.

Claire couldn't wait for Charlie to get home from wherever she was. She was sick of her shit—sick of her sister's life colliding with hers.

Ahbou offered no apologies to Claire. He continued to frown and simply said, "When you see that bitch, tell her she needs to call me. ASAP."

He spun around and left. Claire slammed the door behind him and screamed out in frustration and anger. She wanted to kill her sister for putting her in such a hostile predicament with a jealous lunatic.

Chapter Twenty-Two

Chanel sat impatiently by Mateo's bedside while Nurse Beth gave him a sponge bath. Chanel would often ask if she could be the one to give it to him, but it was against the facility's rules. If something were to happen, then they could get sued. Chanel thought, *What can happen with helping to give my man a sponge bath?*

After the sponge bath, she watched Kyle help Mateo move his legs and arms during therapy. His arms were strong and his legs were slowly catching up. Mateo would sweat profusely while trying to walk and do things that most people take for granted. Early on, Mateo was embarrassed, but he pushed those feelings aside because it was all for him and Chanel to get back to normal. He wanted to become a hundred percent whole for her.

He was a fighter. He was determined to get well.

Once everyone left the room, Chanel crawled into bed with Mateo and snuggled against him. He wrapped his arms around her and said, "I know it's hard right now, baby, but I'm gonna get there."

"I know, baby. I see you're trying, and I love that about you. You never give up."

"Yeah, but all this shit is expensive, and Pyro—I know this shit is a lot on him." He sighed.

"He's your friend, your brother, and he's not giving up on you just like I'm not giving up on you," she said, stroking his arm.

"That means a lot to me."

"I know it does, baby. I know."

He paused for a moment before asking her, "Do you still see a future with me?"

Chanel looked offended by the question. "What kind of question is that, Mateo? Of course I still see a future with you. Why would you ask me that?"

"Lately, it seems like your mind has been distant—on something else. And for a moment, you weren't coming to see me on a regular like you used to."

She sighed. "I just had some things going on."

"Like what?" he wanted to know.

"Just things, Mateo."

"I understand. You don't want to talk about it right now."

"I would rather talk about us."

"Us?"

"You still wanna marry me?" she asked him.

"Of course I do, Chanel. I love you. You're my world."

She smiled. They locked hands and stared at each other. Though parts of his body were still impaired, he was still the same, she felt. The way he gazed at her, she never had to guess how he felt about her.

"You want a big wedding or small wedding?" he asked her.

"You know me; something simple," she replied.

"And kids? How many?"

"You can give me four kids—two boys and two girls."

He laughed. "Four?"

"Oh, that's gonna be a problem?"

"Nah."

"I know you're gonna have fun making them," she joked.

He laughed. "You got that right."

"I know, and I wish we could start now," she teased.

"No doubt."

They talked about their future, movies, family, and life. Their conversation flowed effortlessly, and Mateo loved hearing her voice. It was comforting to him in so many ways. He wanted Chanel to lay with him forever. With her by his side, he felt like he could take on the world.

Chanel saw with her own eyes that Mecca and Pyro were back together again when they both walked into the apartment smiling and laughing. Chanel was caught off guard by their reconciliation. The last she heard, Mecca was feeling neglected and used, and she thought Pyro was ready to move on. But that wasn't the case.

"I'm done with him, Chanel," she remembered Mecca telling her.

Pyro had his arms wrapped around Mecca lovingly. They seemed like the "it" couple. He was happy and she was happy. They were up on each other so tight, not even gravity could pull them apart.

"Wow. How did this happen?" Chanel asked with a smile.

"He missed me and I missed him. That's what happened," said Mecca.

"Yup. Real talk," Pyro cosigned.

Pyro had met Mecca at her university carrying a bouquet of flowers and a sincere apology. He swept her off her feet, took her on a shopping spree, and then to dinner at an eloquent restaurant in the city. Now they were at his apartment ready to have make-up sex.

"It's good to see y'all together again," Chanel said.

"Thank you. Now if you don't mind, Chanel, my baby and I got a lot of making up to do," Mecca said gleefully.

She and Pyro kissed passionately for Chanel to see. Mecca was googly-eyed for her man, and Pyro couldn't keep his hands off of her. He massaged her booty and held her firmly in his grasp.

"Well, I baked a cherry pie," said Chanel.

"Oh word? You baked?" asked Mecca.

"Yeah. Y'all hungry?"

"Shit girl, you know I love your cooking, especially your baking," Mecca replied excitedly.

Putting their make-up session in the bedroom temporarily on hold, the two decided to keep Chanel company in the kitchen as they nibbled on her mouthwatering cherry pie and drank some Bailey's liquor. It was the three of them sitting at the table, chatting and laughing, and Chanel couldn't help but to wish that Mateo was there too. She wished they could all go out on a double date.

Mecca was seated on her man's lap, and the two continued to flirt, touch, and kiss on each other. Chanel simply smiled at their affection in the kitchen. Mecca even fed her man some cherry pie, and Pyro glided his hand between her thighs and rested his touch against her pussy. They kissed fervently again, and it looked like they were ready to fuck each other right there in the kitchen. Mecca wanted to cut their threesome short and go make love to her man. She began hinting and looking at Pyro sexily.

"I guess you want me for dessert next, huh?" Mecca asked.

He smiled widely and replied, "With a cherry on top."

The two stood up, and Pyro embraced Mecca from behind, kissing the side of her neck. They said goodnight to Chanel. She didn't want them to leave. Their company kept her mind off certain things, but there was no stopping them from getting their freak on.

The couple hurried into the bedroom and closed the door behind them. Chanel remained in the kitchen cleaning up their dishes. She had nothing else to do. Soon, she heard the passionate sounds coming from the bedroom—Mecca moaning and groaning.

Chapter Twenty-Three

KB's black Beamer came to a stop on black 20" rims in front of Charlie's apartment building. The two were all smiles as they continued to be affectionate toward each other in the front seat of his car. Charlie kissed him intensely and even massaged his dick.

"Yo shawty, ya too much. I had a good time wit' you," KB said.

"I did too, baby."

The two had just returned from the Bahamas, where they had fucked passionately every night. Charlie swore she was going to have to take a pregnancy test after the vacation. Not once did they use any protection, and KB wasn't a big fan of pulling out.

"Da pussy too good for me to pull out, shawty," he had said.

The two locked lips and wrestled tongues for several minutes, while Charlie conjured up another erection in his jeans. Finally pulling away, KB joked, "Damn, you ain't get enough in the Bahamas?"

"No. It was too good. Shit, I might have you come upstairs," she said.

He grinned. "Shawty, I gotta make moves, ya know? Been away from the streets a bit too long."

"I feel you. So when I'm gonna see you again?"

"I'll be back north sometime next week."

"Business or pleasure?" she teased.

"Ya know I'm down fo' both."

They kissed passionately once again before her exit from the vehicle. KB smiled her way; they were like two teenagers in love.

"Be safe out hurr, shawty," he said to her before driving off.

"I will."

She watched his Beamer turn the corner and headed inside. The New York City cold was a direct contrast to the Bahamas. It was paradise out there, and Charlie was grateful that KB whisked her away to someplace she had never been before. KB was fun and exciting. He was different and funny, and she couldn't stop thinking about him.

Charlie came sauntering into her apartment after her blissful week on vacation with KB. She was tanned, cheery, and finally loving her life again.

However, the moment she stepped foot into her place, she was confronted by an angry Claire.

"Where the fuck were you, Charlie?" Claire shouted.

"What, you Bacardi now? I gotta tell you my fuckin' whereabouts?"

"You were gone a week!"

"And?"

"And that crazy cop you're fuckin' kept coming by here looking for you, and he even assaulted me," Claire exclaimed to her, waiting for her sister's reaction.

"I'm not worried about that fool," Charlie replied.

"What? I told you, he came here and fuckin' assaulted me."

"Obviously, he didn't do a good job at it. You look like you don't have one scratch on you," Charlie replied.

"Are you serious? After everything I did for you—after everything you put me through, you stand there nonchalant about Ahbou assaulting me? I had your back against our parents and got put out because of you, and you can't have my back over a nigga!"

Charlie remained unaffected by the speech. "Ain't nobody ask you to have my back, Claire. I know how to handle my own."

In that moment, Claire realized that she meant just as much to her sister as Chanel did. She stared at Charlie with disgust, having nothing else to say to her. She turned around and left the apartment. She needed to go for a walk—clear her head and get Charlie out of her mind. She wanted to punch Charlie in her face, but she kept her composure.

Charlie was over Claire's tantrums and wished she would grow up.

The loud and impulsive banging at the apartment door came after midnight. Claire and Charlie were both asleep, but the reckless knocking ricocheted through the apartment and stirred both girls awake.

"Charlie, open the fuckin' door!" Ahbou shouted.

Charlie sighed with contempt for that man. He was relentless, and she knew he wasn't going away. She grabbed a long T-shirt and went to confront him. She angrily swung open her door and shouted, "Nigga, you know what time it is?"

They had matching scowls. He pushed his way past Charlie and into the apartment and shouted, "Where the fuck were you this past week?"

"I was busy!"

"Busy doing what, Charlie?"

"Like that's your business," she retorted.

"It is when you're fuckin' with me," he countered.

"Muthafucka, who you? You don't own or control me."

"Bitch, I run shit here," he yelled. "So who you fuckin' out there?"

"Fuck you, Ahbou. That's none of ya business."

"You think I'm playing with you?"

Claire grimaced at their confrontation from her position on the couch and threw the pillow over her head. She had to get up for work and school the next day.

"I'm gonna ask you again, who you fucking?" Ahbou was desperate to know.

"I told you, I was fuckin' busy!"

"You lying-ass bitch!" he screamed.

"You the bitch!"

Things were becoming intense. It looked like Ahbou was ready to strike Charlie, but then the unexpected happened. His tone softened and he became apologetic.

"Look, baby, I'm sorry for coming at you fucked up like this, but I love you, Charlie, and I get jealous just thinking about you being with another nigga."

She stood there listening with her hands on her hips.

"I missed you, baby. You know I did. And it drives me crazy when I don't see you on the regular," he continued.

"You need to stop being so jealous, Ahbou. I told you, I was out of town takin' care of some business," she said.

"I know you're a busy woman."

"You know that, so stop comin' at me wit' your insecurities. It's a turn-off," she said.

"I know what turns you on." He smiled and reached out and took her hand.

She looked at him uninterested.

He continued. "I'm tired, Charlie. I worked a double shift. Could I stay the night?"

"Don't start no shit, Ahbou. I'm warning you!"

In a hot minute, they were inside Charlie's bedroom fucking their brains out. Claire could hear their loud sex noises like bells ringing in her ear. She was back to living in hell.

The following morning, Charlie lay naked between Ahbou's arms, the side of her face nestled against his hairy chest. It seemed like last night's argument between them never happened. The two looked loving together, but Charlie was working her magic on him. She wanted an update on Landy's criminal situation.

"The ADA is trying to get her to plead guilty and do six months," he informed her.

Charlie was pleased. *Teach that bitch to be in my business*, she thought.

"Then do me a favor—give me the date she'll go before the judge if she cops a plea. I definitely want to be there so that bitch can know that I had a hand in her demise—that I did this to her."

"I definitely will," he assured her.

For some reason, Charlie still wasn't satisfied. There was someone else that she wanted on her hit list.

"I need another favor from you," she said to him.

"Like what?"

"I need you to find an address for my sister. Her name is Chanel Brown. Can you run her name through your system or through the DMV? I know she drives around in a white Range Rover Sport," said Charlie.

"I didn't know you had another sister."

"We're not close," she said.

"Oh? And why not?"

"It's a long story that I'm not tryin' to get into. But we got beef and you can help me solve my issues wit' her," she said.

"I got your back, baby," he said.

Anything for Charlie.

Chapter Twenty-Four

Chanel was on the couch watching TV and minding her business when Pyro came out of his bedroom with a smile on his face.

"Come and take a ride with me," he said.

"A ride? Where to?" she asked.

"It's a surprise."

At first, she was skeptical. He and Mecca were an item, and Mecca had been at the apartment nearly every day since they had gotten back together. Every night, Chanel could hear them in the bedroom, probably having some of the best sex they ever had. Chanel couldn't help but to be a bit envious of their relationship and their sex life. Hers had been put on hold for a while.

"So, you're not going to tell me?"

"Like I told you, it's a surprise," he repeated.

A surprise for me or Mecca? she thought.

"Let me get my coat," she said.

She stood up and went into her bedroom, closing the door behind her. She went to the bedroom window and gazed outside. It was a cold day, and each day it seemed like the world around her was becoming colder. For some reason, Claire came into her thoughts. Chanel didn't know why she started thinking about Claire, but she wondered if she was okay. Though they didn't always see eye-to-eye, they had both been through some shit.

Chanel threw on her Moncler jacket and joined Pyro out in the hallway. He was still all smiles.

"This better be worth my time, Pyro. I got things to do, you feel me?" she joked with him.

"It will be."

As Pyro drove, he remained in a high spirits.

Mecca's pussy must be good. It has him grinning like the Cheshire Cat, she joked to herself.

"I see you're in a very good mood today, Pyro. Why's that?"

"What, I can't be in a good mood?"

"Yeah, you can, but you seem a bit extra with it today."

"I'm just happy, that's all."

"Well, it's good to see you happy," she said.

"Things are going great with Mecca."

"Yeah, I can see that."

"I mean, she's smart, beautiful, and ambitious, and we can make a great life together," he stated.

"Mecca is a great person. I can definitely cosign on that. So, you're in love with her, huh?"

"I do love her."

"And she really loves you too."

Pyro continued to smile and drive to their destination.

"I went to see Mateo again. He asked about you," Chanel said.

"How's he coming along?"

"Every day is a blessing for him. And he's coming along really well."

"Damn, I've been meaning to go visit him, but I've been so caught up with everything . . ."

"He understands, Pyro. He's grateful for everything you've done for him, including keeping up with his medical expenses," she said.

"Yeah, but I need to start being there for him more. I've been distracted," he said.

"You're in love. That's a reasonable distraction," she replied.

Pyro was grateful to have Chanel as a friend. He knew that he could talk to her about anything. She was a good listener and she gave good advice. Their conversation continued freely until Pyro arrived at his destination in the city.

Chanel was confused. She wondered why they were in the Diamond District. Pyro looked at her with a smile, and he picked up on her confusion.

"I bet you wanna know why we're here," he said, pulling into a parking garage.

"Yeah."

"I need your help in picking out an engagement ring for Mecca."

Ah-Ah, what...? she thought. Chanel was shocked and speechless.

"Are you serious?"

"The utmost."

She didn't know what to say or how to react, so she just smiled. She glanced down at her own empty ring finger and swallowed a host of emotions—jealousy being one of them. It looked like Mecca was going to get married before her. Her friend's life had changed for the better, and she felt that her life had been destroyed.

"She deserves it, Chanel. Mecca is great woman and I'm not trying to lose her," Pyro said as he got out of the car.

Chanel reluctantly followed him out of the garage and into the quaint jewelry retailer. Right away, they were greeted by an orthodox Jewish man with a grizzly beard who was dressed in black clothing and long curls.

"Welcome. I'm Seth. How may I help you, my friend?" the man asked.

"I'm here to buy a diamond engagement ring for my girlfriend," Pyro said.

Seth immediately assumed that Chanel was his lady. He smiled at her and said, "Well, congratulations."

"Oh, it's not me," she quickly corrected. "I'm just here to help him pick out the perfect ring for my friend."

"Well, tell me what you're looking for and we can take things from there," said the jeweler.

"No doubt," Pyro happily replied.

Chanel pretended to be happy and excited for the couple as Seth showed them different styles and cuts of beautiful and expensive rings. Each ring was remarkable and flawless, and they all came with a hefty price tag. But for Pyro, money wasn't an issue. He was willing to spend whatever on a ring for his woman so she could flaunt it to her university friends.

Chanel tried to pick a modest ring for Mecca, stating that her friend wasn't flashy and that she admired the simple things. But Pyro felt the opposite. He wanted his woman to have the biggest and gaudiest diamond ring ever.

Pyro ended up picking out a 7-carat platinum setting diamond ring that was truly gorgeous. The ring even made Chanel envious. She wished Mateo was putting it on her finger. And it didn't come cheap. Pyro dropped $90,000 onto the counter like he was Floyd Mayweather, and the jeweler was all smiles.

"Anything for my lady," he proudly proclaimed.

"She is a very lucky woman," Seth replied.

Leaving the jewelry store, Chanel tried to smile and be happy for Pyro and Mecca, but it was becoming difficult. The engagement ring Mecca was about to receive was sinking into her mind like quicksand. She thought, *Why am I hating on my best friend? I should be happy for her.* But it continued to feel like the opposite no matter how hard she tried.

She climbed into the passenger seat of Pyro's car and sat there gazing out the window, lost in her own troubling thoughts.

"You think she'll like it, right?" Pyro asked.

"Yeah. She's gonna love it," she replied faintly.

Picking up on her aloof response, he asked, "You good, Chanel? Everything okay wit' you?"

"I'm fine, Pyro . . . just thinking about some things."

"Like what? Mateo?"

"That and other issues that I got going on."

"You know you can talk to me about anything, Chanel. I'm there for you like you're here for me," he said.

She smiled. "Thanks."

"So, you good?"

"Yeah. I'm fine."

"Listen, I wanna make this proposal really special. I want to set up something nice for Mecca, and I'm gonna need your help wit' this."

"And what do you have planned?"

"That's the thing. I don't know," he said. "That's why I need you in my corner right now, Chanel. I don't wanna mess things up. I want this proposal to be really memorable for her."

"I'll see what I can come up with," she replied halfheartedly.

He grinned. "I would appreciate that so much. You're the best."

Chanel didn't feel like she was the best. It felt like she was drowning in jealousy, sorrow, and displeasure. It felt like she was misery and she wanted to drag her friend along for some company.

Chapter Twenty-Five

Wanda was sprawled sloppily across the couch in Charlie's living room. She was tipsy and high and looking for an escape from her troubles. She and her man, Wisdom, had gotten into a major fight earlier. Wanda swung on him several times and threw a bottle at his head. Her temper had gotten the best of her, and Wisdom threatened to kill her. So she left in a hurry, escaping to Charlie's place to hide from him.

It was a Wednesday night and Charlie didn't care that it was a weekday. Wanda had become a regular guest, and the two of them frequently hung out in the living room, which doubled as Claire's room. They would have their own private party with drugs and liquor and talking shit. Wanda had become something like a leech in Charlie's life. She loved the area that Charlie was in, she loved the apartment, and she loved cruising around town in Charlie's SL Benz—along with being affiliated with someone who was on the rise. Charlie was making money and she was making a name for herself on the streets, and Wanda wanted to be a part of that.

Wanda didn't know it was Charlie who sent the cops to kick in her front door looking for stolen merchandise.

Charlie took a swig of Hennessy straight from the dwindling bottle. "You and ya nigga always fighting and breaking the fuck up, and then y'all get back together like the shit ain't happen."

"Fuck that nigga this time, for real. He ain't shit," Wanda griped.

"Bitch, please. You say that now, but next week, you gonna be riding his big black dick and forgettin' about y'all fight. Shit, I see why you keep goin' back to him. He knows how to fuck right—especially in doggystyle," Charlie said, taking a deep pull from her weed vape pen.

"What? How you know my nigga got a big dick? And how . . . how you know he likes to fuck doggystyle?" Wanda slurred.

"Cuz he looks like a nigga that can handle bitches like us," Charlie replied, exhaling the vapor into the air.

Suddenly, Wanda wasn't too tipsy or high to ask questions and put two and two together. Charlie was speaking too freely about Wisdom—especially about his dick game and how he liked to fuck a bitch. Though she and Wisdom had their issues, Wanda loved him.

Wanda stood up from the couch with a frown. "Is there sumthin' you ain't tellin' me, Charlie?"

"Sit ya dumb ass down, cuz I ain't in the mood for your drama right now, Wanda," Charlie retorted. "You really gonna trip over Wisdom? He ain't shit—he *been* out there fuckin' everything that moves. So don't start trippin' over that nigga right now."

Wanda became incensed. "Bitch, you fucked him, didn't you? You fucked Wisdom!"

"And if I did, so what? That nigga a ho," Charlie replied nonchalantly.

Wanda stepped threateningly closer to Charlie, getting in her face with her hands moving around wildly. "What, bitch? You a trifling-ass ho—fuckin' cunt bitch!"

"Fuck you!" Charlie shot back. "You better step back, bitch, and get the fuck outta my face."

"Or what? What the fuck you gonna do?" Wanda dared her with a hard stare.

And then it happened. Wanda coughed and spit out a loogie in Charlie's face. The nasty phlegm latched on to the side of Charlie's right eye and her cheek. Charlie reacted in a heartbeat and punched Wanda so hard that it looked like her face exploded. Their argument escalated into a fierce fight with yelling and screaming, strong punches, and hair pulling.

Charlie struck Wanda several times with a combination of blows, but Wanda's rage matched hers. They wrestled inside the living room, knocking over furniture, glasses, and pictures from the walls. Charlie grabbed a handful of Wanda's hair and tried her best to pull it out from the roots, wanting the bitch to become bloody and baldheaded. Wanda counter-attacked by thrusting her elbow into the side of Charlie's face and her chin. Charlie stumbled and Wanda lunged at her like a pouncing lion.

"Bitch! Fuck you, bitch!" Wanda shouted.

Wanda was stronger than Charlie thought—aggressive too. Knowing Charlie had fucked the man she was in love with ignited such a ferocious rage inside of Wanda that she started to have strength like she was Luke Cage. And since Claire was at work, there was no one around to break it up.

Wanda started to get the upper-hand on Charlie. As with her brawl with Chanel, Charlie was quickly finding herself on the losing end of a fight. She was determined not to lose to Wanda, though. She managed to escape Wanda's grasp and made a beeline for the kitchen. Wanda chased after her, determined to finish what they had started. Rage and hatred had completely overwhelmed her.

"I knew you was a snake-ass bitch, Charlie!" she shouted. "I'ma fuckin' kill you!"

Wanda was coming for her like a runaway train. However, the tide was about to change. Charlie grabbed a glass jar full of liquid from the kitchen cabinet and hastily opened it. When Wanda came near her to stomp her out, the clear liquid, which looked like water, was swiftly tossed into Wanda's face. Wanda immediately screamed and grabbed her face and fell to her knees. She was in unbearable pain. What looked like water inside the glass jar was in fact industrial grade acid. Charlie had bought the chemical weapon for Chanel, but any enemy would do.

Wanda continued to clutch at her face, feeling her skin melting away. Charlie's chest heaved up and down, and she gazed down at Wanda coldheartedly.

"What now, bitch! I told you don't fuck wit' me."

As she watched Wanda thrash around on the kitchen floor, hollering and screaming out in excruciating pain, the front door opened and Claire walked into the horror. She was shocked to see Wanda's face melting away.

"Ohmygod, what the fuck, Charlie! What happened to her!" Claire shrieked.

"Fuck that bitch," Charlie growled.

The screams coming from Wanda were so piercing that they echoed from the kitchen and into the hallway. Wanda was now running through the apartment crashing into furniture and the walls, not able to see. She was frantic and panicking. She was able to reach the kitchen sink and desperately tried to wash away the acid from her face, trying to save what was left of her beauty, but it was too late.

Claire tried to help too, but the damage was already done.

The screams coming from the apartment alerted her neighbors and they called the cops. Charlie was arrested and Wanda was rushed away in an ambulance to the nearest hospital with her face looking like melting wax. She was still in agonizing pain and the paramedics tried their best to soothe her. They had seen a lot of gruesome things, but in their eyes, this was a full-scale horror show.

Two uniformed cops escorted a handcuffed Charlie into the Brooklyn 77th precinct. Charlie didn't look worried at all. She remained cool and kept her mouth shut. In fact, she smirked at the cops as they arrested her and brought her into the building to be placed into a holding cell. Ahbou was shocked to see Charlie in handcuffs and being dragged into the precinct. The two briefly locked eyes but pretended that they didn't know each other, and when Charlie was out of his sight, Ahbou quickly went into action. He removed himself from the busy area inside the precinct and made an urgent phone call to Mona.

"Hey, it's me. They just arrested Charlie for something. I don't know what, but you need to get down here immediately," he said to her.

"I'm on my way," Mona replied.

Mona and Ahbou worked feverishly on Charlie's charges and her case. They were dumbfounded that she would do something as stupid as tossing acid in a friend's face during a fight. They had a lot to lose, and Charlie's reckless actions were costing them time and money. The two dirty cops were able to snag the case, and within hours of her arrest, she was released.

No charges.

But that didn't mean that Charlie was out of hot water yet. She was still on the stove. Mona and Ahbou needed to do some persuasion and coercing of the victim. They went to pay Wanda a visit at the hospital.

"Charlie Brown has been released," Mona told her.

Wanda became perplexed by the news—angry too. "Do you see my fuckin' face?! That bitch is a fuckin' maniac!"

Calmly, but assertively, they explained that they had two witnesses who gave statements saying Wanda had brought the acid to Charlie's apartment once she found out that Charlie had sex with her boyfriend. The statement continued to say she had somehow tripped and the acid fell over on her.

Wanda was stunned by the bullshit statement. "What? Are y'all fuckin' serious? Look at me, do it looked like I did this to myself by accident?"

Mona coolly asked her, "Did Charlie and your boyfriend have sex?"

"Yes, but—"

"Did y'all have an argument over it?"

Wanda hesitated and reluctantly replied, "Yes . . ."

She observed them taking down notes. She was unaware that the detectives were connected to Charlie—that they were business partners in the drug trade. However, it was obvious that they were taking Charlie's side for some reason and were turning things around on her, making it appear as if Charlie was the victim to a horrendous crime.

When it became clear to Wanda that Charlie wasn't going to be prosecuted and pay for what she did to her, she flipped out. She started screaming and crying hysterically for the detectives to see. The nurses had to rush into her room to calm her down by sedating her.

Before leaving the room, Mona told Wanda that they had dusted the glass jar for fingerprints and found none belonging to Charlie. She also mentioned Wanda's long rap sheet.

As Wanda was calming down from the sedative and was gradually drifting off to sleep, she couldn't understand why any of this was happening to her. It was a bewildering situation that made Wanda want to commit suicide—because she looked hideous and Charlie was going to go on with her life without any consequences.

Chapter Twenty-Six

The lights in the auditorium were dimmed and the audience was quietly engrossed in what was happening on the stage. They were watching a Columbia University student performance of *Aida*. Once a popular Broadway musical, this rendition of the play was being shown in two acts. Among the audience in the packed house were Mecca and Chanel. They were immersed in the play, mesmerized by the phenomenal singing and acting.

Chanel was amazed by the campus and Mecca's life. Mecca was accomplishing big things, but it made Chanel feel like life was passing her by. She continued to carry the guilt of what happened to Mateo, feeling that he was fucked up because of her. Mecca's situation made Chanel want to press the fast-forward button on her life to her own wedding date. It felt like she was just existing—trying to survive day by day.

She sat next to Mecca watching the play with a smile on her face, but she couldn't fully enjoy the experience. Chanel knew she was constantly thinking selfish thoughts and she didn't like herself much for it. With Pyro and Mecca's new love, Chanel felt insignificant again. It was now all about Mecca, as it had always been about Charlie or Claire. Mecca had the man. She would have the ring. And Mecca would have the wedding. Although Mateo was on the mend and they undoubtedly would have a future together, it was her present rut that kept infiltrating her thoughts.

After the play, the two girls decided to go get something to eat at a popular university hangout called Hang Time. They took a seat at a tetragon table and ordered two drinks.

"I'm glad you were able to come out and spend some time with me," said Mecca.

"It's my pleasure. I loved the play," Chanel replied.

"*Aida* is one of my favorites, and the school did an amazing job reenacting it."

"They did."

They took a sip from their drinks and smiled at each other.

"So, how are you holding up, with Mateo still in the hospital?"

"I got my good days and bad days," replied Chanel.

"Don't we all?" Mecca said.

Chanel felt slighted. She thought, *What bad days are you experiencing right now?* She wanted to say something sarcastic, but she replied, "We just gotta have faith that things will get better, right?"

"Of course, and they will for you, Chanel. I know you're strong."

They ordered their meals and continued with their chitchat. When their food was brought out, Mecca said to Chanel, "Sooo, I need to talk to you. It's important."

"What is it?"

Mecca took a bite of a fry. "I think Pyro is going to propose to me."

"Propose? What makes you think that?"

"There have been so many hints, and lately, he's been talking about kids and a family, and things have been moving swimmingly with us."

"Swimmingly?" Chanel laughed at the word.

"Girl, it means we're flowing."

"I know what it means." Chanel quickly recognized that her voice sounded a little more assertive than she wanted to come across, so she softened her response with a smile.

"Anyway," Mecca continued, "I believe him when he tells me there's no one else."

Chanel believed it was true. There hadn't been any women sleeping at the apartment but Mecca.

Mecca didn't know if she should celebrate or become worried. What if Pyro did ask her to marry him? Was she ready for marriage?

"Well that's not entirely true, is it?"

Mecca nearly choked on her drink. "What do you mean? Is he seeing someone else?"

"How should I know?" Chanel looked bewildered by the question.

"You just said that Pyro is seeing some bitch."

Chanel smirked. "Oh, I just meant that Sheree will always be in his life. She is that someone else that you'll have to deal with should you two get married. Just something to think about."

Mecca exhaled. "Girl, you had me going for a second. I can handle Sheree. What I can't handle is Pyro fucking Sheree, but I'm confident that he's not, so that's a non-factor."

Chanel nodded.

Mecca stared at her friend for a beat, looking serious about something.

She started with, "Listen, Chanel, we really do need to talk about something."

"I thought we were talking," Chanel said, giggling a little.

Mecca didn't laugh. She continued with, "Once Pyro and I are married, he probably won't be able to take care of Mateo anymore. You have to admit, Pyro has spent a lot of money on Mateo's hospital stay and his physical therapy. I mean, it just wouldn't be financially sustainable with him having a wife and hopefully more children coming."

Chanel couldn't believe what she was hearing—especially coming from her best friend. The smile on her face was gone, replaced by some shock and resentment.

Mecca saw the offended look on Chanel's face and said, "Listen, and let me explain. I know Mateo has his own money that Pyro hasn't dipped into yet, sitting in banks and safety deposit boxes and most likely collecting interest."

"So he tells you everything?" asked Chanel.

"I mean, isn't he supposed to? He's my man, and maybe soon to become my fiancé."

"You won't have to worry about Mateo anymore. He's pulling through just fine," said Chanel with a slight attitude.

"I'm so glad to hear that. And one more thing, Chanel," Mecca said with her attention fixed on her friend. "Once Pyro and I are engaged, I really want you to move out. I mean it's cool for now, with him looking out for you. But I'm his woman and I would like to walk around the place naked for my man, and have sex with him throughout the place . . . you know, like giving him some head in the living room, or having sex butt naked on the kitchen counter. And real talk, having you around is gonna fuck up our kinky-ass sex life."

"So tell me how the fuck you really feel?" Chanel retorted.

"And why would you get offended by that, Chanel? I'm just keeping things real with you."

Chanel pushed her plate to the side. Her appetite was suddenly gone. "It must be great to be on top of the world, right? Boss your friends around."

Mecca waved her hand in the air and caught the attention of their wait staff. It was time for the check. She was ready to go. She didn't know how much longer she could listen to Chanel play victim.

"Are you serious? You think I'm bossing you around for not wanting you living with my man?"

Chanel pointed out, "There would be no you and Pyro if it wasn't for me."

Mecca heartily disagreed. "Do you really think that?"

"I made that happen."

Mecca countered with, "You can bring a horse to the water, but you can't force it to drink. Pyro hollered at me because of what I brought to the table. It had nothing to do with you, Chanel."

Chanel's nostrils were flared. She looked Mecca up and down and for the first time in their friendship she wanted to punch her in her conceited face. To Chanel, Mecca had changed. The Mecca she knew would never toss her out on the street.

She asked, "You really believe that, don't you?"

"I know it."

"Whatever, Mecca. You're different—sitting there thinking you're better than me," said Chanel.

Mecca smirked. "What? Why would you think that?"

"It's true. Your man is healthy and my man is fucked up right now."

"Chanel, you really need to chill and think about what you're saying. You sound like a hater right now."

"I'm not hating on you, Mecca."

"Well, the way you're coming at me, you could have fooled me."

Chanel expressed with finality in her tone, "Look, let's just agree to disagree. Okay?"

"Fine then," Mecca snapped back.

The waiter came over with the check, which was promptly paid. Mecca asked that her food be placed in a doggy bag, which added additional tension between them. They couldn't even look at each other. In fact, Chanel was ready to leave, but Mecca wanted to take home everything on her plate. She didn't want to waste anything, and Chanel felt she was being petty. Their time together had ended in disaster.

Chanel continued to stew as she dropped Mecca off on the campus. They didn't say a word to each other. Mecca climbed out of the Range and didn't look back at her friend. She strutted onto the campus while Chanel rolled her eyes and sighed.

"Bye then, bitch."

Chapter Twenty-Seven

*B*acardi was in the kitchen smoking a cigarette and chatting on her cell phone when she heard the loud and familiar knocking on the apartment door.

"Let me call you back," Bacardi said to the person on the other end of the phone.

She ended her call and stood up huffing and puffing with an attitude. Her cigarette dangled from her lips and her robe was slightly opened, revealing the bra and granny drawers she was wearing underneath. She glanced through the peephole and saw what she expected—two detectives standing outside in the hallway. Bacardi moaned with displeasure. She was in no mood to deal with them, but she knew that they weren't going to go away.

She reluctantly opened the door and greeted them with a puckered brow. "What y'all want now? I'm tired of fuckin' police comin' to my door. Ain't this harassment or sumthin'?"

"We're sorry to bother you, ma'am, but we're here looking for a Charlie Brown," said Detective McKnight.

"She's not here," Bacardi responded. "She don't live here anymore."

"Can we come in and look around?" asked his partner, Detective Greene.

"I told you, she's not here."

"Well, we have a few questions to ask her," said McKnight.

Bacardi felt like her back was against the wall. The detectives were stern faced and persistent.

Someone had called the tip line for the $2,000 Crime Stoppers reward, and the DNA results from Chanel's rape kit had finally come in. They found that the Godfrey Williams was the perpetrator. The tipster alleged that Charlie Brown had set the whole thing up. Charlie was also listed on God's bail and she was Chanel Brown's sister. The detectives felt that they had something. Charlie's name kept coming up in several investigations, from robbery to homicide, and they needed to have a serious word with her.

The murder suspect, Kymberly Stephens, adamantly swore that she saw Godfrey's ex-girlfriend, Charlie, leaving his place only moments before she arrived—and that she found God already dead when she got there. Her defense team was testing for DNA and any trace evidence.

Bacardi allowed them into her home, but she wasn't making them coffee. Their guard was up; they looked around to confirm that her daughter wasn't home.

"I told you that I don't fuck wit' my daughter. I kicked her ass out."

"We just needed to make sure," said Greene. "Someone called in a tip saying that she lived here."

Bacardi fumed. "These fuckin' snitches out here need to mind their fuckin' business."

Butch joined his wife in the living room, and he was angry to see the detectives inside his home. Enough was enough. Even with Charlie gone, she was still bringing trouble to their home.

Seeing that there were no signs of Charlie's presence, the detectives made their exit. But it didn't come without a tongue lashing from Bacardi.

"Like I told y'all muthafuckas, my daughter don't live here anymore. So I would appreciate if you would stop comin' around here and makin' trouble. I don't need the stress, got-damn-it! And if you got a case against Charlie, then so be it, but leave me and my fuckin' husband out of it. Go bother someone else and go arrest some real fuckin' criminals!"

She slammed the door behind them.

Butch looked at his wife with appreciation. "That's telling them, baby. I love you."

Bacardi didn't smile or reply to his words. She stood there by the door pissed off and wondering who had called in the tip. She knew it wasn't about the reward, but it was about getting Charlie arrested.

Chapter Twenty-Eight

The chiming of her cell phone made Charlie frown and curse. She had been sleeping all day after partying all night and popping bottles in VIP with Ahbou. She wanted the world to see her—and they were taking notice. Last night she was the fiercest chick in the club in her Alexander Wang cocktail dress and knee-high boots, her reddish hair in long curls. She and Ahbou did it up on the dance floor, acting a fool, grinding and kissing and feeling on each other like they didn't have a care in the world. They had money to burn and were living it up. After the club, the two were drunk and animated, and they continued to paint the town red by hitting up after-hours spots in the city. An hour before the sun rose, they were fucking in a bathroom stall.

Charlie came stumbling through her apartment door two hours after the sun came up. The only thing she wanted to do was sleep all day. But that dream ended abruptly with her ringing cell phone. She ignored it once, and twice, but the third time sent her over the edge. She leaped from her bed and snatched the cell phone into her hand and shouted, "Who the fuck is this?"

"I need you to come get me," said Claire.

"What? Why?"

"Because that hooptie you gave me to drive to work broke down."

"And this is my problem?"

"How I'm gonna get home?"

"You in New York City—buses, trains, and automobiles," Charlie wisecracked.

"Charlie, stop playing with me. You know I got classes tonight and I can't be late," Claire griped.

"Damn it, Claire—"

"I need to get home, Charlie. Don't do this to me. It's cold out here," she exclaimed.

"Okay! I'll fuckin' be there, just chill—and you better not keep me waiting."

Charlie huffed as she removed herself from the bed to sluggishly get dressed to do her sister a favor. The alcohol from last night had her feeling heavy and sloppy. It felt like her legs were concrete and rooted to the floor.

Half an hour later, Claire got into the car and she right away smelled the liquor on Charlie's breath. Claire sighed. Charlie had been driving under the influence. Lately, Charlie felt that she was untouchable with her dirty cop connections. She started to believe that she was above the law.

"You happy, sis?" Charlie asked.

"Just take me home."

Charlie got on her cell phone to talk to Ahbou. They had their fun last night, but now it was time to get back to business.

"Did you find that bitch's address yet?" she asked him.

"I'm still on it," he replied. "But that acid incident was stupid, Charlie. I meant to say something last night, but we were having too much fun."

"It wasn't meant for Wanda. It was meant for my sister. She thinks she pretty now and can fuck niggas on my level. I wanted to teach her pretty ass a lesson and scar her fuckin' face."

"You'd do that to your sister?"

"I said we ain't close, right?"

"Just be smart out here, Charlie. You become too reckless and we won't be able to protect you," Ahbou warned her.

"I hear you."

"Charlie, listen. I got your back, boo. I love you, and I don't want you lying to me about anything ever again. You feel me? Because I got my ways of finding out shit. You scratch my back and I scratch your back."

Charlie rolled her eyes. "Find that address, detective."

His odd statement baffled Charlie for a moment, but she didn't think anything of it. It was just him talking tough and foolish.

"I will. I'll do anything for you, baby—even kill a nigga," he said recklessly through the phone.

Claire was glaring at her sister. "Damn, Charlie, just when I thought you couldn't get any colder. You just can't leave shit alone. You're going after Chanel now?" Claire fussed.

"Not your business," Charlie snapped.

"You think just because you're fuckin' a cop that you're untouchable? This shit ain't gonna end well, Charlie. I can feel it. Stop while you're ahead!" Claire shouted.

"You know what, Claire? As much as I do for you, you still wanna judge me and take everyone's side except mine. I'm the only one who has always had your back. Not Butch, Bacardi, and especially not Chanel. When she got put on by Mateo what did she do for you? That bitch ain't give you a crumb. She walked around sporting new shit, driving an expensive whip. Did she ever toss you the keys? Or buy you a pair of kicks?"

"This ain't about money!"

They argued with Ahbou still on the phone.

"I'm sick of your shit!" Claire continued to rant. "You are the worst!"

Charlie ignored her sister's ranting and continued to stay on the phone with Ahbou, who heard Claire's rants too.

161

"What's wrong with your sister?" he asked her.

"She's being a bitch right now," said Charlie.

"Oh, *I'm* the one being a bitch!" Claire shouted.

Claire continued to fuss, and Charlie remained on the phone with Ahbou until she reached her block and saw KB's Beamer parked in front of her place. She smiled. It was unexpected, but she was glad he was there. Ahbou was fun to be around, but KB was the nigga she loved and the nigga who rocked her world, made her toes curl, and put a genuine smile on her face. It had been over a week since he was in New York. She knew that he was here for both business and pleasure.

"Ahbou, I'm gonna call you back."

Charlie ended their call, double parked, and got out of her Benz with Claire following her to KB's BMW. From her position, she could see his silhouette behind the steering wheel. Claire continued to fuss at Charlie, but Charlie had her mind on KB. Claire threatened that if Charlie touched Chanel again that they were going to have a problem. Enough was enough. Claire was standing up for her little sister. Chanel had been through enough, and she was determined not to let Charlie put her through any more pain.

Charlie eagerly approached the Beamer and knocked on the driver's side window, but KB didn't open the door. The car windows had a light tint, so it was difficult to see what was happening inside. She reached for the door handle and swung it open. Right away, she got the shock of her life. KB had been shot in the head and was slumped in the seat. His blood was spilled across the dashboard and the leather seats.

Charlie's eyes grew wide with shock and she cried out, "What the fuck!"

Claire shrieked when she saw the body inside the car and slowly backed away from the crime scene. She was utterly shocked at what she saw. Though she didn't see the murder or know the guy, another dead body was troubling enough. Her life had become a continuous reel of monumental lows.

After Charlie setting Chanel up to get robbed and raped, murdering Melanie, disfiguring Wanda with acid, and now seeing another dead body connected to her sister, Claire was coming unhinged. She looked into her sister's eyes and said, "I can't do this anymore."

Like a zombie, she walked away, not sure where she was going. There was no destination in Claire's mind. The only thing she wanted to do was get away from the body and get away from Charlie.

Charlie couldn't worry about her sister. KB was dead, and she wasn't going to call the police. She took a napkin and wiped away her fingerprints from the door handle, but not before removing his Rolex watch and his pricey gold chain.

Charlie was sure that this was Ahbou's handiwork. Ahbou was a dirty cop with plenty of connections, and it was foolish of her to believe she could keep her affair with KB a secret from him. He was dangerous, and she was seeing it firsthand.

Chapter Twenty-Nine

*C*hanel woke up to memories of the horrific ordeal flooding back to her. She and Mateo were having the time of their lives. There were gifts and laughter and promises, and they were planning a trip to Hawaii to get married. And then they weren't. Funny how circumstances change within a split second. But life moves on, and time moves on, and today she wanted to spend her time with Mateo.

She got dressed in thick leggings, a nice top, and winter boots and drove her Range to the city to see her man.

"Hey, baby," Mateo said with a smile when Chanel walked into the room.

Chanel smiled back and replied, "Hey, you."

She climbed into his bed and hugged him lovingly. He was so brave. Not too long ago he had to piece words together to make conversation, and his emotions were flat. He was unable to carry out small tasks that people take for granted like holding a utensil or sitting up in bed by himself. He had come so far. Their conversations were back to normal, his muscles were strengthening, and he was getting better. Mateo was more awake and aware, and it wouldn't be long before he would be able to leave the place and function on his own. In fact, she felt he was ready for checkout.

She tested him. "Do you remember what we talked about the first day we met?" she asked.

"Yeah . . . I do."

"You sure?"

"Of course. How . . . how can I forget?" he said thinly as his mind searched for the answer.

But the look in his eyes was telling Chanel a different story. The trauma had left some gaps in Mateo's memory, and though he remembered certain things, there were events that were completely black to him—simple memories that Chanel was cherishing alone, for now.

She spent the day with him. They had lunch together and watched a few movies in his room. Chanel was grateful for the quality time with her man.

That evening, she left his bed to return to Pyro's place to get some rest. She kissed Mateo goodbye as he drifted off.

When Chanel walked into Pyro's apartment, she was shocked to find that Pyro had ordered them an expensive dinner and some pricey champagne.

"Surprise," he said. "You've been down lately and I wanted to do something to cheer you up."

"Wow. Thank you."

"It's the least I could do. I know you've been through a lot, and seeing you this morning, how sad you were . . ."

"I appreciate this, Pyro."

"C'mon, what are friends for? We look out for each other, right?"

She nodded. "No doubt."

Pyro had decorated the kitchen table for her with lit candles and they feasted on lobster tails, grilled scallops, and salad. Chanel had a thing for seafood, and Pyro went all out.

He asked about Mateo and she replied that he was doing fine. They joked and laughed and were working on their second bottle of champagne.

"So, any plans this weekend?" he asked her.

"Seeing Mateo," she said.

"Good to hear. But I got you a gift too."

"Pyro, a gift? Why?"

"Because I wanted to. It's just something to put a smile on your face, that's all. And I know if Mateo were here he'd be showering you with gifts left and right. Let me do this for my man," he said with the warmest smile.

Everything was genuine about him, and Chanel loved that. Mecca was a lucky woman.

Pyro got up from the table and went into the next room. He soon came back into the kitchen carrying a perfectly wrapped gift for her.

"Here you go."

Chanel was smiling and couldn't wait to see what he got her. She started to tear away the wrapping paper like a kid on Christmas Day, anxious to see her gift. It was a cookbook by Chrissy Teigen.

"I love it, Pyro. Thank you. I'm definitely gonna use it. Maybe I'll cook something for us tomorrow," she said.

"Hey, I wouldn't mind that. Your cooking is the best."

She chuckled at his compliment. Their evening together consisted of playing backgammon, sipping more champagne, joking and laughing, and then sharing stories about family, love, and their future. And then it happened—the lingering stare and the champagne blurring their boundaries. He leaned intimately close to her and pressed his lips against hers. She didn't resist, and the two of them shared a passionate kiss.

They both pulled away, knowing it was wrong, though it felt so right. They looked stunned by what just happened—no words for a moment, only silence between them with their eyes speaking volumes. It was a mistake.

He spoke first, saying, "I'm sorry."

"No. It's my fault."

"No. I shouldn't have tried to take advantage of you," he said.

"Pyro, I'm fine. It was just a kiss. It's not the end of the world."

He stood up and removed himself from the volatile situation he had put himself into without saying another word, going into his bedroom and heading straight for his shower. She did the same.

While showering, Chanel couldn't help but to think about the kiss. It was nice, though it was short. Pyro was a good kisser, but she hated that she was even thinking about how well he kissed. Chanel didn't want to make a big deal out of it, but she felt like she had let three people down; Mateo, Mecca, and herself. After showering, she donned a T-shirt and crawled into her bed, and instead of closing and locking her door like usual she left it ajar—just in case he wanted to talk. She placed her head against her pillow and tried to get some sleep. But she couldn't. The only thing on her mind was kissing Pyro.

Meanwhile, in the master bedroom, Pyro couldn't sleep either. He was up thinking about Chanel and their shared kiss. He wrestled with an unnerving thought. It stuck to him. It kept him up. And after an hour of trying to resist what he felt was inevitable, he got up from his bed and headed toward Chanel's room. Seeing her door ajar, he tapped on it and then slowly made his way inside.

"Hey, are you still up?" he whispered to her.

"Yeah," she faintly replied.

He crawled into her bed and moved close to her with no resistance. They stared at each other briefly, neither one saying a word as he abruptly disappeared underneath the covers, maneuvering his frame between her legs. She was wet, and so hot, and he burned to sample her nectar. Poised between her thighs, he lifted her bottom off the bed and hitched her legs over his shoulders so her pussy was directly in front of his mouth. He dipped his tongue inside of her and sucked and licked her sweet spot while she squirmed in his grasp.

Chanel knew it was wrong, but it felt so good. She was tired of having her only memory of sex be of her rape. She moaned and continued to squirm as Pyro swirled his tongue around inside of her and softly rubbed her clit with his thumb.

"Ooooh . . . uhh . . . ahhh . . ." she moaned.

The moans that were escaping from her full lips turned him on. He wanted to make her come. He wanted to feel her sweet juices gushing against his mouth.

Chanel panted and clutched the sheets as Pyro ate her out passionately. She closed her eyes and tried to fight the guilt, but it was a losing battle. Everything inside of her screamed, "You need this. Your body needs this."

After giving her ten minutes of oral pleasure, Pyro moved up from between her thighs and readied himself into the missionary position. Without a condom, he slowly penetrated her. He slowly made love to her and he was gentle, his strokes caring but masterful at the same time.

Chanel moaned against his ear. "Ohhhh. . ."

Right before she was about to come, he stared intensely at her and told her to open her eyes and look at him. She did so. The transfer of energy that passed between them was undeniable.

"Pyro," she moaned his name.

Soon, she had multiple orgasms. It was mind-blowing for her. Her body quivered in places she didn't know she had. She was breathless and spent, and Pyro held her tightly as they both fell asleep nestled against each other. Chanel didn't want to be let go. She wanted Pyro to hold her all night. It was a blissful moment for them both. The guilt they had both felt earlier was a distant memory.

When Chanel woke up the following morning, Pyro was gone, leaving her to face their situation alone. The feeling of ecstasy was replaced with a feeling of betrayal.

Chapter Thirty

Bacardi and Butch were sleeping like hibernating bears. It was 6:20am, and their bedroom was dark and silent. The house phone was the first to ring, and when they failed to answer that, Butch's cell phone started to ring nonstop. And then Bacardi's. Someone was desperately trying to reach them, and they didn't care how early it was.

Groggily, Bacardi got up and turned off all the phones in the room and then got back into bed and turned over to go back to sleep. She had a late night with Butch, and it was too damn early in the morning to be answering phone calls.

Thirty minutes later, she heard the banging on their front door. Now the entire apartment was up. The two female renters had to go to work soon, but the heavy banging at the door had them worried. The banging was consistent, and it sounded desperate.

Bacardi shot up from the bed with an attitude and threw on her robe and slippers and marched out of the bedroom looking like she was ready to go to war. She grumbled to herself and was ready to give whoever it was that was knocking loudly so early in the morning a strong piece of her mind.

Bacardi swung open the door to find her neighbors, Lester and Tisha, standing there looking strange. "Now why the fuck would you two be knocking on my door at the crack of muthafuckin' dawn?"

"Bacardi, didn't you see the news?" Lester asked her.

"What? No, I didn't see the news, Lester. It's six in the goddamn morning," she said.

The look her neighbors exchanged told Bacardi that something was wrong. Lester's look was sorrowful, as was Tisha's. Her anger transitioned to concern.

"What's on the news, Lester? What happened?" she asked fretfully.

By now, Butch had joined his wife at the front door. "What is it, Bacardi? What's going on?" he asked.

"I don't know, but it's something fucked up—I know it," Bacardi said.

Tisha was the one to say it, because it seemed Lester was too shaken up to spill the news.

"NY1 is reporting that Claire Brown, the student expelled from Harvard University, took her own life last night by jumping in front of a subway train," she informed them with a quivering lip.

Bacardi and Butch stared at Tisha in disbelief before Bacardi broke the trance.

"What? No! Stop lying to me, bitch! My daughter isn't dead," Bacardi hollered.

Butch spun around and moved toward the TV and hurriedly turned it on and changed the channel to NY1. And there it was. The news story was running with Claire's graduation picture and the heartbreaking headline in the lower third of the screen.

Bacardi ran to see it too. Both were overwhelmed with grief, and Bacardi felt her knees weaken. No, this wasn't happening. Not their daughter. Not Claire.

"I'm so sorry, y'all," Tisha expressed with profound sympathy.

They didn't hear her. They both were in shock. How could this have happened? Why did she do it? Suddenly, Bacardi was torn with guilt and anguish. Claire had called and begged to come back home, but Bacardi had treated her coldly and held firm to her grudge. Now their middle child was dead.

Bacardi nearly fainted, and Butch raced to catch his wife from falling.

The renters and their neighbors were all trying to console Bacardi. She screamed at the top of her lungs in agonizing grief. It was a bone-chilling mother's shriek that would become eerily embedded in the memories of those who heard it. No mother should lose her child, regardless of what kind of relationship they had.

Chapter Thirty-One

*C*hanel wanted to lock herself inside her room for the day. She didn't think she could face Pyro without the awkwardness they both deserved. Visions of him spending the day with Mecca ate away at whatever dignity she felt she had left.

Last night wasn't supposed to happen. Her first consensual sexual experience was supposed to be with her fiancé, Mateo. Chanel was at an age when you still believed in relationship fairytales—when you believed in Prince Charming and happily ever after. It was the fantasy mindset where you remained a virgin until marriage and raised your two-point-five kids in a house with a white picket fence. Now those dreams had gone up in flames thanks to God and his perversion.

Chanel felt like a slut. She wondered if the rape had changed her, or if this was who she truly was. She was Mecca's best friend, who had slept with her soon-to-be fiancé. She was also Mateo's fiancée who had slept with his best friend. She had done that. But wasn't that kind of thing Charlie's MO? Charlie was the remorseless one who would do something just like this.

By noon, she felt like she was suffocating. Her guilt was shutting off her air supply. She got dressed looking extra modest in a loose-fitting turtleneck dress and trench coat. Her face was bare—no blush, lipstick, mascara, eyeliner, or eye shadow. Her first stop was St. Benedict's Roman

Catholic Church for afternoon mass. Chanel wasn't Catholic or Baptist or any denomination, but she was in pursuit of absolution. Quietly she slid into a back pew and grabbed a Bible as the priest read his sermon. The verses didn't matter to her. Chanel clutched the Bible, looked at the numerous statutes of white Jesus and the other saints, and began to cry her eyes out.

Later, Chanel went to see Mateo. When she walked into the room, she perched herself on the side of his bed and kissed him deeply and passionately. It was a sensual kiss that probably could have created a miracle in his pants. It was something she hadn't done since before the invasion.

Mateo stared at his lady and worriedly uttered to her, "Have you been crying?"

Chanel's eyes widened. "No. Of course not. Why would I be crying?"

Mateo grew concerned. His eyes weren't deceiving him. Chanel's face was flushed, and her eyelids were low, red-rimmed, and puffy. And although she smiled widely, it never quite made it to her eyes.

He moved his shaky hand to grasp hers. "Something's going on. Something has changed about you."

Chanel's bottom lip was now visibly trembling. It took all her strength to not burst into tears. "It has? What, baby?"

"I don't know. You seem so sad, Chanel. Has something happened?"

"I'm happy, baby. I'm excited to see you."

"You don't seem happy. You seem different," he continued to probe.

"Different? Please, Mateo, that's obvious. I *am* different. Things have changed for the both of us, but I don't want to keep talking about it."

"Do you still love me, Chanel?" he asked her.

"I do. You know I do, baby. I love you so much."

"Just checking. Ya boy can't be too sure. You come, you don't come. When you leave I never know if it's the last time I'll see you." Mateo tried to have levity in his voice, but she knew her actions had made him insecure.

Chanel blurted out, "Let's get married."

"We will. As soon as I get out of here."

"Now. Let's go and get married now. We don't need a destination wedding. We can go back to our original plan and go to City Hall. Let's get married before this month ends."

Mateo's reaction to her proposal was tentative. "Babe, we can't. I feel we should wait just a while longer. At least until I'm feeling stronger and can stand before you on my own two feet and not have to be held up."

"Baby, if I'm going to be your other half, you can lean on me—we'll lean on each other," she replied.

"I love you, Chanel. I do. But if you give me a little more time, I'm going to fully recover. I'm gonna walk again on my own—watch and see."

She managed to smile. "I know you will."

Mateo became emotional. "Chanel, I'm sorry that I couldn't do anything to stop what happened to you. I should have been there to protect you—to stop it. But I wasn't."

"Mateo, it's not your fault. I told you so many times already."

"I should have stopped them."

"You did your best."

"No. What they did to you—"

She didn't want to talk about it. She wanted to forget about it. She was finally starting to feel normal again.

"Please, Mateo, don't bring it up again! I don't want to think about it. I told you, let's forget what happened and move on with our lives. You and I, together, that's the only thing that matters to me."

He nodded. "You're right. We can't change the past, but we can create our future."

"Yes. So let's do that—create a wonderful future together."

"We will, baby. We will."

Chanel didn't want to be trapped in one room with him. She wanted Mateo to get out, and she wanted to try and get her mind off of the thoughts of Pyro sinking deeper inside of her—his muscular body, strong arms, and soft kisses. A light perspiration formed on her upper lip and around her hairline. Soon she felt like she was in a sweatshop. Chanel wheeled Mateo around the facility as he spoke optimistically about their future.

"I can't wait until our wedding day, Chanel. I can't wait to finally hold you in my arms all night. I want to watch you sleep peacefully, no fear. I promise I'll love, honor, cherish, and protect you forever and one day."

Chanel looked deep into Mateo's hopeful, love-filled eyes and burst into tears. She sobbed uncontrollably until he was able to get her to calm down.

"Baby, what's wrong? What's wrong, Chanel?" he repeated.

Chanel kneeled near his wheelchair and took his hands into hers. She was so ashamed of herself that she could hardly hold his worried stare, but she did.

"I-I-I have something to tell you," she began. "I don't know where to begin."

"Shhhh," he soothed. "Are you ill?"

"Ill? No, that's not it."

"Are your parents okay?"

She nodded.

"Look, Chanel, how about this? Whatever you need to tell me, wait. Go home and sleep on it and if tomorrow you still think it's something that I should know, then we'll talk. How does that sound?"

Chanel saw the fear in his eyes and she just couldn't break his heart, not while he wasn't one hundred percent back to normal. How could she destroy him and then leave him alone to process her hurtful revelation in a rehabilitation center? She had to ask herself honestly, was this something he should know or was it about clearing her conscience? She wasn't sure. Thank God he stopped her.

For the remainder of their time together, Chanel perked up. She wheeled him around each floor talking about their future and the first thing he wanted to do when he was released was go to Spanish Fly Barbershop and let his barber, Bolo, cut the Patriots logo in his hair. He missed the little things.

She warned, "Over my dead body will you cut your hair."

After her time with Mateo, Chanel drove back to Pyro's place, and she was rapidly plagued with embarrassment and guilt again. It hit her swiftly—like lightning striking her—her shame came flooding back. She was parked on the Bronx street but remained frozen in the driver's seat looking lost. She sat there and cried her eyes out for hours. She cried so hard that her eyes were nearly swollen shut. All she could think about was Mateo.

How could I do that to him? And what about Mecca?

She felt like a whore. Pyro was paying all her and Mateo's bills. Was last night her repayment? Her mind kept replaying how Pyro made sweet love to her and how good it felt. It was making her go insane. She told herself that it would never happen again.

Chanel worried if Mateo would be able to tell that she willingly had sex. It happened only once, and God had already taken her virginity.

She stared at the building and gazed up at Pyro's apartment floor. The lights were on, so that meant he was home. She didn't want to go up. She didn't want to see Pyro at the moment.

Chanel sighed. She didn't have much money on her, but she did have enough for a hotel room. She thought about it. She would get a room and spend some time alone, collect her thoughts, and try to quell her guilt.

She was about to pull off when there was a sudden tap on her window, startling her. It was Pyro. She looked at him and rolled down her window.

"You okay, Chanel?" he asked. He could see that she had been crying, and he noticed that she was about to pull off.

"I'm fine."

But he knew she wasn't. He felt like a piece of shit. He had taken advantage of her knowing how much she missed Mateo. But them having sex wasn't the worst thing for now.

"I guess you heard what happened," he said.

"No. What happened? What's going on?"

She hadn't heard yet, which made it more difficult to tell her. Seeing her crying, he assumed Chanel had heard about her sister.

Bacardi couldn't get a hold of Chanel. She had turned off her phone when she visited Mateo, because she didn't want any interruptions from anyone, especially Pyro. She hadn't checked any of her voice messages yet.

"It's about your sister," he said with premature sympathy.

"My sister? Who, Charlie?" Chanel assumed, knowing her oldest sister was foul.

"It's Claire . . ."

"Claire?" There was panic building in her tone. "What about her?"

"She's dead. She jumped in front of a moving train down in the subway."

"What? What are you talking about, Pyro? No! Are you lying to me!"

"Yo, I wish I was."

His eyes were telling her the truth. There was great sadness and pain in them—pain and sadness for her. Chanel started to lose it.

"No! Why would she do that? Why would she kill herself?" she hollered with anguish in her voice. "Ohmygod. No! Why the fuck would she do that?!"

"I don't know."

She wondered what had set her sister off this time. She was devastated by the news, so devastated that it looked like she was having a panic attack.

"Chanel, move over. We need to go see your peoples right now," he said, jumping into the driver's seat of her truck.

Chanel couldn't stop crying. Her heart was broken. Claire's suicide was overwhelming and she was still in disbelief about it. She had to hear it from her mother—to confirm the tragedy from her flesh and blood. While Pyro raced her to her parents' place, Chanel dialed her mother's phone. Once she heard her grieving mother on the other end, it was confirmed that Claire was dead.

Chapter Thirty-Two

When Chanel and Pyro walked into Bacardi's apartment, they were both were surprised to see Charlie and Ahbou seated in the living room, looking cozy. Immediately, Pyro noticed Ahbou's holstered gun and badge clipped to his jeans. Pyro instantly grew uncomfortable. A cop and a career criminal in a relationship? Both men tried to be cordial, but there was instant and underlying tension.

Chanel right away went to her mother and hugged her strongly. They both were in heavy tears. Her parents were torn up. Chanel was fucked up too, but she knew that she needed to be strong for her parents. Claire was gone, and it was hard for them to fathom that.

Even with her sister's suicide, Charlie couldn't stop herself from being an asshole.

"Isn't this a tender moment?" she said, her voice dripping with sarcasm.

Chanel cut her eyes at Charlie, warning the bitch not to start anything. When Bacardi's two renters came home after a long day of work, Charlie started talking slick and greasy to them, calling them every foul name in the book. It was upsetting to see two pretty strangers now occupying her and Claire's old rooms, and she had something to say about it, despite the grief everyone was going through.

"You got these dumb-ass lookin' bird bitches stayin' here now. Them the hoes you kicked us out for?" Charlie griped.

The two young girls ignored Charlie's insult and went into their bedrooms. They didn't want any trouble. The vibe in the apartment was thick with tension and sorrow, and Charlie was adamant on trying to make things worse. She tried to talk slick to Chanel and Pyro, and she kept whispering something to Ahbou, who would stare uncomfortably at Pyro.

Ahbou rubbed Pyro the wrong way. It wasn't just that he was a cop; it was that he was spending time with Charlie, and birds of a feather flock together. She was grimy, so he knew Ahbou had to be grimy too. He was a shifty looking muthafucka. Pyro knew to be on guard.

The question on everyone's mind was, what had triggered the suicide? Something had to have happened between Charlie and Claire to push Claire over the edge. Whatever it was, Bacardi felt partly responsible. She would give anything to go back in time and be a mother to her.

It didn't take long for Bacardi to start mentioning burial money.

"I need to bury my daughter, and I need help. I ain't got nothing for her funeral or a cemetery plot," she said, her gaze moving around the room and landing on one person at a time.

"Don't worry about it. I'll help pay for the cost of her funeral," Pyro offered.

"Nigga, you didn't know my sister like that, so don't worry about it," Charlie chimed. "I'll cover her funeral, Bacardi, so stop begging. She was my little sister."

Bacardi's ears perked up, but she was skeptical. "You can pay for Claire's entire funeral?" she asked in disbelief.

"I told you, I got it. Whatever it costs, don't worry about. It's the least I could do for Claire. And I want nothing but the best for her," Charlie said sincerely. "When I lost her, I lost half of me."

Bacardi and Chanel stared at Charlie with mistrust, knowing that she was probably up to no good again. Bacardi hated to take money from her because people had probably died over it. But she knew that one day Charlie was going to have to answer for her crimes, and she needed the help, no matter where it came from.

"Yeah, Ma, don't worry about the cost. We got it," Ahbou confirmed.

Ma? Who the fuck is he calling Ma? Bacardi thought. But she kept her mouth shut. She didn't want to stir up any trouble, and Charlie's new man looked dangerous and sinister. His eyes were black and icy. He was lounging on her couch like he had known them for years, and his badge and gun were intimidating. NYPD inside her living room, giving his creepy condolences. Who would have guessed?

Bacardi stared at Charlie sideways. She was hesitant to accept her help, but she agreed to take the money. And in doing so, Charlie started talking really big and cocky. She grinned and said to her mother, "I'll bring over twenty thousand in the morning."

Twenty thousand? Shit. What the fuck is she into to have that much money lying around? Bacardi wondered.

Charlie and Ahbou didn't stay long. They left, and Pyro and Chanel decided to stay longer to comfort Bacardi and Butch. Bacardi was grateful to see Chanel, and she continued to hug her daughter tightly. She excused herself and asked Chanel to come into her bedroom to talk while Butch and Pyro remained in the living room.

Bacardi closed the bedroom door and first asked her daughter, "How's Mateo doing?"

"He's doing fine," she said.

"Good. Now, are you fuckin' Pyro?"

Chanel was taken aback by the question. Bacardi wanted to ask her that at a time like this? But that was her mother; she said what was on her mind, no matter what.

She wanted to lie, but she couldn't. With her mother's eyes fixed on her, she replied, "Yes. We had sex. But it happened just once."

She would have confided in Mecca, but for obvious reasons, she couldn't. Chanel's eyes started to well up with tears and then she started to cry.

"And I feel so guilty about it. I don't know what to do. It just happened, and I got feelings for him. But I'm still in love with Mateo," she cried out.

Bacardi sighed. One daughter was dead, one was the devil, and her youngest was confused. She sat with Chanel at the foot of the bed and placed her arm around her. She knew what Chanel was going through far too well.

"Listen to me, Chanel. We all make our mistakes in life—some more than others, and you've made yours and you're gonna have to deal wit' them. But a little warning to you, if you want to continue your relationship with Mateo, then don't tell him about you and Pyro. Men are different creatures than us. He will dwell on that until the end of time. Keep it a secret and take it to your grave."

Chanel nodded, taking in her mother's advice. She did leave one thing out. She didn't tell her mother about Mecca and Pyro being in a relationship.

"Chanel, I'm gonna tell you something, and I tell you, it needs to stay in this room," said Bacardi.

Chanel nodded and hung her head, awaiting the sermon she figured she was about to receive.

"I had an affair on Butch a long time ago," she confessed.

Chanel's head snapped up and her eyes locked onto her mother's.

Bacardi stared at her daughter and continued with, "In fact, Butch isn't your real father. I was once in love with your biological father."

Chanel's eyes narrowed as if Bacardi was pulling her leg. "What? Are you serious?"

"It's one of the reasons why I gave you such a hard time growing up. Your father broke my heart, when I wanted to run away and only be with him. But he didn't want that. He didn't want me. He left me—left me pregnant with you—and I took out that anger and hatred I felt toward him on you," Bacardi confessed.

It was a lot for Chanel to take in. She was speechless, but the outpouring of emotion came instantaneously. She closed her eyes and deeply inhaled, and as she exhaled the angst and pain of the situation, the tears rolled down her cheeks.

Bacardi was broken up inside. She had caused all this pain and then some. What kind of parent was she? She gave birth to Charlie—a real menace; Claire—who ended up mentally unstable; and Chanel—the victimized product of an affair. Bacardi decided then and there that she and Butch needed to have an introspective talk about parenting the two children they had left.

Finally, Chanel pulled herself together and asked, "Does Butch know?"

"About the affair? I just said no."

"That's an assumption, Bacardi. Do you think he knows that I'm not his daughter?"

Bacardi shook her head. "He thinks you're his without a doubt."

"What about Charlie and Claire? How everyone treated me, they had to have suspected this, right? They always said that I wasn't their sister."

"Those spoiled bitches—" Bacardi had to bite her tongue. Claire was dead. "Chanel, their disrespect was all my fault. They picked up on my negative energy toward you and ran with it, but I promise you they didn't know. It's our secret now. Just you and me."

Despite the tragedy that brought them together, Chanel and Bacardi enjoyed their mother-daughter time, even though it was under such traumatic circumstances.

Two hours later, Pyro and Chanel left the apartment. Chanel exhaled. She was still sad and troubled by Claire's suicide, but the talk she had with Bacardi was needed. She even smiled when she got into the passenger seat of her Range Rover.

"You okay?" Pyro asked her.

"Yeah, I'm fine now. My mother and I had a meaningful talk in the bedroom," she said.

"That's good to hear."

Pyro started the SUV and drove off.

"She just told me that Butch isn't my father."

"Oh, word?"

"You're not shocked, are you?" she asked.

He shrugged. "Not really. I mean, you don't look like your sisters, so most would say your moms spit you out. It could go either way. So, how do you feel about that?"

"Butch will always be my dad. I love him so much even when he's mean. I think when Bacardi told me, I realized that somewhere deep inside, I always suspected it. And now I know."

"Will you ever reach out to your real father?"

Chanel shook her head. "Nah. Butch is my father, flaws and all."

"I understand," was Pyro's response. But as a father, if he had a child out there, he would want to know no matter what.

"This conversation doesn't go past you and me."

"Not even Mecca?"

"Please, Pyro. Give me your word."

"Chanel, you can always trust me." Pyro felt special she would entrust him not only with her first consensual sexual experience but now also this.

As they drove home, Chanel wished she was having this conversation with Mateo. It should be him sharing these life-altering moments.

Chanel stared out the window, looking a bit distant for a moment. Then she said out the blue, "I can't believe that she's really gone."

Pyro's attention was on something else, though. He continually glanced at his rearview mirror, carefully scrutinizing something behind them. "I think we're being followed."

"What?"

"Red Benz."

He continued to glance in his side and rearview mirrors at the red Benz following them. Pyro rode past his exit and stayed on the highway. He coolly removed his pistol from his coat and placed it on his lap. He was ready to go ham on someone if it came to it.

Chanel looked back to see what he was talking about, but all she could make out were several headlights from various cars traveling behind them. "Are you sure we're being followed?"

"Yeah, I'm sure. They've been on us since we left your parents' place," Pyro said.

Pyro continued to drive, keeping his composure. Two miles later, the Benz exited off the highway. Pyro figured they realized he had spotted them and backed off. Still, he kept an eye out in his mirrors.

When he finally arrived home, he hesitated to park. Instead, he circled the block several times, making sure that there was no one posted up nearby and that they didn't have unwanted company. When he felt the area was secured, he parked and they quickly headed upstairs.

Pyro wanted to talk to Chanel, but she wanted to be alone so she could call Mateo and tell him the sad news. She went into her room and shut the door, locking it behind her.

"Why did you back off them?" Charlie shouted to Ahbou.

"Because the muthafucka knew we were following him," he replied.

"You shouldn't have exited off the highway. I want to know where that bitch stay."

"And we'll find out, but not tonight."

They were both pissed that they couldn't follow Chanel and Pyro home. Her plates were registered to a PO Box, which was smart on Mateo's behalf. Charlie wanted to fuck Chanel up real good—destroy her life. She hated to see her little sister happy and thriving.

"I know one thing for sure—that bitch fucks wit' me and I might end up making myself an only child," Charlie said coldly.

Chapter Thirty-Three

It was early morning when Pyro buzzed Mecca upstairs. He barely slept the night before. He had a lot of things on his mind, one of which was Chanel. Their sexual experience replayed in his mind every day. It was good—really good, and he enjoyed it. But it was wrong—so why did he want to do it again? But he couldn't, right? Mecca was his girlfriend and Mateo was his best friend. Chanel was emotional because of Claire's suicide, and he wanted to be there for her—to console her whenever she cried or felt alone.

Mecca came into the apartment and stared at her man with mixed feelings. There he was, standing in front of her in his boxers and shirtless while Chanel was still inside her bedroom.

"You always come out your room looking like that?" she asked him without greeting him with the usual hug and kiss.

"What's the problem? It's my place," he said.

"Yeah, it's your place, but did you forget you have Chanel staying here too? You don't feel like it's inappropriate to walk around half-naked?"

Pyro frowned. "What's wrong wit' you, Mecca? Why the attitude?"

"I heard that you were with Chanel at her parents' apartment. I heard what happened to Claire, and that's fucked up, and I'm sorry she did that to herself. But I'm confused. Chanel didn't call me to tell me about her sister," said Mecca. "You know how I found out? By seeing the news."

"Well, I didn't know. I thought she would call you," Pyro said.

"Well, she didn't. And you know what? When I did find out about her sister, I called her multiple times and she never called me back. And when I called you, you didn't answer or return any of my phone calls either. It seems like y'all both froze me out."

"Didn't nobody mean to freeze you out."

"So what's going on then?"

"Chanel is going through some shit. She just lost her sister."

As if on cue, Chanel's bedroom door opened and she exited dressed in a T-shirt, scowling at Mecca. Sexual guilt had now turned into anger. Chanel was mad with herself, she was mad at God for taking her sister, and last, she was overwhelmingly mad at Charlie. Chanel felt that Charlie had done something to provoke Claire. And all that anger was now transferred to Mecca.

"Why are you here?" she snapped at Mecca.

It was unexpected coming from Chanel. Even Pyro was shocked by her tone.

"Chanel, are you serious? This is my man's place—what do you mean, why am I here? And I came to see if you were okay. I knew Claire too," Mecca replied.

Mecca didn't match Chanel's anger because she knew the weight of the situation. Her friend was upset, and she could easily lash out at anyone.

Chanel backed off, knowing it was wrong to go after Mecca. None of this was her fault.

Mecca stayed a few hours to try and comfort Chanel, even though she felt some kind of way about her living with Pyro. But she put that aside for now, knowing Claire's suicide was weighing heavily on her.

"Why would she do that to herself?" Mecca asked.

But there were no answers. There most likely would never be an explanation on why Claire would commit such a ghastly suicide by throwing herself in front of a moving subway train. Her death was hard enough, but how she killed herself was the most troubling part for the family.

While the trio were inside the kitchen talking, both Mecca and Pyro tried to keep Chanel in an upbeat mood. Mecca paid close attention to Pyro and Chanel's behavior toward one another. She noticed that sometimes he looked a little too deeply into Chanel's eyes and vice versa. There was even some minor contact between them at the kitchen table. Pyro would touch Chanel's hand slightly and then pull away, or he would gently brush his fingers across her cheek for some reason—maybe trying to wipe away a tear. It bothered Mecca. Something was going on, but she brushed her gut feelings to the side because of the situation with Claire.

It seemed like the entire neighborhood came out for Claire's funeral. Her tragic suicide had been airing on the local news for several days. Chanel's only wish for that miserable day was that Mateo was well enough to be there beside her. Mecca had Pyro, Charlie had Ahbou, and Bacardi had Butch. The somberness of the day made her feel isolated and more alone than ever. Chanel wanted to be held for emotional support; to cry in her man's arms. When she had visited Mateo at the rehab facility and told him about Claire's suicide and Butch's paternity, through his eyes, she saw his heart break into pieces. He felt this was yet another moment he couldn't shield Chanel from the hurts of life, but she assured him there was nothing he could have done to prevent any of it.

Bacardi planned an all-white funeral and requested that everyone wear white to celebrate her daughter's life, not her death. A white horse and carriage carried her casket to the funeral home, white roses decorated the place, and white doves were to be released. It was all compliments of Charlie's drug money. Charlie wanted her little sister to have an extravagant funeral that would rival a famous celebrity's. Claire's last days on earth were troubling, so Charlie wanted her home-going service to be special. It was the best that money could buy.

It was a sunny day, but breezy. Chanel and Bacardi stood at the burial site in their white clothing and dark shades to cover their crying eyes. Each held a white rose as the pastor gave his eulogy. Butch was there to comfort Bacardi, and Pyro and Mecca flanked Chanel.

As Mecca stood by Chanel's side, she glared at Charlie, who was standing next to Ahbou. Pyro continued to stand protectively near the two ladies. He didn't trust Charlie or her new man.

Wanda also came to the service to pay her respects, regardless of being disfigured. She looked like a burn victim. She too glared at Charlie. Wanda got the shock of her life when she saw her with the same cop that investigated her assault case. It all made sense to her now. She wanted her revenge, but it wasn't the place or the time. Even if she did attack Charlie, Charlie's cop boyfriend would be there to protect her.

Claire's white casket was lowered into the ground, and everyone tossed their white rose on top and walked away as the white doves were released and circled the area. There were teary eyes and sad faces, knowing Claire was gone from this world permanently, but she would be forever remembered.

Pyro, Mecca, and Chanel walked away from the gravesite and climbed into Pyro's car. They came together and they were leaving together. Chanel climbed into the front seat of his car, and though Mecca felt some kind of way about it, she remained silent. Chanel had just buried her sister and Mecca didn't want to make an issue of it.

As he was driving back to the Bronx, Pyro noticed the marked police car following behind them and right away, the blue and red lights started to flash in his rearview mirror, indicating for him to pull over.

"Shit," Pyro cursed. "We gettin' pulled over."

The girls glanced behind them, seeing the cop car approaching closely.

"What did you do, Pyro? You ran a red light?" Mecca asked.

"I ain't do shit. I ain't break no traffic laws."

"Then why they pulling us over?"

"I don't know."

Unbeknownst to them, the cop car was implementing the traffic stop at the behest of Ahbou. He still needed an address for Pyro and Chanel.

Pyro coolly pulled to the side of the road and kept the engine idling. He watched two uniformed cops exit their vehicle and cautiously approach his car with their hands against their holstered weapons.

Pyro rolled his window down and asked the cop at his window, "What's wrong, officer? What did I do?"

"License and your registration," the cop said.

"You gonna tell me why you pulled me over?"

"License and registration," the cop said again in a demanding tone.

"Just give it to him, Pyro," said Mecca.

Pyro huffed, but he acquiesced to their demands. He slowly reached over to the glove compartment and unhurriedly removed the information that the cop asked for. The last thing he wanted was to become another minority gunned down by the police. He handed the cop his information, and his partner went to run Pyro's license and vehicle information. While doing that, the look on the first cop's face was indicative that it wasn't enough. He wanted to harass the driver.

It didn't take long for everything to come back clean.

However, the questions came. Where y'all coming from? Are there any drugs or weapons inside the car? Pyro answered them firmly and convincingly, but he knew the inevitable was coming.

"I need for you to step out the car, please," said the cop.

"What? Why?"

"Listen, let's not make this shit difficult. You do what I say, and you might get to go home to your barrio," the cop replied rudely.

Pyro frowned at the insult. "Are you serious?"

"What did I say? Get the fuck out the car before you make it worse on yourself and these bitches," the cop continued with his verbal abuse.

"Bitches?" Mecca griped.

Pyro glared at the cop and reluctantly removed himself from the driver's side. He was immediately tossed against the hood of his car and manhandled by the white cop, while his partner kept an eye on Chanel and Mecca.

"In fact, you two bitches need to get out the car too," the partner instructed.

Reluctantly, the ladies did what they were told. All three were held at gunpoint and harassed while the second cop rummaged through Pyro's vehicle searching for drugs or guns. Pyro was roughly patted down for a gun, and like his car, the search on him came up empty. Both cops were annoyed that he was clean.

Knowing there wasn't anything else they could do to them, the cops had to let them go. They had nothing—no information about him. His license and registration listed a PO Box, so they had no idea where he laid his head at night.

Pyro grimaced at the officers but kept his composure, knowing now wasn't the place or the time for payback.

"Y'all have a nice day, officers," he said nearly mockingly to them.

They ignored him and went back to their marked cop car.

Pyro predicted the harassment from the cops. When Charlie and Ahbou had waited for him and Chanel for two hours at their parents' place and tried to follow them home, he knew there was more to come. It didn't take a rocket scientist to know it was Charlie and her cop boyfriend tailing them that night. Pyro knew that Charlie's man was a dirty cop by the way Charlie was tossing around twenty stacks for the funeral like it was nothing to her. And dirty cops never played by the rules.

Pyro purposely didn't bring any guns with him to the funeral, and he took a chance riding clean for once. However, he had a contingency plan. He had shooters on his payroll that subtly followed behind them. They were at the funeral, unseen and watchful. Pyro wanted an address on Charlie's man, Ahbou.

Pyro sent a text to the shooters, instructing them to follow Ahbou home after the funeral. It was time to remind Charlie who she was dealing with. Pyro was not a man to be fucked with.

When Ahbou got out of his car and walked to his front door, two masked gunmen came out of nowhere and lit him up brighter than Times Square at midnight. Several slugs tore into his body—including a gunshot to the head, and Ahbou was dead before he hit the ground. They didn't give a fuck that he was a cop—a dirty cop was a criminal like them. He violated, and the underworld dealt with him accordingly.

Chapter Thirty-Four

*I*t had been twenty-four hours since Claire was laid to rest in the earth. Charlie kept herself locked inside her apartment, needing some solitude. Although she was bitchy and cold to everyone with her tough-girl persona, half of her died when she buried Claire. Charlie knew it was mostly her fault. Her shenanigans had pushed her sister over the edge. Charlie fondly remembered how people would ask if they were twins when they were younger. As they aged, the bond between the two deepened. Charlie took her sister for granted, and now that she was gone she wondered if Claire knew that she deeply loved her. She didn't always show it—but she did.

Her solitude wouldn't last. There was a knock at her door. Charlie opened the door and greeted Mona halfheartedly.

"Can I come in?" asked Mona.

Charlie stepped aside and Mona walked inside. With Claire gone, the place felt different and cursed.

"What do you want, Mona?"

"Listen, I have some bad news to tell you. Ahbou is dead."

"Dead? How?"

"He was gunned down right after your sister's funeral."

It was tragic news, but Charlie wasn't too broken up about it. She wasn't in love with him. And she knew he killed KB. Maybe it was karma coming back for him.

"That's fucked up," Charlie said with fake outrage.

"I know. And I figure you shouldn't be alone after everything that's happened to you," said Mona. "Whoever killed Ahbou, they're gonna pay. Believe that, Charlie. The entire force is out there investigating his murder, and someone will be held accountable."

"Good," Charlie replied.

She pretended to grieve for Ahbou, but inside, she was cracking up that Mona actually believed that she cared.

Mona got comfortable on the couch and started rolling up a blunt. She looked up at Charlie and said, "Look, Ahbou's death isn't the only reason why I'm here."

Charlie was listening.

"They—my partners—want you to know that this will not hinder our business relationship with you, and they want you to stay focused on what really matters. We need to keep things flowing, especially the money."

"I know. I understand. I'm always gonna be 'bout my business, no matter what. You know that."

Mona stared at her, looking for any signs of change or weakness with Charlie, but she saw nothing but the same coldhearted get-money bitch from when they first met.

"Good. It's what we wanted to hear from you," Mona said.

"So, we good, right?"

"Oh, we good. You stay focused and we all stay gettin' paid."

"No doubt."

The two ladies shared a blunt together, but Mona couldn't stay long. She had a job to do and a murder to solve. She left Charlie's place after an hour.

Charlie shut herself inside her apartment for days, moping. She had no one. She had no man. Her parents were still giving her the cold shoulder, she hated her only living sibling, she had no friends with Claire dead, and even her frenemies were long gone. Thinking that the fresh air would pull her out of her funk, she decided to drive to her old neighborhood to conduct a drug transaction with a local dealer. He had requested two kilos from her, cash on delivery. Charlie came through, made the transaction with the dealer, and got her money, but she decided not to leave the hood right away. Near her old stomping grounds, she saw a few dudes she knew shooting dice on the side block, near the bodega. One of the men shooting dice was a fine brother named Daquan, and she'd had her eyes on him for a minute.

Charlie drove up to the dice game in her Benz and got out looking extra sexy in her tight jeans, stilettos, and reddish hair. For a moment, all eyes were on her.

"My niggas, what's poppin'?" Charlie asked, walking toward the group.

"Nuthin' poppin', Charlie. Just tryin' to get this money out here," Daquan replied.

"I see that," she replied, "and I'm tryin' to get money wit' y'all niggas."

She pulled out a wad of hundred-dollar bills to buy in to the dice game with the goons, but the mood toward her was aloof. She picked up on their unfriendly attitudes right away—especially Daquan's. She was ready to fuck him if he wanted the pussy, but he didn't even look at her.

"What the fuck is wrong? Y'all got beef wit' me?" she asked with roughness in her voice.

"Nah. We good, Charlie. Ain't no beef wit' you," a young goon named Smack replied.

"I'm sayin', y'all niggas actin' all funny and shit, like y'all don't want me around." She stared at Daquan, because he was the main one who looked like he had a problem with her.

"Look, we just out here minding our business, Charlie. That's it," said Daquan.

Knowing Charlie's reputation, at first no one wanted to tell her what the streets were saying. But Charlie was adamant in finding out.

"Nah, fuck that. If y'all muthafuckas got a problem wit' me, then spit it the fuck out and don't be pussy about it. I see that shit on y'all fuckin' faces," Charlie griped.

"Look, the streets are talkin', Charlie," a hustler named Dope blurted out.

"Talkin'? Talkin' 'bout what? I ain't no fuckin' snitch."

Daquan finally looked her in the eye. "It ain't 'bout you being no snitch, Charlie. It's about you being cursed," he said.

"Cursed?" Charlie repeated. "What the fuck you mean, I'm cursed?"

"Look, I'm gonna keep real wit' you, Charlie. The streets are talkin', and they calling you 'suicide pussy,'" Daquan informed her.

"Suicide pussy? What the fuck y'all niggas talkin' bout?"

"Three niggas that you used to fuck wit' are now dead—God, KB, and that fuckin' cop," Daquan said.

Charlie couldn't believe what she was hearing. Suicide pussy? She scowled at the disrespect to her name.

"Look, I ain't mean no disrespect to you, Charlie. I'm just the messenger," Daquan added.

"Fuck you and fuck all y'all muthafuckas! See if all y'all make another fuckin' dime on these streets again," she shouted.

"C'mon, Charlie. It ain't even like that," said Dope.

"It's *just* like that, Dope. Y'all don't want me around and don't wanna fuck wit' me, then fuck it—suffer the fuckin' consequences, cuz I'm the head bitch in charge out here," she continued to shout.

Charlie pivoted and marched away from them. Once again, her name was mud on the streets.

Chapter Thirty-Five

*C*hanel couldn't sleep. How could she after seeing her sister lowered into the ground last week? She tried to block everything out, but it felt impossible. After seeing that casket go down into the dirt, the horrific events of the home invasion came flooding back. Her rape felt like it happened yesterday. Claire's suicide and her burial had triggered something inside of Chanel, and it was becoming harder for her to shake it off. It could have easily been her and Mateo being buried. God and Charlie were two dangerous people. Chanel felt lucky to be alive, but she felt haunted by some creepy entity. She felt that something was coming after her—chasing her. She felt cursed almost.

She tried to get some sleep, but it wasn't happening. It was after midnight and her bedroom felt too still—too quiet. It felt like something was in there with her. Maybe it was her mind playing tricks on her, but she didn't want to be alone tonight. She wanted some comfort, and she knew exactly where to find it. She got up from her bed and exited the room.

Pyro was shocked when he heard the faint tapping on his bedroom door. He got up from the bed wearing only his boxers and opened it. There was Chanel in her T-shirt with a sad look on her face.

"You okay?" he asked her.

"Can I sleep with you tonight? I can't sleep. I'm having these upsetting visions, and they're bothering me."

"Yeah. Sure," he said.

Chanel crawled into Pyro's bed and snuggled against him. She wanted to be held. She wanted to be protected by him. Pyro was the only person who made her feel secure. She laid her head against his chest and exhaled. Eventually, she felt at ease and secure in his arms. She could feel the warmth from his body. She wasn't seeing any more upsetting visions while lying with Pyro.

She felt so soft and curvy against him. He didn't want to let her go. Her smell was enticing. His dick was hard for her. He wanted to feel her again. He couldn't stop thinking about the way she made him feel and the way she made him come. Mecca was good, but sex with Chanel was something completely different.

He didn't want to make a move on her unless she wanted the same thing too. Unfortunately for him, Chanel quickly fell asleep.

The next morning, Pyro was awakened by Chanel softly rubbing on his chest and stomach. Groggily, he gazed into her eyes.

"Thank you for holding me last night," she said.

"You know I got you, Chanel."

"I know. You're always there for me."

"Whenever you need me," he assured her.

She smiled and continued to massage his chest and stomach. Pyro cupped her face into his hands and a deep and passionate kiss ensued. Soon, the little bit of clothes they had on came off, and their flesh met once again. Chanel was on her back looking into Pyro's eyes, her legs wrapped around him. Once again, he thrust himself inside her without a condom and she moaned. His hard dick was hitting her spot and he was about to make her come. He fucked her slowly and with conviction, and the wet, lathered juices coating his dick told him that she loved every second of it.

"Ooooh, Pyro . . . I . . . I love you," she whispered to him as she felt his hard dick steadily move in and out of her.

He heard the words, but he didn't respond to them. Instead, he continued to please her. He drove deeper into her flesh, and her cries became primal as she felt herself about to come.

Pyro gave Chanel her first orgasm of the morning, but they weren't done. It was one of several that she was going to have this morning. The two twisted around on his bed, subsequently becoming knotted underneath the sheets.

The more pleasure he gave her, the more she gave him. Now the sheets were on the floor and they were fucking on the bare mattress. He continued to thrust inside of her, feeling his orgasm brewing. At first, Pyro was tempted to come inside of her without a condom. He wanted to finish off strong and not pull out, but he knew it would be a mistake. He pulled out just in time as his semen spilled onto Chanel's smooth stomach. He watched her body react with tremors from another orgasm. They collapsed together on the bed, sweat covering their bodies. They were both exhausted.

Chanel gazed into Pyro's eyes and smiled warmly.

"I love you too," he said.

Chapter Thirty-Six

*C*harlie gulped from the bottle of 1800 tequila like it was a bottle of water. She was lounging on the couch in the dark, trying to drink her troubles away. She was supposed to be living her best life, but muthafuckas kept getting in her way. She was frustrated, lonely, and she had no man and no one to harass, kill, or bully. Claire was dead, and she couldn't get a location on Chanel. She wanted to set Chanel's pretty white Range Rover on fire and watch it burn. She wanted to slice her sister's face to shreds and have Pyro and Mateo murdered.

Those were her twisted and demonic wishes.

She was furious that the NYPD couldn't get an address on these Bronx muthafuckas. There seemed to be some kind of hedge of protection surrounding Chanel that she couldn't penetrate.

She had just taken another hearty swig of tequila when the familiar hard banging at her door startled her. She frowned and got up and opened the door to see two New Jersey detectives. The moment they flashed their badges, Charlie's stomach did a somersault. She knew exactly why there were there. God AKA Godfrey Williams.

Fuck!

"Charlie Brown?" the detective queried.

Charlie knew she couldn't lie about her name. It would have been stupid. "What do y'all want?"

"Can we come in?"

"Whatever," she grumbled, stepping aside.

She realized that changing her temperament toward them would be wise. She asked with a polite smile, "Y'all want coffee or something?"

The tough talking, slick mouthed gangster bitch diva that she was became muted. This was murder, and she wanted to get out from under suspicion and investigation.

"No thanks."

The detectives told her that her name had come up in a murder investigation and they started to ask her a few questions. The one question that gave Charlie pause was, "Have you ever been to 576 Little Town Road, apartment 3f in Middle Village, New Jersey to see a Godfrey Williams, or God, as the streets called him?"

Charlie knew that if she denied being there and they found her DNA on the scene, she would be fucked. But, if she said yes and no DNA was found, she would be opening the door to additional questioning. She inhaled to buy herself some time to think. She remembered the number-one rule—don't snitch—and she certainly wasn't going to snitch on herself.

"No, I never been there. We broke up some time before he was killed," she lied.

"Was there any animosity between you two?"

She watched as they jotted down notes to her answers. Again, another question to stump her. She was trying to play chess with the detectives. Why not build some trust by giving them some truth?

"Honestly, there was. I broke up with him because I had reasons to believe he might have had something to do with my sister's rape," she said.

She figured it would be a huge revelation, but she was stunned when one of the detectives said, "Yeah, we've heard about that, and the DNA has come back conclusive. He did rape your sister. But we also heard that you were the mastermind behind it."

Wait? What? She was taken aback by their reply. They already knew. New Jersey? *These sneaky muthafuckas!* Now she wondered what their true intentions were. Were they there for God's murder, her sister's rape, or Mateo's attempted murder? Charlie started to feel foolish and wondered if it was stupid to talk to them without a lawyer.

"I didn't know," she replied, appearing to be somewhat offended. She pushed back from the table and she started to sob. "I could never do such a thing to my baby sister!" she wailed.

The detectives were unaffected by her outburst. They weren't there to give her any sympathy. They were there to solve a case. They continued to press.

"Do you know why you would be implicated?"

"No! Of course not. Just ask Chanel, she'll tell you."

"We are trying to find her. Could you give us your sister's address?"

Charlie stammered, "I-I-I don't have an address for her."

"No. Why not?" They were confused.

"I mean, I do have an address for her, but I can't give it. She went into hiding after that nasty pervert raped her."

"But you're facing serious charges, so I'm sure your sister will understand you giving us her address to help us clear your name."

It felt like the questions from the detectives would never end. They kept coming for her, like they wanted her to slip up and say something incriminating. Them challenging her brought out the real Charlie.

"You know what? I think I'm done here," she snapped. "Y'all can leave now, and next time I talk to y'all, I will have a lawyer present."

They were dumbfounded by the sudden change.

"We'll have a warrant next time," one of them replied.

"Get the fuck out!" she shouted. "Fuckin' pigs!"

Calmly, they left the place. Charlie was upset and nervous at the same time. A few minutes later, she realized that she had played her hand wrong.

She let her temper get the best of her. They were New Jersey detectives and most likely they didn't have any jurisdiction over Chanel's case in the Bronx. Chanel's rape was just a ruse to upset her, and she fell for it.

Charlie retrieved her bottle of 1800 tequila and took a mouthful from it. She dropped against the couch and took another swig. She needed to think. Ahbou was gone, but she still had Mona to watch her back.

Charlie needed her cop cronies to take care of her problem. She wanted them to make the investigation go away permanently. What good was it to have NYPD connections if some inept New Jersey detectives could come fuck with her? They had their suspect, so why they were bothering her?

"Fuck 'em," she cursed. "Let them try to put me in jail. I got another thing for they bitch asses!"

Meanwhile, outside the apartment, the detectives walked to the car. They weren't upset about Charlie's outburst. They pushed and pushed until the bubble finally popped. They knew that she had a hand in both the rape and God's murder. But God's death was their case, not her sister's rape. Charlie had guilt written all over her face, and the detectives would do what they could to prove it. It wasn't too late to drop the charges against Kym before she was convicted of a crime she didn't commit.

Chapter Thirty-Seven

It happened again, and then again and again. Chanel and Pyro were having an affair. Chanel didn't want to be consumed by guilt, but Pyro made her feel so good. She couldn't stop thinking about him. The sex was great—really great—and Chanel even went down on Pyro several times. Things were escalating between them. They couldn't get enough of each other, and they were having sex right under Mecca's nose.

Chanel lingered in the hot shower, feeling the water cascading against her skin. She wished Pyro was with her, holding her, caressing her, and making love to her in the shower, which had happened before. But then her mind shifted to Mateo and how emotionally supportive he was when she told him about Claire's suicide and Bacardi's paternity admission, and the pang of guilt she felt ended her steamy fantasy.

She got out of the shower and toweled off. She stared at her naked image in the mirror and thought about how her mother had told her to never tell Mateo about her and Pyro.

Pyro wasn't home, and she had no idea where he was. She didn't keep tabs on him, but she did care about him—a lot—and she sometimes worried about him. He was a hustler, and the streets were a dangerous place for a man like him. Pyro knew how to take care of himself, but Chanel couldn't help but to think what would she do if something were to happen to him.

Her cell phone rang, knocking her back to reality. It was Mecca calling. *Shit.* She didn't want to answer. Chanel hadn't talked to Mecca in over a week, and even when she did, it was hard knowing she and Pyro had a thing. She decided she needed to answer. Otherwise, Mecca would start to wonder why she was avoiding her.

"Hello?"

"Chanel, can we talk?"

"What's going on, Mecca? You okay?"

"No. I'm not. I really need someone to talk to," she said.

"Come by then. I'm here," Chanel said.

"No. Can you come to my place?"

"Yeah, sure. I can be over there in about two hours."

"Okay."

Mecca ended the call.

As she got dressed, Chanel felt nervous about meeting Mecca at her apartment. *What if she found out about Pyro and me? What if she wants to fight me?*

Mecca buzzed Chanel up, and she took the elevator to the third floor. Her nerves were shot as she approached her friend's door. She had her guilt. Two days ago, she and Pyro were together in his bed.

She took a deep breath and knocked.

The door opened, and Mecca appeared in front of Chanel looking like she had been crying. They looked at each other. Chanel thought, *Are we still friends or not? Did Pyro tell her about us? No—he wouldn't.*

"Just come in, Chanel," she said.

Chanel entered the apartment. Mecca looked tired and distraught. Something was definitely bothering her.

"Mecca, what's going on with you? What happened?"

"I'm just trying not to trip or flip out, Chanel," she replied.

"Flip out over what?" Chanel asked nervously.

Chanel remained standing as Mecca took a seat. She needed to be on guard just in case things went left. She still had no idea what her friend was upset about.

"It's Pyro . . ."

"I figured it had to be about him. What did he do to you? Y'all broke up or something?" she asked sheepishly.

"No."

"Mecca, just talk to me. I'm here for you. You know you can tell me anything. I got your back."

Mecca looked at Chanel with teary and troubled eyes. "I thought Pyro was going to propose to me. I was so sure about it. But he hasn't yet. And lately, he's been acting distant. Like, we haven't had sex in two weeks, and every time I call him, he's busy. I mean, c'mon, Chanel, he's supposed to be my man and suddenly he doesn't have time for me?"

"Mecca, you know he's a busy man."

Mecca shook her head. "Bullshit. That's not an excuse."

Chanel replied, "I know."

Mecca dried her eyes and looked at her friend. "Chanel, I want you to be honest with me . . ."

Shit! Please don't ask me if I'm fucking Pyro.

Chanel didn't want to lie to her friend, but she was bracing herself for the inevitable.

Mecca continued with, "Is Pyro fucking somebody else? Does he have another bitch in his life? Have you seen someone else over there? And please, don't lie to me. I need to know."

"Mecca, you know I don't want to get involved with y'all business."

"You're my friend, Chanel, and Pyro is Mateo's friend. Your loyalty is to me. I need your help—your advice."

"Why don't you just sit down with Pyro and tell him your issues? He loves you, I know it. And I assure you, there is no one else in his life. If there was, I would definitely tell you," Chanel said.

"But I don't get it. Why is he suddenly so distant from me?"

"Why did you think Pyro was going to ask you to marry him?"

Mecca shrugged. "I don't know. I thought I was reading his signals correctly, but maybe I was wrong."

"Sometimes we want something so badly, that we make ourselves believe it will come true. And I'm not saying Pyro's not going to marry you, because I know he loves you, but maybe just give it some time and it will happen."

"I love him, Chanel. He's my world and I don't know what I would do without him—or if he was fucking someone else. I would die if that was the case," Mecca uttered.

Chanel sighed. "He's not. I know he's not."

Mecca stared at her friend and replied, "I guess you would know, right? You're always with him."

And what that's supposed to mean? Was Mecca hinting at something?

"But you're right, Chanel. I will talk to him about our future. I can't assume anything anymore; it needs to come from the horse's mouth," Mecca said.

"Right."

Again, Chanel thought Mecca was implying something, but she couldn't jump to judgment. Her friend was upset and wasn't thinking rationally. So, she decided to leave it alone. Unless Mecca came at her directly about it, it was useless to bring the issue up.

Chanel spent most of the day with Mecca. They continued to talk, but it wasn't about Pyro. It almost felt like the old days when Chanel would visit Mecca to escape her hellish home life. They talked about old friends and old times, the neighborhood, and even Claire.

"I know it must be hard, Chanel, but if you ever need me, I'm here for you," said Mecca.

"Thanks, Mecca. You always have been."

Chanel didn't leave Mecca's place until late that night. As she was walking to her SUV, her cell phone rang, and it was Pyro calling her. At first, she didn't want to answer, feeling it wasn't right for Pyro to be calling her instead of Mecca, but she couldn't resist.

"What's up?" she answered.

"Where are you?" he asked her.

"I'm leaving your girlfriend's place," she said.

"You were at Mecca's?"

"Yes."

"Why?"

"Because she needed to talk. And you need to call her, Pyro," she said.

"I will."

"No—like right now."

"I said I will," he repeated sternly. "What did she need to talk to you about?"

"She's worried about your relationship."

"There's nothing to worry about. I love her."

"Like you love me too?"

"I love you both, but the way you make me feel, Chanel, it's different. It's special."

She shook her head. "Pyro, we both should be worried. We have made love and now are in love and we also love others, your best friend and mine. It's tongue twisting and mind bending. We're lying, Pyro. We're liars, and I'm starting to scare myself because it's getting easier for me to deceive them. I lied in Mecca's face and she had no clue. But the worst part is, I felt no guilt."

"Chanel don't ruin it, don't ruin us. Together we'll figure it out."

"What does that mean?"

"Come home, Chanel. I wanna be with you tonight," he said.

Chanel sighed again. It wasn't supposed to be like this. It was supposed to be a onetime thing—a one-night stand. Now, they had developed strong feelings for each other and shit had become complicated. She didn't want things between everyone to become complicated. Mateo was the love of her life, and Mecca was her best friend. It was that simple. Unfortunately, it wasn't.

Chapter Thirty-Eight

*Y*ou need to fix this, Mona. These New Jersey cops are so far up my ass, I'm starting to shit brass. I don't know why they're fuckin' wit' me, but I need this shit to go away. They got their killer, so why are they still investigating the fuckin' murder? Who are these muthafuckas anyway? And now they wanna bring up this rape shit wit' my sister, saying I had something to do with that? Fuck! Can you make these cops disappear?" Charlie rambled as she paced around Mona's living room.

"Just calm down, Charlie," Mona replied from her position on the couch.

"How can I calm down when these fools are fuckin' wit' me? I swear, these muthafuckin' pigs—they need to get got!"

"I said calm down! Have a seat and calm the fuck down."

Charlie had gone to Mona about her visit from the cops and she was a bit hysterical about them. In fact, she was a bit too hysterical for Mona's taste.

"What did we tell you, Charlie? To keep your cool and keep your mouth shut, right?"

Charlie took a seat in a chair and said, "I didn't tell them anything."

"And you're sure?"

"You ain't gotta worry about me, Mona. I'm fuckin' solid. I'm no fuckin' snitch. I know a good thing when I see it, and this shit wit' y'all is the best thing that ever happened to me. I'm makin' money and all I wanna do is make money," Charlie replied.

"Good."

"So what now?" Charlie asked.

"What now? You just chill, keep a low profile, and let us handle it."

"How?"

Mona shot a hard stare at Charlie. "You don't need to worry about the how. Just know that things will be taken care of."

Charlie wanted to believe her.

Mona already knew about the New Jersey case, but the New York rape case was news to her.

Mona went to her impromptu bar and poured Charlie a shot of tequila and told her to relax and have a drink. Charlie downed the tequila and wanted another shot.

"There's nothing to fret over, Charlie. It's fuckin' New Jersey," Mona said. "I'll have some people look into the case and see what new developments there are."

"I would appreciate that."

Mona smiled. "Listen, we look out for our own. We won't let you fall."

Charlie smiled.

Mona started to roll up a blunt. She wanted Charlie to relax. However, Mona felt that Charlie was now becoming more of a liability than an asset. She needed to have a meeting with other members of the organization. They needed to make a decision.

Mona pulled up to the New Jersey warehouse at dusk and climbed out of her BMW. She had called a special meeting with the other eight members of the organization. She entered the warehouse and saw she was the last one to arrive. The other officers were there and waiting. Everyone took a seat at the round table to discuss Charlie's future with them.

"She's becoming a liability to us, and with everything that's going on, can we afford the risk?" Mona asked them.

"What's the alternative, Mona?" Captain Halstead asked her.

"The only alternative there is to this kind of situation," Mona replied.

"So, you want us to have Charlie killed because of speculations against her right now?" Lieutenant Davis chimed.

"Can we afford to keep her around?" said Mona.

"She's bringing in a lot of money," Lieutenant Graham mentioned.

"More money than all the others combined, Mona. She's profitable, smart, and she's been loyal so far," Sergeant Whyte added.

"But the investigation against her is heating up. She's becoming nervous, maybe too nervous for my taste, and with nervousness always comes recklessness," said Mona.

She continued to explain in detail what they were up against, especially if New Jersey decided to move forward with prosecuting Charlie.

"Are you sure it's not paranoia on your end?" asked Sergeant Whyte.

"I'm just concerned," she replied.

"As we should be," replied Lieutenant Graham.

"Then we need to come to a vote," Mona said.

Before Ahbou's death, there were ten members. If their vote was tied 5-to-5, then it would be the call of the founding member who had vouched for that person. Now there were only nine of them, so there would be no ties.

The process started, and the count was eight against one. Mona was the only person who wanted Charlie dead. The others decided to give her a stay of execution.

Ironically, Mona, the only female and supposed friend of Charlie, voted to murder her—yet, the remaining eight men didn't see it her way.

Mona knew that if Charlie wasn't so uniquely beautiful and profitable for them, then she would have been a dead bitch.

"Fine. She lives." Mona removed herself from the table, bit her tongue, and made her exit from the warehouse.

She didn't like their decision and felt it was going to come back to bite them.

Chapter Thirty-Nine

April

The sun was brighter than it had been in months. Winter was finally over. The spring breeze was gentle and the days were longer. It was goodbye to the snow and ice, the slush and the cold. The trees and flowers were blossoming, and things were changing with Chanel and Pyro. Today was a new day for Chanel, an exciting day. Mateo was being released from the facility.

Finally! Chanel was over-the-moon excited.

Pyro sat in the living room waiting for Chanel. He wanted to have a talk with her before she left to pick Mateo up. Something was bothering him, and he couldn't shake it.

Mateo would be released from the facility in a few hours, and his expenses totaled in the hundreds of thousands of dollars. But Pyro felt it was worth it. Mateo was healthy and alive, and the last thing Pyro wanted was drama with his partner.

Pyro assumed Chanel was going to tell Mateo the truth about them. It was a daunting thought. He felt that they should tell Mateo together. He wanted Mateo to understand that it wasn't planned—that things just happened with Chanel. He wasn't a predator. He wasn't trying to stab his friend in the back and fuck his girl. No. He wanted to explain to Mateo that he loved Chanel too. *Deeply.* He was tired of sneaking around, but he wanted Mateo to be fully healthy when the truth about them came out.

Chanel came out of her bedroom looking stunning in a blue spring dress and heels. Her hair was long and flowing, and she looked radiant this morning. She was all smiles and in a very good mood. She looked at Pyro and said to him, "Ohmygod, I'm so nervous right now."

"Why?"

"I mean, it's been months—nearly a year since it happened, and finally, he's coming back to me a healthy and whole man. I can't wait to walk with him out of that facility," she said.

"I'm excited too."

Pyro's eyes lingered on Chanel's sexiness and her curvy figure. She was alluring, and the only thing he could think about was being with her again. It almost felt as if Mateo's coming home was a problem for him.

"Do you want me to come with you?" he asked her.

"No. I'm fine, Pyro. I can pick Mateo up alone. And I want to have some quality time with him so we can talk," she said.

"Chanel, before you leave. Can we talk?"

"Yeah. Of course," she replied.

"Look, I wanted to be there with you when you tell Mateo about us."

Chanel looked surprised by his words. "About us? Are you serious? No. I don't plan on telling him about us, Pyro."

"I thought you wanted to."

"And why would I do that?"

"I just thought that with him coming back to you that you may not want to keep any secrets from him."

"Like you've come clean to Mecca?"

Pyro smirked. "I just figured you'd want transparency, that's all."

"Pyro, I don't ever plan on ever telling Mateo about us. Never. I love him too much to hurt him like that. And I want to be with him. So no, there will be no confession. What we had together will stay between us. I plan on taking our secret to my grave and I hope you feel the same way." Chanel was annoyed that Pyro was trying to control how she handled her business with her man.

The revelation floored him.

Pyro was in love with Chanel and he thought that she was in love with him too. In fact, he felt that if it came to it, he would leave Mecca for her and she would follow suit and leave Mateo for him.

"So, are we good, Pyro? You're not going to feel some kind of way with me and Mateo?" she asked him.

"Yeah, I'm good. I just wanted to clear some things up," he replied, masking the hurt and disappointment he was feeling.

"Good. Because I don't want any trouble with us or Mateo. I love you, but I love Mateo so much more. If you understand what I'm saying."

"I do, Chanel. I'm with Mecca and you're with Mateo. Let's keep things simple like that."

She smiled. "Thanks."

Before she left, she gave him a kiss on his cheek.

Pyro was heartbroken. He had to pull himself together.

Mateo had made a full recovery, and he had Chanel and Pyro to thank for that, the two people he loved the most. Pyro had paid for everything and taken good care of his fiancée. From what Pyro had told him, he had murdered Fingers in cold blood for him too.

Mateo was escorted out of the rehabilitation facility in a wheelchair, but outside, he was able to walk to the Range Rover without any difficulty. Chanel was proud of him. She hugged him lovingly and they kissed for what seemed like forever. Her arms stayed around him like it would kill her to let him go. Today, they would finally be moving into the condo he had bought for them.

He was looking good and he was feeling good. His barber came to the rehabilitation center earlier and gave Mateo a fresh haircut with the Patriots logo. His favorite team. The team logo also showcased where the bullet went in. His hair wouldn't be able to grow back in that spot.

Along with his haircut, Mateo had new clothes and shoes. Pyro had called him and said, "Yo, I can't have my bro leaving that place looking like a bum. Nigga, you gonna be fresh out the door."

Mateo was grateful.

Chanel continued to shower him with kisses from the time he left the center, to the SUV, and even while she was driving. She would come to a stop at a red light and she couldn't help herself. She would lean toward him and kiss him at random moments. Her eyes were bright and smiling.

"I missed you," she said.

"I missed you too."

She held his hand and continued to drive to the address Mateo had given her. It was hard for her to focus on the road because all she wanted to do was stare at him. He looked so cute with his fresh haircut and new clothes. He was talkative and joyful. Her man had even gained some of his weight back since the shooting.

"I promise you, baby, I'm gonna get back on my feet again."

"I know you are."

"I owe you and Pyro a lot—too much—and it's time to get back out here and repay what I owe."

"Baby, you don't owe me anything."

"Yeah, I do. If it wasn't for y'all, I wouldn't be here today," he said.

"We did it because we love you."

"I know."

They soon arrived at a fancy glass high-rise in the Bronx.

Chanel's eyes scanned the area. "What's this?"

"This is ours. I bought this condo for us to live in after we were married. I hope you like it."

"You had this for us all along? You're so sneaky and I love it!" she squealed.

Mateo grinned. Her enthusiasm was infectious.

The condo was in an area away from everything—from a harsh past to a new beginning and a bright future. They were starting over, and Chanel didn't want to look back. Excited, she and Mateo approached the front door hand-in-hand with the condo keys.

They walked into a fully furnished, three-bedroom condominium apartment with two and a half baths and a small laundry room. The décor with the leather furniture, the artwork, the television mounted on the wall, the parquet flooring with the sprawling area rug, it all blew Chanel away. Her man was everything.

"Wow. It's amazing," she complimented.

"Thanks. I hired an interior decorator to help blend my masculine taste and your femininity."

"They did a great job, babe," she said.

He grinned.

"Why so many rooms? I mean, it's just us."

Mateo walked up and hugged Chanel from behind. "For now one is an office that I can use for business and you could use once you enroll in college. The other is a guestroom, and eventually we can convert it to a nursery. This apartment is an investment, so the more rooms, the more marketable it will be should we put it up for sale."

"That's my money man." Chanel beamed. "Always thinking smart."

"Definitely. And speaking of money, I've been down for too long and I need to get back out here and start making this money. I need to pay Pyro back and take care of you."

"I'm good, baby. As long as I have you next to me, I don't need anything else," she said.

"Nah. You held me down while I was fucked up and in physical therapy. You kept me motivated. I want nothing but the best for you."

"And I want the best for you. That's why I want you to take it easy, Mateo. Don't go out there and kill yourself trying to play catch-up."

"I'm not. But I need to start making things happen again."

"I know."

"It's time to start making things right, and I need to start that with you, baby."

"What you mean?"

"I mean this." He got down on one knee in front of her. "I want you to marry me."

She grinned. "What?"

"I want you to marry me, Chanel. And I know I don't have a replacement ring to present to you right now, but best believe I'm gonna get you one twice the size of the first one."

She stood there looking down at him, her eyes matching the smile on her face.

"But here," he said. He tied a piece of red string around her ring finger. "Let's this do for now—until I can brighten that finger up with a big-ass stone."

She continued to grin. "Baby, you don't have to do all that."

"I want to. You're my woman and I love you."

Those words and the way he said them with meaning and confidence made Chanel melt inside. But it also made her feel extremely guilty. Life was so strange with its unpredictability. Mateo was first in line for Chanel's virtue, but he would end up being lucky number three.

Chapter Forty

*C*harlie kept her promise to herself. She wanted to see the damage
she had created firsthand. It was a warm spring day with a bright
sun shining down on the city when she entered the courthouse. She took
a seat front and center inside the courtroom while Elandy Slogenberg,
AKA Landy, stood stoically in front of the judge to plead guilty to drug
distribution. Standing next to her was her attorney, Michael Bernstein, a
middle-aged white male with bushy hair and a shabby suit. He looked like
he had seen better days and was working on little sleep.

Charlie sneered. *If that's the fool representing Landy, then she is doomed.*
She loved it.

Even though it was Landy's first offense and she was an honor student,
the prosecutor wanted to make an example out of her. Prior to his death,
Ahbou had worked with the ADA and convinced Landy's inexperienced
attorney that she was a real menace to society operating a major drug ring
throughout the projects.

Landy's own attorney didn't believe in her. He wanted her to take a
plea deal. He didn't want to spend too much time on her case, which he
felt was open-and-shut for the prosecutor. In fact, he was appalled by the
young white girl who came into his office with her urban gear and slang
talk. Right away, he figured her to be a "wigga," a slave to the black culture
and black men. *Such a damn waste,* he had said to himself.

"Can you get me off? Cuz I didn't do it. I don't sell or do drugs," she had said to him.

"The prosecutor has a strong case against you," Bernstein had told her.

"And I'm telling you, somebody is setting me up. I'm a college student! I've never hugged a block in my life."

"Hugged a block? What's that? I'm confused."

Landy exhaled her frustration. He wasn't getting the full picture here. She felt he was stuck in a time warp. Landy needed someone who understood the culture; someone more liberal. She needed CNN, and his vibe was Fox News.

"It means that I've never sold drugs and you need to believe that, cuz it's true. I need a miracle, Mr. Bernstein. You have to get me off so I can go back to my life."

"I can't make you any promises."

"What can you make then? I can't go to jail. This isn't me!"

His reaction to her outburst was expressionless. Landy had her hair in cornrows and a scowl on her face, looking the part of a thug. He thought of her as one of his own who had been brainwashed by the niggers with their street swag and ghetto troubles. She wanted to be with them and look like them, and it bothered Bernstein.

"It's not what you're telling me; it's what it looks like to the judge and the prosecutor and a jury if you decide to take this case to trial. Which I wouldn't advise."

"But I don't have a criminal record."

"This is an election year, and politicians up for reelection don't hold any sympathy for criminals, especially drug dealers," he had warned her.

Landy had frowned. Her lawyer's words already had her defeated.

Bernstein had continued with, "Sentencing for drug distribution and trafficking can generally range from three to five years to life in prison."

The little color in Landy's face drained, and she had appeared paler than she already was. Her earlier scowl transitioned into a worried pout.

Michael Bernstein continued to advise her about the harsh New York City drug laws—the Rockefeller Laws. Drug trafficking and distribution was a felony and a more serious crime than drug possession, and they wanted to hit Landy with intent to sell charge.

"It's not fair," Landy had cried out.

Bernstein continued to express apathy to her plight. He felt, if you lie around in the mud with pigs then eventually, you're gonna get dirty and be slaughtered. And now she had nigger charges.

"Take a plea deal. I can arrange something with the ADA, and you might do a year in jail."

"A year!" she hollered. She didn't want to do a day in jail.

"Right now, it's the best deal you're gonna get from the ADA."

Landy felt like this was all a nightmare. This wasn't happening to her. She was a good girl. She was in school trying to get a degree and next thing she knew, all hell broke loose when plainclothes narcotics officers suddenly sprung on her with their guns drawn. They spewed out threats and demands, subsequently searching her and finding the unexpected in her book bag. Now her life was ruined.

Landy stood inside the courtroom flanked by her inept attorney and gazed at the gray-haired and stern-faced judge who looked to be in his early fifties. Her cornrows were replaced with long, spiral curls, and her urban attire became a loose-fitting dress and ballerina flats. Landy looked like a young lady from the Long Island suburbs who didn't know a thing about staying in the ghetto.

The judge asked her how she pleaded to the charges against her, and she reluctantly replied, "Guilty, Your Honor."

Charlie was truly enjoying the show. When Landy turned around and glanced at Charlie sitting in the courtroom observing her sentencing, it didn't register. She knew that she had been set up, but she didn't know the who or the why.

The judge continued with his courtroom jargon, but now Landy wasn't paying too much attention to what he was saying. She once again glanced back at Charlie seated two rows behind her, and it dawned on her.

Landy glared at the bitch. This had to be Charlie's doing. She didn't know anyone else grimy enough to plant drugs on her and have her set up—and Charlie was fucking that cop.

To add insult to injury, Charlie pointed to herself and then to Landy and mouthed to her, *"I did this to you. I put you in here."*

The hard, stoic look on Landy's face suddenly cracked. *How could I have been so stupid and naïve?* she thought. Charlie had singlehandedly destroyed her life. She started to weep openly, which turned into heavy sobs with her shoulders heaving up and down. No one cared for her tears. She did the crime and now she was about to do the time, they all believed.

The judge sentenced Landy to a year in jail. With good behavior, she would most likely do a little more than half that. It was a slap on the wrist to Charlie, but the punishment would do.

Michael Bernstein felt that he had done a remarkable job with Landy's case. A year in jail and eligible for release within six months, she should be kissing his ass.

Landy continued to sob. It looked like the judge had sentenced her to life in prison instead of a year.

Before the bailiffs could escort Landy into the bullpens below, Charlie stood up to leave, but before doing so, she yelled a threat to Landy. "I'm not done wit' you!"

The judge demanded order in his courtroom and shouted a harsh warning to Charlie. If she continued with her outburst, then she would be held in contempt of court. But she was done. She had gotten her point across. She wanted to teach Landy a lesson, and she had. Anyone who came against her would be dealt with accordingly.

Charlie marched out of the courtroom with a self-righteous attitude. Landy was going to jail and she was going to continue to enjoy her freedom. Ahbou had proven worthy to her. She almost wished he wasn't dead. Having a cop at her beck and call was useful.

Outside the courthouse, Charlie smiled and took in a whiff of fresh air—a whiff of her continued freedom. She was satisfied with how her plan had come together so perfectly. But her satisfaction felt short-lived because Chanel came into her mind. Landy was lightweight compared to whose life she truly wanted to ruin. She had heard that Mateo had fully recovered and now he was home. Chanel was back with her true love and it sickened Charlie to think that bitch was happy again. Charlie had a deep-seated hatred for her little sister. Why did she hate the bitch so much? Jealousy? Resentment? Whatever the reason, there was no way Charlie was going to allow her younger sister to live her best life.

She got into her convertible Benz and put the top down. She lit a cigarette and connected her phone to the car, loading up a Spotify playlist that kicked off with Nipsey Hussle's "Victory Lap." It was back to the block—back to business and making money. But it was also time to plot Chanel's demise, along with Mateo's.

Chapter Forty-One

*C*hanel couldn't reconcile the irritation that shot through her body when she heard the news. A few hours ago, Mecca had called her screaming into the phone excitedly.

"Ohmygod! Ohmygod, Chanel! He did it! He did it!" Mecca had exclaimed. "He finally proposed to me. We're getting married, Chanel! Ohmygod, I'm getting married!"

Chanel tried to feign excitement when she congratulated her. "I'm so happy for you, Mecca. You deserve it. Y'all are gonna make a wonderful married couple."

"I can't believe this is finally happening. I'm getting married. And of course, I want you to be my maid of honor, Chanel."

"Of course," she answered, swallowing the lump that had formed in her throat.

"I want a huge wedding if he can afford one. And I'm going to need my best friend's help. You were right, Chanel. I just needed to be patient with him. And you should see the ring he gave me. It's so beautiful and expensive," Mecca had boasted. "I love him so much."

Chanel had already seen the ring—helped picked the bitch out. But it was a secret she would keep to herself.

"I told you," Chanel had said. And then she sighed.

The story that Mecca gave her was that Pyro came down to her university, somehow found her classroom, and got down on one knee and proposed in front of all her classmates.

It was the perfect story—the picture-perfect marriage proposal.

"I love him, Chanel. Ohmygod, I'm getting married!" Mecca squealed.

Chanel wanted to shout to her, *I heard you the first time.* Now it felt like Mecca was parading her proposal in her face. She couldn't believe that Pyro had done it—that he asked Mecca to marry him after all this time.

"So, where do y'all plan on having the wedding and the honeymoon?" she asked Mecca.

"We haven't talked about that yet. But I want to have my wedding in a massive cathedral church and I want to go to Hawaii for our honeymoon."

"Hawaii?"

"Yes. I always wanted to go there, and once Pyro and I get married, it will give us the opportunity."

This bitch! Chanel thought. Hawaii was where she and Mateo had planned on getting married and honeymooning. Now she felt that Mecca was trying to emulate her dreams.

"How you gonna even consider going to Hawaii and that's where Mateo and I had planned to go?"

"But y'all didn't though."

"What?" Chanel shrieked. She was pissed off. "You know why we didn't, Mecca. That was very hurtful to say."

"I'm sorry. All I meant was that you and Mateo don't have exclusive rights to Hawaii. It's basically every woman's dream, and I shouldn't have to stop my fairytale wedding because your family fucked yours up."

Mecca was really feeling herself. The engagement had emboldened her to say things Chanel didn't know were in her. She briefly wondered if Mecca knew about the affair.

Chanel ended the conversation with, "You're absolutely right. Whatever you decide, I have your back. And again, congrats."

That night, Chanel and Mateo were snuggled in their bed together, talking. Moments like this were what Chanel yearned and dreamed for. There were no more hospitals, facilities, physical therapy, or staff. It was an intimate setting inside their home. Chanel was all smiles, laughing and joking with him. And although he wasn't a 100% himself yet, it still felt great.

"Let's get married," she blurted out.

"We are getting married," he replied.

"No. I mean right now."

"Now?"

"Yes."

"But I assumed that you wanted to keep our original plans to get married in Hawaii with Pyro and Mecca by our sides, but this time on your nineteenth birthday."

"I don't want to wait, Mateo. I love you and I want to marry you now. We've waited long enough. I don't need to get married in Hawaii. I almost lost you and I don't want to lose you again. So, let's just go down to the Justice of the Peace and do it—get married."

He chuckled. "Damn." He was flattered.

She stared at him, waiting for his reply. She genuinely wanted to become his wife, and he couldn't tell her "no" again. She had already been through so much.

"Fuck it! Let's do it. Let's get married right now," he said with certainty.

She smiled and hugged him. "I love you."

"I love you too. And how about this . . . let's have our honeymoon in Hawaii then," he suggested.

She sweetly replied, "I want to keep everything between us, Mateo."

Mateo lifted his eyebrow. "What you mean?"

"I mean no Pyro or Mecca; just us."

Mateo could understand her wanting to keep things simple, but he was adamant that they would both regret it later if they didn't have their best friends with them during the ceremony.

"If Pyro's not there with me, then I'm not doing it, Chanel. He's my brother, and Mecca is your best friend. What kind of friends would we be if we didn't invite them to our wedding?"

She knew he was right. She sighed. "You're right."

"I know I'm right. And why wouldn't you want them there in the first place?"

"It's just that you and I have been through so much, that . . . it's nothing important, Mateo. It's just stress," she explained.

"You sure you're okay?"

"Yeah. I'm okay."

Pyro wrapped his arms around Mecca and held her affectionately in the bubble bath. They were sipping on wine, eating strawberries, listening to R&B music, and having a romantic time together in the scented bathroom.

Mecca lifted her hand and smiled at her ring. It was truly beautiful.

"I love you, baby," she said.

"And I love you too."

"So, how many kids do you want me to give you?" she joked.

"Oh, so you want a number?"

"Don't be going crazy with it, either. We're in the twenty-first century, not the nineteenth century."

He laughed. "Okay, shit . . . you're so beautiful and fine, I might fuck around and put six kids into you."

"Six?" She shrieked with laughter.

"You said give you a number."

"You want me to give birth to the Brady Bunch?"

"Hey, I wouldn't mind a big family," he joked.

"Well, three at the most, and you better look into adoption for the rest." She laughed.

"Adoption?"

"You know what giving birth to six kids will do to my body?"

"Yup, make you even finer," he said sweetly.

She beamed. He always knew the right thing to say to her to boost her confidence. She hoped their chemistry continued until the end of time.

As they lingered in the warm tub, Mecca's cell phone rang, and it was Chanel calling her.

"Damn, she got perfect timing," Mecca said. "Give me a minute, baby, and let me see what she wants."

She climbed out of the tub and Pyro grinned at her wet, succulent ass. He wanted to bite her butt. Mecca grabbed a towel and stepped out of the bathroom. Just then, Pyro's cell phone started to ring too. It was Mateo calling him. Each was getting a phone call from their friend at the same time. Before Pyro could answer his phone, he heard Mecca squealing her happiness into her phone.

What the fuck is that about? he thought.

"Mecca hollering all crazy and happy," he said to Mateo.

"That's because she got some good news," said Mateo.

"And what's that, my dude?"

"Chanel and I are gonna get married soon. We decided to just do it—go down to the Justice of the Peace and say our vows there," Mateo said.

"Oh word? Y'all gonna just do it—get married just like that? Man, congratulations," Pyro returned, trying to project that same happiness Mecca had squealed to her friend.

"And you know I want you there by my side when I say 'I do' to her. I love her, Pyro, I truly do. I don't know what I would do without her," Mateo said.

"Well, I'm happy for you."

"I'm happy for you too, Pyro. You and Mecca make a great couple."

"Thanks."

"Look at us, two engaged hustlers from the block moving on up wit' our lives and about to get hitched. Damn, Pyro. We sprung, my nigga?"

Pyro laughed. "We're something," he replied.

"One, my nigga."

"One."

Their call ended, and as if on cue, Mecca came back into the bathroom. She was smiling and happy for Chanel. Pyro's mood about their friends' wedding didn't match hers.

"You think Mateo will be disappointed? Cuz we probably won't be able to make their wedding," he said.

Mecca looked at him like he was crazy. "What are you talking about? Of course we're gonna make it. There's no way we can miss it."

"But it being short notice, them getting married at the Justice of Peace, and I got so much to do."

"So much to do? Pyro, Mateo is your best friend, and when it comes to something special like this, it should be your priority to be the best man at his wedding."

"I'm happy for him."

"Are you sure?" she asked. "Wait a minute. What's this really about? Because the Pyro I know would kill to make it to this wedding. They are our best friends and they've been through so much and lost so much—nearly their lives. And if you don't think this is important, then I don't know what to tell you."

Pyro exhaled. There was no getting out of it.

Chapter Forty-Two

High-profile defense lawyer D'Angelo Bratcher and his legal team, along with the New Jersey detectives, were disappointed that they weren't able to find any third-party female DNA in God's apartment. The cops were able to get a photo of Charlie's license plate as she traveled over the George Washington Bridge several days before they found Kym in the apartment with the murder victim, but they weren't able to place Charlie at the residence. No witnesses saw Charlie, and she was hard to miss with her red hair.

Kym was devastated. She was going to go away for a crime she didn't commit. Her attorney had a knack for spotting liars, and he believed in her innocence. D'Angelo had been a lawyer for twenty-five years, starting out as a Brooklyn prosecutor and then transitioning into a defense attorney because there was more money in it and he wanted to help those who couldn't help themselves. D'Angelo Bratcher had seen his fair share of overturned verdicts—mostly black and brown men and women convicted of a crime because they couldn't afford a good lawyer.

He didn't want to see Kym fall victim to that flaw in the justice system. He believed she was being set up—that the detectives had arrested the wrong person.

"I'm not giving up on you, Kym," D'Angelo said.

"Then what's our next move?" she asked him.

"My office is working closely with the detectives on the case, and right now, things are looking promising for you. The detectives investigating the homicide believe in your innocence too."

"They do?" she asked, her eyebrows going up.

"The case against you is circumstantial at best, and with your clean record, your family background, and no violent history with the victim, the ADA will have a hard time convincing the jury of a guilty verdict. But this Charlie character, she has a criminal history and a rap sheet longer than the constitution. Hey, if O.J. Simpson can get off, I know I can get you off. So, I'm going to have a talk with the ADA," he said.

Kym felt somewhat relieved by those words, but she knew she wasn't out of the woods yet. "Thank you."

"Don't thank me yet. Thank me on the day of your acquittal or when the case against you is dropped," he replied.

For D'Angelo, it was a long shot to try and convince the ADA to drop the charges against his client. But it was worth trying.

The detectives wanted to pull Charlie's cell phone records to see if it had pinged off any cell phone towers closer to God's home, but she didn't have a phone in her name. They assumed that she had a pay-as-you-go disposable phone or a phone in someone else's name. Charlie was a career criminal. She was smart.

Finally, Bratcher subpoenaed the recording of the 911 call reporting the murder. You could clearly tell it was a female disguising her voice.

They were working feverishly on the case. The detectives were also in constant contact with the Bronx detectives regarding the rape of Chanel Brown and attempted murder of Mateo Hernandez. They had even less of a case. Right now, it seemed that Charlie was literally getting away with murder. Now the tide was turning, though, and the more the detectives investigated Charlie, the more they saw she had motive and opportunity to kill God.

It was a damp spring evening when Charlie got into Mona's car. She handed Mona a bulky envelope filled with cash, the organization's cut from her street profits. Charlie had more money coming in than she could count.

"Business is good," Charlie said.

"I see. You were born to hustle, Charlie."

"And y'all need to remember that. That's why I feel I need y'all to increase my cut," she said.

"We'll vote on it. But there's something else I need to discuss with you," said Mona.

"And what's that?"

"New Jersey didn't find anything connecting you to God's murder."

"Are you fuckin' wit' me? Seriously?"

"Yes. So, the case is now at a standstill."

"Standstill? Meaning?"

"The ADA also decided to drop the murder charges against Kym."

Charlie was livid. "What? How is that fuckin' possible?"

"It is possible, and it happened. Somehow, the detectives on the case convinced the ADA to drop her charges."

Fuck me! Charlie thought. She took it as a loss. She hated losing, and now Kym had somehow managed to untangle herself from the nasty web and was free again. Charlie wanted that bitch to end up like Landy, locked up. Now Kym was placed on her mental payback list as number three, with her sister and Mateo holding the top two slots.

Chapter Forty-Three

You look so beautiful, Chanel," Mecca complimented her friend. "And it still fits!"

Chanel chuckled. "Thank you, Mecca."

Chanel smiled at her image in the large mirror, gazing at the Monique Lhuillier wedding dress she was wearing. It was still beautiful. It was still white too, something that had lost its meaning. She sighed.

"What's wrong?" asked Mecca.

"Nothing. I'm just . . . I'm just nervous."

"Girl, this is your best day. You're only a few minutes away from saying 'I do' to the man you love—the man you want to spend the rest of your life with. I can't wait until Pyro and I get married," said Mecca.

Pyro. Chanel didn't want to think about him. She saw him earlier and, for some reason, she had gotten butterflies in her stomach. She felt that it was best to keep her distance from him although he was Mateo's best man.

Chanel and Mecca exited the bathroom and went into the Justice of Peace where their wedding ceremony was to be performed by a judge inside the spacious room. The groom was looking handsome in his black suit and white tie, and Pyro looked equally handsome wearing a black suit. Standing near the groom and the best man were Bacardi and Butch. There was also a surprise guest. Mateo's mother, Silvia, had come down from Boston to attend her son's impromptu wedding. She was a former drug addict and had just come out of a six-month rehab.

It was Chanel's first time meeting Silvia. She was a chubby woman with a massive amount of long, dark hair, and she showed nothing but warmth and kindness toward her soon-to-be daughter-in-law.

"You're beautiful," Silvia said to Chanel.

"Thank you. And I'm so happy to meet you," Chanel said. "You have a wonderful son, and I promise I'm going to always take care of him."

"I know. I've heard so many wonderful things about you. He told me how you were there for him during his recovery while I was going through my own recovery." She looked down at the floor, thinking about her drug addiction. "I've never seen him so happy. He's a lucky man to have you."

Chanel smiled while Mateo appeared to be blushing. "Okay, stop embarrassing me, Ma," he said.

"Boy, let me talk to my daughter-in-law and get to know her better," Silvia sassed at her son.

He sighed and groaned. "Oh boy."

Chanel and Silvia continued their warm and polite conversation and, surprisingly, Bacardi enjoyed Silvia's company too. Bacardi and Butch warmly embraced Mateo and were genuinely happy for the couple.

Everyone was socializing and laughing before the couple was to say their vows in front of the judge. Pyro and Chanel kept their distance from each other and barely said two words to each other. It was odd in light of how close the two had become since Mateo's shooting and rehabilitation. Now it appeared as if they were complete strangers.

Mateo sensed some uneasiness in Chanel, but he assumed it was pre-sex jitters. Mecca also could sense that something was off with her fiancé, but she couldn't put her finger on it.

A Spanish couple was up next to see the judge. Bacardi approached Chanel and gently pulled her to the side saying, "I need a word with you."

Chanel didn't resist.

"What's up?" she asked her mother.

"You're what's up. Get it together, Chanel, right now, unless you want everyone in here to know that you and Pyro had something goin' on," she strongly whispered in her daughter's ear.

"I'm fine, Ma."

"No, you're not fine. The way you're acting toward Pyro right now, it's clear as day that y'all had something goin' on. And if I can see it, don't you think Mateo and Mecca will see it too?"

Chanel sighed. Her mother was right. She had been acting awkward toward Pyro.

"I'll fix it, Ma. Thank you."

"Just go in there and marry the man you love and don't think about your past," said Bacardi.

She nodded and smiled.

They went back into the room, where the judge was waiting for them.

"Let's do this, baby," Mateo said proudly.

Chanel gazed at her husband-to-be and grinned from ear to ear. Mateo took her hand in his and they approached the judge. Judge Harold Cawthan, an old white man in his early sixties, smiled at the couple.

"Are you two ready?" he asked them.

"Yes, we are," Mateo replied.

"Great. Let's get started.

Pyro flanked Mateo and Mecca flanked Chanel, and the judge looked at the young couple with the Bible in his hands and said, "Marriage is a wonderful thing. I've been married to my wife for over forty-five years."

The judge then got the ceremony started. After Chanel and Mateo exchanged their vows, the judge happily announced, "I now pronounce you husband and wife. You may kiss the bride."

Mateo took Chanel in his arms and they kissed passionately with happy tears in their eyes. Everyone applauded, including Pyro.

"I love you," Mateo proclaimed with all his heart.

"And I love you," Chanel replied with the same conviction.

The married couple left the Justice of Peace and climbed into the backseat of a sleek, black SUV. They were driven to the JFK airport, where they boarded a first-class flight to Hawaii to enjoy their honeymoon.

The newlyweds enjoyed champagne and proudly announced to the other passengers that they'd just gotten married this morning and were on their way to Hawaii for their honeymoon. The pilot even made an announcement through the speakers, and the entire plane erupted with clapping and congratulations.

The resort they had reserved was five stars with breathtaking views of the island and the Pacific Ocean. They had waited so long for this— the Hawaiian music, the warm tropical breezes, and champagne. Because Chanel was underage, she had to sneak drinks, which was fun for them.

On their wedding night, Mateo couldn't wait to make love to his new bride. They had the honeymoon suite with a large king size bed, sitting areas, a balcony, a whirlpool, and two flat-screen TV's.

Mateo wanted to be extra gentle with his wife. He knew she had a traumatic experience and he didn't want to do anything to trigger memories of the rape. He was excited to finally be with Chanel, but he was nervous too. While Chanel was in the shower, he popped open a bottle of champagne. To pass the time until Chanel came out the bathroom, he decided to call Pyro.

Mateo stepped out onto the balcony and gazed out at paradise. The night was tranquil, and the Pacific Ocean was calm and glistening under the moonlit night. Mateo had his phone to his ear and listened to the ringing. Pyro soon answered.

"I know things must not be going right if you're calling me on your wedding night," he joked.

Mateo laughed. "Nah. Everything's going good."

"And you're calling me?"

"I don't know if it's just me or what, but I need some advice."

"Listen, if you don't know by now about the birds and the bees, then there isn't much I can do for you, Mateo," Pyro continued to joke.

"Seriously. Chanel's been through a lot and I don't want to hurt her," said Mateo.

"Man, you'll be fine."

"I just want everything to be special for her. I want her to enjoy tonight."

"She will, man. Believe me, things will be fine. Don't worry; her getting raped and making love to her husband are different. She loves you, so just be confident and stop over thinking shit. It's your honeymoon, and you already wasted most of it by being on the phone with me," said Pyro. This phone call was killing him. The last thing he wanted to know was the exact time Chanel and Mateo would make love. However, he had to suck it up. She wasn't his.

Mateo felt better with Pyro's reassurance. "Yo, you're right. Thanks."

"You know I always got your back."

"You do, and I got yours. One, my nigga."

"One."

Mateo went back inside to see Chanel coming out of the bathroom in a sheer pink teddy and sexy panties. Mateo stood there in awe and thought, *Damn, I'm glad I married you.*

"How do I look?" she asked him.

He was almost speechless. "You . . . you look so damn beautiful."

She smiled. "Thank you."

He sighed and she continued to smile. He felt twelve again—eager and excited like he was having sex for the first time.

"C'mere, you," he said.

Chanel sauntered to her husband, who picked her petite frame up and walked her to the bed that was decorated with rose petals. Gently, he laid her down and drank in her beauty for a moment.

Mateo started at her small feet, sucking her toes and slowly working his way up. He took his time, peeling off her lingerie and positioning his body between her curvy thighs. He began nibbling and sucking on her clit and started to taste her juices. Chanel's hips subtly began to gyrate as he inserted his index finger into her warm pussy. She was so wet and so turned on as her husband tasted her.

"Ohhhhhh….Oooooh," she moaned. Her sweet voice was turning him on. He wanted to please her.

His tongue swirled around inside of her until he was confident that she was ready for more. There wasn't an inch of her body that wouldn't get his attention. His strong hands massaged her thick thighs, tracing her sexy silhouette as he planted wet kisses against her flat stomach. Her large, perky breasts were explored as his mouth sucked her areolas until her nipples were at full attention.

Mateo maneuvered himself on top of his wife in the missionary position, for now. He was still apprehensive about entering her and triggering any negative feelings.

"You ready?" he whispered.

"I am," she sweetly answered.

Slowly he penetrated her and started to make love to his beautiful wife. As his girth spread Chanel's tight walls, she moaned her pleasure. Their bodies connected intimately as Mateo inched deeper and deeper until he had almost fully entered her. He tried to be gentle with her, but Chanel grabbed his ass and guided him farther and faster—helping him pick up the pace.

"Fuck me," she cooed. And he did.

In fact, she wanted to switch positions. She got on top and wanted to ride him. Mateo was caught off guard. She started to ride his dick like a pro—she even reached down for his hands and made them cup and squeeze her tits as her ass gyrated against him. Mateo's big dick had Chanel forgetting about her fling.

Whoa! What the fuck! Mateo mouthed. He wanted to make passionate love to her tonight, but it looked like Chanel wanted to fuck—hardcore too. She began responding in ways that kind of shocked him.

"Ooooh, fuck me, baby," she cooed. "Fuck me!"

Mateo didn't know what to think.

The next morning, as they were lounging by the pool that overlooked the ocean, Mateo was trying to focus on the positive. Yet, something about last night was bugging him. The sex was great—maybe too great. He started to replay her moves in his mind, and he couldn't shake the feeling that she'd had sex before. There was something seasoned about the way she moved that gave him pause. Mateo had been with plenty of women—none of them inexperienced—and not many could take all of his dick the first time he fucked them. But Chanel wanted it—all of it—in different positions and repeatedly. *Was she truly a virgin before she was raped?* Was she with someone else while he was down and out in the rehabilitation center? What was it she wanted to tell him that day before he stopped her?

Something was off, but he couldn't confront his sweet wife and insult her. He felt if he was wrong, then it would traumatize Chanel forever and she would think that the rape had tainted her in some way. So Mateo kept his suspicion to himself.

Chanel emerged from the pool with her long hair flowing off her face and hanging low down her back. Her skimpy yellow bikini had many men doing double takes. Slowly she approached her husband with a distinctive walk—a walk only a long night of fucking could trigger. Mateo knew the walk well.

She flung her wet body on top of his and nibbled on his ear. Instantly his dick grew hard. Chanel then whispered, "Let's go back to the room."

He smiled at his wife, and life went on.

Chapter Forty-Four

The arrest, spending time in jail until her parents could make her bail, and then fighting for her life in the court system had hardened Kym. She was fired from her job, she lost her apartment because her parents couldn't pay the bills, and God was killed while owing her five thousand dollars. She looked and felt like shit. Her life had been snatched from her because of a fraudulent murder charge.

As far as she was concerned, there would always be a shadow of suspicion hovering over her. Her case was dismissed without prejudice, meaning the prosecutor could reopen it and bring it back to the courts. Kym knew she wasn't completely off the hook, because if any new evidence against her came to light, then it was back to hell in the court systems. She also knew that neither she nor her parents could afford to go through that ordeal again. The situation had nearly bankrupted them.

Kym felt that there was one person responsible for everything she had been through. Charlie. She wanted that bitch to suffer, and she wanted it to be painful and slow.

Being homeless, Kym was going from spending the night on one friend's couch to another. And being jobless, she had to beg and borrow money. She found herself at rock-bottom, trying to claw her way out of a hole while Charlie was walking free and living it up.

Night after night, Kym would cry and cry until there were no more tears left. She had nothing left, not even her dignity, and she found herself having sex with an ex-boyfriend just to have somewhere to stay for a few nights.

She felt it was time to go after Charlie. She didn't have to look far to find someone who would help her accomplish her task of revenge.

Kym got out of the cab on the rough-looking street. It was twilight and balmy, and the neighborhood she found herself in was the South Bronx. There was a group of guys lingering in front of the bodega across the street from the projects on Rosedale Avenue and a slowly passing cop car. She stared at the brick projects and felt some apprehension, but she continued toward the six-story building. She made her way into the grungy lobby, got into the elevator, and pushed for the sixth floor. Alone with her thoughts and worries, she wondered, *Am I doing the right thing by going to him?*

The elevator door opened and Kym stepped into the narrow, graffiti-covered hallway that reeked of weed and an unfamiliar ghetto smell. She made her way to the end of the hallway and nervously knocked on apartment 6H.

Shortly after her knock, she heard someone say, "Yo, who is it?"

"I'm here to see my uncle—Uncle Pete," she announced.

The door opened right away and a tall, thuggish looking man with a gleaming bald head and a muscular upper body swathed with tattoos came into view. He had a cigarette dangling from his mouth as he smiled at his niece.

"Oh shit, niecy! Why you ain't tell me you were coming?" he said.

"It was a spur-of-the-moment thing, Uncle Pete."

"Yo, come inside."

Kym entered the ultimate ghetto bachelor pad and drug spot. A shifty looking guy was on the couch puffing on a blunt and talking on the phone.

"Yo, CK, this my niece right here, Kym," Uncle Pete introduced her. CK simply nodded to her and continued with his business.

"Anyway, what brings you by, niecy?" he asked.

"I got a problem, Uncle Pete."

"Fo' real? Yo, just talk to me. You know I got you."

Uncle Pete was her dad's younger brother, and he was just a few years older than her. He was a street dude and was considered the black sheep of the family. But he was proud of his niece. She was a beautiful young girl with goals in her life, and he didn't want to see her struggling or messed with.

"You heard what happened to me?" she said.

"Yo, when I heard that shit, I knew you ain't caught no body. That ain't you, niecy. I know if you needed someone got, then you woulda been came to me to do that shit, cuz you know I got you," he said.

"Well, that's why I'm coming to you."

"Talk to me."

Just thinking about it started to make her emotional. "I was set up."

"No doubt . . . by who?"

"This bitch named Charlie Brown—redhead bitch with freckles. She ruined my life, Uncle Pete, and I want her dead," she declared.

"Oh word?" he grumbled, agitated by what he was hearing. "Just tell me everything you know about this bitch."

There was no way he could refuse his niece's request. Murder wasn't anything new to him. He had several open homicide investigations on him, and he wasn't afraid to commit another one—especially for his niece.

"She needs to pay."

"And she will fo' fuckin' wit' my niece," he said with a clenched jaw. "But I'm on it. Don't even fret 'bout it, a'ight?"

She nodded. Hearing those words gave her some comfort. The look in her uncle's eyes said he wasn't going to rest until the bitch was got.

"Yo, go home and get some rest. I got this."

She exhaled and replied, "Thank you, Uncle Pete."

"They fuck wit' family, then they fuck wit' me."

It didn't take long for Pete to get a beat on Charlie Brown AKA Red Charlie. The more he investigated her, the more shocked he was by her notorious reputation. She was the real deal. She had allegedly done dirt that most niggas wouldn't do. She was well-known on the streets, and she was a pretty bitch, with her reddish hair and attractive features. He was impressed, and he would have gotten with her—had she not done his niece dirty.

He called Kym and told her to leave town for a while, maybe go see some friends out of state. He wanted her to have a solid alibi. He was ready to make his move and take out the infamous Red Charlie.

Chapter Forty-Five

Pyro was sleeping like a baby. He looked so peaceful, like he didn't have a care in the world. But Mecca couldn't sleep. She had been up most of the night thinking. No matter how much she tried to brush it off, the same question kept popping back up into her head.

Why the sudden tension between Pyro and Chanel? At the ceremony, they barely said anything to each other. Bizarre. And why did Pyro ask her to marry him after keeping his distance for so long? His proposal came right after Mateo's release from the rehabilitation center.

Mecca didn't want to think the unthinkable.

Would Chanel, sweet Chanel, fuck her man and Mateo's best friend? Did she and Pyro have something going on? And did it happen right under her nose? Mecca wrestled with the disturbing thought. Lying next to Pyro, she propped herself against the headboard and looked down at the huge rock on her finger and exhaled most of her doubts.

This man loves me, she said to herself. He had to. She was pretty and would soon become a Colombia University graduate. She was ambitious and smart, and she was going places.

Mecca mentally compared herself to Chanel. Chanel was her friend, but she came with issues. She was very pretty, but her life had been stalled. Mecca felt that Chanel couldn't hold a candle to her and her accomplishments. She wasn't in college. Her family was dysfunctional, and to Mecca, Chanel's DNA was tainted. Charlie was a sociopath, Claire was crazy and committed suicide, Bacardi was uncouth and ghetto, and Butch was a drunk.

Mecca felt she was clearly the better of the two. She had her shit together, and there was no way Pyro would be with someone like Chanel.

But there were signs. They lived together for a few months. Chanel knew a lot of things about him, and at one point, the two of them seemed inseparable.

She sat upright in the bed and stared at Pyro again. If only she could read his thoughts or know what he was dreaming about. But she was too afraid to ask him. Her stomach started to churn with emotions just thinking about her man fucking her best friend—and if so, was it a one-night stand, or was it an ongoing thing with them?

Mecca wanted to wake him up and ask him, but what if he told her he did fuck Chanel, and it happened on more than one occasion? Even worse, what if Pyro confessed his love for Chanel? The thought was sickening. Would she be able to walk away from him? Mecca knew she would have to gather her strength and move on from him and end their engagement. The truth would tear her apart, and she knew that she would never forgive Pyro or Chanel if her worst nightmare came true. She continued to wrestle with the upsetting thoughts and heaved a deep sigh. The mere thought of it made a few tears trickle from her eyes.

They say don't ask questions that you don't want to know the answers to, so Mecca decided to remain quiet and keep her suspicion to herself.

Chapter Forty-Six

*P*ete sat behind the wheel of a Chevy dressed in dark clothing and smoking his cigarette. His attention was fixed on Red Charlie climbing out of her red convertible Benz. He was parked across the street, his dark blue Malibu blending in with the other vehicles on the Brooklyn street. It was dark and her quaint Brooklyn neighborhood was quiet. He had been watching Charlie for two weeks now—her comings and goings. He was ready to make his move.

He extinguished his cigarette and donned a pair of black latex gloves. He secured his 9mm Beretta with a suppressor in his hoodie pocket. He wasn't nervous. What he was about to do was nothing new to him. He was relaxed and sure of himself.

Seeing Charlie enter her building, Pete quickly removed himself from the car and hurriedly walked across the street, trying to remain discreet. He glided toward her building and slipped inside. He followed her up the stairwell and onto her floor.

She traveled down the hallway and approached her apartment. Pete, with his gun in his hand, eagerly crept behind her just as she was placing her key in the lock. The plan was to push her inside the apartment and kill her there. He also planned on robbing the bitch to make some extra cash off the hit.

Unfortunately for Pete, he was a few seconds too eager to pounce on Charlie from behind. She spied the threat from her peripheral view and quickly reacted. She immediately pivoted as Pete was inches away and she braced herself for the assault. He was too close for her to reach for her gun at that moment, so she went pound for pound with him. A brawl ensued inside the hallway, and while Pete desperately tried to take her down with brute force, Charlie was urgently reaching for her pistol in her purse. It was life or death for them both—someone was going to die tonight, and they were both determined it wouldn't be them.

Pete continued to try and overpower her and drag her into her apartment, but Charlie knew that meant certain death. She screamed and she fought.

"Help me! Help! Someone help me!" she hollered frantically.

Pete smashed his fist into her face repeatedly, immediately silencing Charlie by knocking her out. With the fight and her screaming, his plans of killing her inside the apartment changed. Cops were possibly on their way, and he was finishing what he'd started. He picked Charlie up from the floor, tossed her over his shoulder, and hurried for the exit.

Epilogue

July

Once again, familiar, hard banging on her front door made Bacardi ready to implode. When was she ever going to find peace?

She was in the kitchen seasoning meat for their 4th of July barbeque downstairs in the park. Her renters were helping load pans of macaroni salad and potato salad into the coolers, along with lemonade, bottled water, sodas, and ice.

Bacardi opened the door to a new set of detectives. Both were white males who looked to be in their mid-forties.

"What now?" she barked at them.

A Detective Henry asked, "Have you heard from your oldest daughter lately? Charlie Brown?"

"What has she done now?" asked Bacardi.

"She's missing."

"Missing?" She was taken aback by that information.

"Yes, and we have reason to believe she was met with foul play," said the partner, Detective Mathews. "A neighbor called it in and said that there was some kind of struggle outside her apartment. There was some blood found on the walls and her door was left open."

Hearing this, Bacardi reached for her cell phone and dialed Charlie's phone, but it went straight to her voicemail.

"When did this happen?" she asked the detectives.

"Two days ago, ma'am. It took us some time to investigate and locate her parents."

Butch came out of the bedroom, and upon seeing the detectives, he asked, "Bernice, what is going on now?"

Bacardi sadly gazed his way. Although Charlie was bad news, the thought of having to bury another child was disheartening.

"Charlie is missing," she said.

Chanel sat alone in her doctor's office and couldn't help but to be nervous. She fiddled with her thumbs and fingers and tried to chase away the butterflies in her stomach. The reason she was hard pressed to quickly marry Mateo was because two days before he was released from the center, she and Pyro had sex. For the first time, he came inside of her instead of pulling out like he usually did.

Chanel didn't know if Pyro did it on purpose or if he was caught up in the moment. Nor did she know at the time if she was pregnant. But eight weeks after her wedding, she was told that she was ten weeks pregnant. History was repeating itself. She knew that the baby was Pyro's and it was also, as her mother had advised her, a secret she was prepared to take to her grave.

IT'S ABOUT TO GET DIRTY

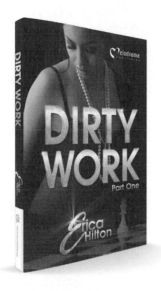 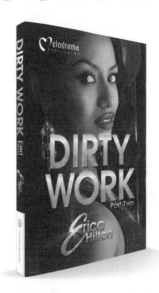

Poisoned Pawn

Harlem brothers, Kip and Kid Kane, are like night and day. While Kip is with his stick-up crew hitting ballers and shot-callers, the wheelchair-bound Kid is busy winning chess tournaments and being a genius.

Kip's ex, Eshon, and her girls, Jessica and Brandy, put in work for Kip's crew as the E and J Brandy bitches. Eshon wants Kip, but Kip is always focused on the next heist—the next big come-up.

When given an assignment by the quirky Egyptian kingpin, Maserati Meek, Kip jumps at the chance to level up to bigger scores. While doing Maserati Meek's Dirty Work, Kip and his crew find that doing business with crazy pays handsomely. But at what cost? Insanity leads to widespread warfare, and the last man standing will have to take down the warlord.

DON'T CALL IT A COMEBACK.